FIXED UP

What Reviewers Say About Aurora Rey's Work

Sweat Equity

"Rey (*Roux for Two*) stresses the importance of building something to last in this torrid home renovation romance. Rey makes the chemistry between Maddie and Sy obvious and immediate, leading naturally to plenty of creative and exciting sex scenes, but tempers the hot-and-heavy goings-on with emotional intelligence that makes the relationship feel as sturdy as a load-bearing wall. Readers will never doubt that a happy ending is on its way, but they'll love watching it come together."—*Publishers Weekly*

Greener Pastures

"I was hooked on this from the very first moment and enjoyed it so much I couldn't put it down. It had everything I want from a romance and everything I have come to know and love in Aurora Rey stories. Definitely recommend this amazing story and for romance readers, it's another must read!"—*LESBIreviewed*

You Again

"*You Again* is a wonderful, feel good, low angst read with beautiful and intelligent characters that will melt your heart, and an enchanting second-chance love story."—*Rainbow Reflections*

Twice Shy

"[A] tender, foodie romance about a pair of middle aged lesbians who find partners in each other and rediscover themselves along the way.

…Rey's cute, occasionally steamy, romance reminds readers of the giddy intensity falling in love brings at any age, even as the characters negotiate the particular complexities of dating in midlife—meeting the children, dealing with exes, and revealing emotional scars. This queer love story is as sweet and light as one of Bake My Day's famous cream puffs."—*Publishers Weekly*

"This book is all the reasons why I love Aurora Rey's writing. It's delicious with a good helping of sexy. It was a nice change to read a book where the women were not in their late 20s–30s…"—*Les Rêveur*

The Last Place You Look

"The romance is satisfying and full-bodied, with each character learning how to achieve her own goals and still be part of a couple. A heartwarming story of two lovers learning to move past their fears and commit to a shared future."—*Kirkus Reviews*

"[A] sex-positive, body-positive love story. With its warm atmosphere and sweet characters, *The Last Place You Look* is a fluffy LGBTQ+ romance about finding a second chance at love where you least expect it."—*Foreword Reviews*

"I caught myself smiling while I was reading this book. Always a good sign. This book is a second chance of sorts since Taylor has been attracted to Julia for years but the focus is on their butch-femme relationship, a dynamic Aurora Rey writes with confidence. Taylor is so well drawn. Rey understands the fragile ego of a butch, the uncertainty behind the bravado. Her books are a pleasure to read."—*Late Night Lesbian Reads*

Ice on Wheels—*Novella in* Hot Ice

"I liked how Brooke was so attracted to Riley despite the massive grudge she had. No matter how nice or charming Riley was, Brooke was dead set on hating her. A cute enemies to lovers story."—*Bookvark*

The Inn at Netherfield Green

"I really enjoyed this book but that's not surprising because it came from the pen of Aurora Rey. This is the kind of book you read while sitting by a warm fire with a Rosemary Gin and snuggly blanket."
—*Les Rêveur*

"Aurora Rey has created another striking and romantic setting with the village of Netherfield Green. With her vivid descriptions of the inn, the pub, and the surrounding village, I ended up wanting to live there myself. She also did a fantastic job creating two very different characters in Lauren and Cam."—*Rainbow Reflections*

"[Aurora Rey] constantly delivers a well-written romance that has just the right blend of humour, engaging characters, chemistry and romance."—*C-Spot Reviews*

Lead Counsel—*Novella in* The Boss of Her

"*Lead Counsel* by Aurora Rey is a short and sweet second chance romance. Not only was this story paced well and a delight to sink into, but there's A++ good swearing in it and has lines like this that made me all swoony because of how beautifully they're crafted."
—*Lesbian Review*

Recipe for Love

"*Recipe for Love* by Aurora Rey is a gorgeous romance that's sure to delight any of the foodies out there. Be sure to keep snacks on hand when you're reading it, though, because this book will make you want to nibble on something!"—*Lesbian Review*

Autumn's Light—*Lambda Literary Award Finalist*

"Aurora Rey is by far one of my favourite authors. She writes books that just get me. …Her winning formula is Butch women who fall for strong femmes. I just love it. Another triumph from the pen of Aurora Rey. 5 stars."—*Les Rêveur*

"This is a beautiful romance. I loved the flow of the story, loved the characters including the secondary ones, and especially loved the setting of Provincetown, Massachusetts."—*Rainbow Reflections*

"[*Autumn's Light*] was another fun addition to a great series."—Danielle Kimerer, Librarian (Nevins Memorial Library, Massachusetts)

"Aurora Rey has shown a mastery of evoking setting and this is especially evident in her Cape End romances set in Provincetown. I have loved this entire series…"—*Kitty Kat's Book Review Blog*

Spring's Wake

"[A] feel-good romance that would make a perfect beach read. The Provincetown B&B setting is richly painted, feeling both indulgent and cozy."—*RT Book Reviews*

"*Spring's Wake* has shot to number one in my age-gap romance favorites shelf."—*Les Rêveur*

Summer's Cove

"As expected in a small-town romance, *Summer's Cove* evokes a sunny, light-hearted atmosphere that matches its beach setting. …Emerson's shy pursuit of Darcy is sure to endear readers to her, though some may be put off during the moments Darcy winds tightly to the point of rigidity. Darcy desires romance yet is unwilling to disrupt her son's life to have it, and you feel for Emerson when she endeavors to show how there's room in her heart for a family."—*RT Book Reviews*

"From the moment the characters met I was gripped and couldn't wait for the moment that it all made sense to them both and they would finally go for it. Once again, Aurora Rey writes some of the steamiest sex scenes I have read whilst being able to keep the romance going. I really think this could be one of my favorite series and can't wait to see what comes next. Keep 'em coming, Aurora."—*Les Rêveur*

Crescent City Confidential—*Lambda Literary Award Finalist*

"This book blew my socks off… [*Crescent City Confidential*] ticks all the boxes I've started to expect from Aurora Rey. It is written very well and the characters are extremely well developed; I felt like I was getting to know new friends and my excitement grew with every finished chapter."—*Les Rêveur*

"This book will make you want to visit New Orleans if you have never been. I enjoy descriptive writing and Rey does a really wonderful job of creating the setting. You actually feel like you know the place." —*Amanda's Reviews*

Built to Last

"Rey's frothy contemporary romance brings two women together to restore an ancient farmhouse in Ithaca, N.Y. …[T]he women totally click in bed, as well as when they're poring over paint chips, and readers will enjoy finding out whether love conquers all."—*Publishers Weekly*

"*Built to Last* by Aurora Rey is a contemporary lesbian romance novel and a very sweet summer read. I love, love, love the way Ms Rey writes bedroom scenes and I'm not talking about how she describes the furniture."—*Lesbian Review*

Winter's Harbor

"This is the story of Lia and Alex and the beautifully romantic and sexy tale of a winter in Provincetown, a seaside holiday haven. A collection of interesting characters, well-fleshed out, as well as a gorgeous setting make for a great read."—*Inked Rainbow Reads*

"One of my all time favourite Lesbian romance novels and probably the most reread book on my Kindle. …Absolutely love this debut novel by Aurora Rey and couldn't put the book down from the moment the main protagonists meet. *Winter's Harbor* was written beautifully and it was full of heart. Unequivocally 5 stars."—*Les Rêveur*

Visit us at www.boldstrokesbooks.com

By the Author

Cape End Romances:
Winter's Harbor
Summer's Cove
Spring's Wake
Autumn's Light

Built to Last
Crescent City Confidential
Lead Counsel (Novella in The Boss of Her collection)
Recipe for Love: A Farm-to-Table Romance
The Inn at Netherfield Green
Ice on Wheels (Novella in Hot Ice collection)
The Last Place You Look
Twice Shy
You Again
Follow Her Lead (Novella in Opposites Attract collection)
Greener Pastures
Hard Pressed
Roux for Two
Her Brother's Girlfriend (Novella in All for Her collection)

Renovation Romances:
Sweat Equity
Good Bones
Fixed Up

Written with Jaime Clevenger:
A New Leash on Love
Frosted by the Girl Next Door
A Convenient Arrangement
Love, Accidentally

FIXED UP

by

Aurora Rey

2025

FIXED UP
© 2025 By Aurora Rey. All Rights Reserved.

ISBN 13: 978-1-63679-788-5

This Trade Paperback Original Is Published By
Bold Strokes Books, Inc.
P.O. Box 249
Valley Falls, NY 12185

First Edition: April 2025

Credits
Editors: Ashley Tillman and Cindy Cresap
Production Design: Susan Ramundo
Cover Design By Inkspiral Design

Acknowledgments

I've been in love with Jack since the first of the Renovation Romances, and I was excited to have him finally meet his match. I knew he needed a sunshine to balance his grumpy, but I had no idea that Ellie would take me on such a journey or that she'd wind up so close to my heart.

Having a parent with mental illness is a unique experience, and it was healing for me to craft a character who learns that being easy isn't always all it's cracked up to be. A huge and heartfelt thanks to my editor Ash, for seeing the squishy parts of me in Ellie. Thank you for being gentle with her, and with me.

Thanks as always to Cindy and the folks at Bold Strokes Books who create the books and get them out into the world. I am so grateful for the passion and energy that goes into getting so many important stories published.

And you, the readers. None of this would matter without you, so thank you. Thank you for reading and reaching out and being a part of my life. It's a thousand times better with you in it.

Dedication

For all the tender-hearted sunshines
who are afraid to let the messy show

CHAPTER ONE

As usual, at least these days, Jack arrived at the Barrow Brothers office first. Well, not first, but within a few seconds of his parents. "Nice to know some of us make a point of getting to work on time," he said without any real bitterness.

"The honeymoon phase is meant to be enjoyed," his mom said. "You'll see, when it's your turn to fall in love."

He let out a dismissive sniff at the prospect. "Please don't tell me I have to put up with this until everyone is actually married and honeymooned."

His sister Maddie's wedding was in the planning stages. She'd been with Sy more than a year now. And his other sister, Logan, had only recently settled into relationship bliss. Marriage would probably happen eventually, but damn. That was a long time to endure goofy grins and daydreaming on the job.

He was spared the knowing yet pitying smile his mother often gave him when he complained about such things by the arrival of both Maddie and Logan. In reality, both remained perfectly responsible when it came to their work in the family business. He considered it his brotherly prerogative to grumble—had since before he even understood he was trans—and at this point, it was sort of expected.

"Look who decided to join us," he said on principle from his usual spot at the table, cup of coffee in hand.

He got little more than eye rolls in response. It was, after all, only 8:04.

Coats were hung and coffee poured. Computers booted up and planners opened. By ten after, the weekly meeting of the Barrow Brothers Construction brain trust was underway.

Dad ran through ongoing projects, and everyone gave their updates. Mom noted a few holes in the schedule and wondered if any soft inquiries regarding small jobs might be converted and squeezed in. At the unanimous murmurs of agreement, she said she'd make some calls.

Maddie raised her hand. "Is Rich going to do any work while he decides if he's going to bother working anymore?"

Their uncle technically owned half of Barrow Brothers. And while he'd spent most of the last twenty years or so as the face—and mouth—of the business rather than the crew, even that had gone out the window when he'd gone to a trade show in Florida, fallen in love, and decided to retire. The specifics of how all that would play out remained to be seen, but he'd managed to throw everyone into a state in the meantime. The whole thing had been going on for the better part of a year.

"He and Cherry are planning to be back in Vermont before the Burlington Home Show in April," Mom said.

Jack shrugged. He didn't put a lot of stock in flashy events like that, but they did matter, especially when it came to getting visibility and securing jobs in the neighboring towns. And he'd rather poke himself in the eye with a voltage tester than stand around some booth and schmooze potential clients. "Better him than me."

"Better them." Mom grinned. "Cherry is going to help with the logistics and swears the two of them can manage the whole thing."

Cherry, Rich's fiancée, happened to be an event manager. She'd turned out to be far more of a delight than anyone expected given Rich's smarmy personality. But the prospect of her jumping into Barrow Brothers operations implied a lot more than sharing a few hours of her time and expertise. He quirked a brow. "Win?"

"We shall see," Mom said.

Everyone else nodded their noncommittal agreement.

"Oh, and one last thing. We got a call from the New England Historic Preservation Trust," Mom said.

Eyebrows went up around the table.

"We did?" Maddie asked.

"They're advising on the restoration of Hampstead House."

Maddie's eyes went up. "Holy shit. Do they want us involved on the project?"

Mom spared a token glare for the cussing, then said, "Not exactly."

"It is a bit beyond our scope of expertise." Logan, ever the magnanimous one, shrugged.

It was Maddie's turn to glare.

"What? It is." Logan folded her arms. "Not that I wouldn't love to get my hands on a house that grand."

It was grand. A mansion, even. Built in the mid-1800s by a Boston banker whose wife had wanted a more pastoral life. It was a marvel at the time, one of the first houses in Vermont to have electricity. Jack had vivid memories of taking a field trip to see it in the third grade. It had fallen into disrepair when the owner died and there wasn't a local historical society with the funds to purchase it.

"Well, someone with deep pockets has bought it. They're renovating it to be a private residence but working with the Trust to preserve as much of the historical integrity as possible."

A chorus of whistles and whispered wows went around the table.

"Did they call just to gloat?" Maddie asked.

Jack laughed. He might have the grumpy sibling reputation, but it was Maddie whose sarcasm could cut like a knife.

"No." Mom's stern expression left Maddie looking effectively cowed, but then her features softened, and she looked to Jack. "They need an electrician."

"They do?" he asked, more than a little surprised.

"The one their project manager lined up fell through. And it seems you, my son, have a reputation."

He did good work and took pride in it. But most of what he did fell squarely in the arena of what any licensed electrician could do. Well, what he did on the clock. He did plenty of mad scientist stuff in his free time, but the only people who knew about his penchant for rewiring old appliances and electronics were the people who bought them. Or so he thought.

Getting to tackle the wiring of a historic mansion would be a bucket list thing—personally and professionally. Even without knowing the current state of things or the scope of the work needed, the prospect got his juices flowing.

"It's an hour from here, though. Are you willing to take on that sort of commute for a month or more?"

It would make for long days, but he'd be hard-pressed to complain about the time to himself, with nothing but music or a podcast or perfect quiet to keep him company. "Sign me up."

Mom smiled. "I already did."

Ellie hadn't gotten past the foyer but already had to remind herself not to gawk. The intricately carved wood could use a good polish and some repair but looked magnificent nonetheless. The wallpaper along the staircase had faded and begun to peel but didn't seem beyond redemption. Of course, all that was just basic appreciation. The thing that really caught her eye—that literally made her heart flutter in her chest—was the mural.

It covered the wall to the right of the stairs, from where the wainscoting ended all the way to the ceiling. The imagery was traditional for the time period the house was built. The pastoral scene featured women in long dresses delicately arranged on blankets under a tree. A couple of men joined them, and a few more sat on horseback nearby. The colors had faded and yellowed through the years, but the heart of the work remained intact.

She couldn't wait to get her hands on it.

Pablo, the project manager for the renovation and her tour guide for the initial walk-through, breezed into the adjoining room, so she cleared her throat and hurried along, only to find even larger and more exquisite murals in the dining room, sitting room, and study. She'd seen pictures, but nothing digital and the size of a computer monitor could do justice to the real thing. Even in their current state. She gestured to the hunting scene in front of her. "These are stunning."

"Aren't they just?" Pablo turned, arm swishing to the side with a level of flair Ellie couldn't even pretend to possess. "The owner wants all of them saved, if possible."

It would require closer investigation to understand the scope of the damage, the integrity of the plaster behind the still vibrant colors. "I'm certainly going to do my best."

"She doesn't want it to be like a museum, though. No plexiglass walls or climate-controlled boxes."

Ellie couldn't help but laugh. "If she did, I'd tell her she should be hiring someone far more qualified than me."

Pablo mocked offense at the notion. "You are what she wants."

And what she was willing to pay for. "She" being Beatrice Castleton, the eccentric pickle heiress who'd bought Hampstead House and wanted to preserve it. But also renovate it. And also live in it. Ellie had yet to meet the woman, but something told her she should be grateful for the buffer of a project manager. Especially since part of her contract included staying in the servant's quarters tucked at the back of the house. "Well, I'm flattered, and I can't wait to get to work."

"That's what I like to hear, Ms. Lancaster." Pablo glanced at the iPad he carried like a security blanket. "Water and heat are on, but only your room and the kitchen currently have electric. Those rooms were upgraded this century at least. Work lights and such for the rest of the house will run off the generator."

She nodded. It was further into the weeds than she needed for the walk-through, but she'd take whatever she could get. The more she knew, the easier it would be to work around the carpenters, plumbers, and electricians doing the rest of the work. She'd learned the hard way many of them considered her work the frosting to their perfectly constructed cake. Hell, one guy on a job in Worcester literally told her to "get out of the way, sprinkles." Though, in hindsight, he might have been going for something crass that went over her head. Fortunately, she didn't anticipate crossing paths with him again.

"Will that work for you?" Pablo asked.

Crap. What had she just missed? "I'm sorry?"

"Oh, I was going over the schedule. You're clear to move in whenever. I have a key for you. I think the electrician is coming sometime this week to do a walk-through of his own, but the rest of the crew won't be onsite until next Tuesday."

A full week away. A full week for her to get her bearings, prioritize her projects, and figure out how to work around dozens of gruff guys who wouldn't take her seriously. "Sounds perfect."

"Do you think you'll be able to do your initial assessment by then? I know Bea is anxious about the state of things." Pablo angled his head and gave her a once-over, like he was gauging her fortitude more than the reasonableness of his request.

"Absolutely. I may need to cut a couple of holes in walls to check the integrity of the plaster and lathe at the back. As long as you're okay with that, I should have a complete report, with options and any additional budgetary considerations." Ellie held her breath after the last bit.

Pablo tapped at his iPad and gave a brisk nod. "Of course. I'm not sure Bea will want to hash through specifics when she's here, but if you send them to me, I can present them when she's in a space to take it all in."

Ellie nodded, again relieved that she'd be dealing primarily with Pablo. She had experience with difficult and volatile people, not to mention a lifetime of experience shielding her mother from unnecessary stress. But it would be nice to have Pablo running interference on the inevitable snags along the way and get to play artist instead of mediator. "I'll plan to have that to you ASAP."

They finished the tour of the main house and ended in the small room that would serve as her eating, living, and sleeping space for the next two months. Modest, to be sure, but it had a tiny private bathroom attached and a big window that faced the backyard. Considering she'd spent the decade after college living at home to help her mom manage living independently for as long as possible, having it all to herself felt almost magical.

"I'd forgotten how Spartan it is. Are you sure you want to stay here?" Pablo's face made his opinion on the matter abundantly clear.

"It's totally fine." Especially considering she'd just gotten her mother moved into assisted living, sold her childhood home, and was technically otherwise homeless.

Pablo didn't even pretend to hide his repulsion. "If you say so."

"Some nice linens for the bed, a cute chair and rug." It wasn't hard to envision making it her own. "Trust me."

"You're the artist." He flicked his wrist, and Ellie decided to take it as a vote of confidence rather than doubt.

"I most certainly am."

Chapter Two

Jack drove up to Hampstead House, stopping briefly out front. It remained grand, to be sure, but smaller than he remembered. Sadder, too, with one shutter sagging and two others missing entirely. Time had not been kind to her—a fact that made him feel both old and oddly nostalgic.

He chuckled at his own sentimentality and pulled in, surprised to find two vehicles in the small gravel lot at the back of the house. The silver BMW he imagined belonged to Pablo, the project manager hired by the owner to oversee the work. The SUV looked far less fancy, but not beat up enough to belong to any worker. Someone from the trust, perhaps. That's who'd tracked him down and recommended him for the job in the first place.

He checked his reflection in the rearview mirror before getting out of his truck, grateful he'd taken the time to shower and tame the mass of red hair a couple weeks past due for a cut. He reached back in for the messenger bag that held the scope of work his mom printed out for him, along with the budget he and Maggie worked up. Both had been approved but were subject to change after he got a firsthand look at the state of things. Not that he expected any discrepancies or pushback. He simply liked being prepared.

Since the path to the back door had been shoveled, he headed there rather than the front. After a moment of hesitation, he entered without knocking but made enough noise stomping the snow from his boots to announce his presence. He needn't have bothered. The dilapidated kitchen was empty, and no one appeared when he called out a hello.

He grumbled a bit under his breath, more irritated over having to do small talk in the first place than the project manager not sitting around waiting for him to arrive. *Just pretend you're Logan.*

The reminder to channel his affable sister diffused his ire. Not ire, exactly. Reticence. He loved the prospect of this job. Having to do it for and with people he didn't know? Less so.

He adjusted the bag strap, squared his shoulders, and ventured further into the house. No sign of Pablo. No sign of anyone, actually. "Hello?"

A thump came from the closet in the foyer, followed by an "ow" and then a "fuck."

"Sorry." He strode over to investigate and apologize. "I didn't mean to startle you."

A sprite of a woman—petite but with curves—emerged from the wall of the closet. Literally, her entire torso had been buried in a two-foot hole in the wall. Most of her face was obscured by a mask, but her hair and clothes were covered in what looked to be plaster dust. She pulled the mask away, revealing a circle of skin only slightly less pale than the alabaster dust. "It's okay. I wasn't expecting anyone. Hi."

Jack blinked a few times, feeling foolish but so startled by her presence that words proved difficult. "Hi," he eventually managed. "I'm guessing you're not Pablo."

The woman laughed, and Jack had to work to ignore what a lovely sound it was. "Good guess. He's around here somewhere, I think."

Jack waited a beat, but she didn't say anything else. "And you are?"

"Oh." Her eyes got big, drawing attention to how impossibly blue they were. "I'm Ellie." She yanked a leather work glove from her right hand and extended it.

He accepted the handshake and, again, waited for elaboration that didn't come. "So, are you working in there or looking for treasure?"

She laughed again. "Both. I'm in charge of the plaster work and I was trying to get a sense of the state of things from behind." She hooked a thumb at the mural now behind her.

He appreciated the commitment to preserve and restore things like delicate plaster, or at least that's what he told himself even if the process of it seemed messy and more trouble than it was worth. "I bet."

"Gotta get my bearings before the contractors start jockeying for position and try to shoo me out of their way." Ellie winked.

Jack winced because that's exactly how most contractors were, especially when jockeying with a woman doing work they considered trivial. And maybe because he'd been guilty of that himself once or twice. Though, to be fair, it was his sister more often than not, trying to sort the finishing touches before the guts of the house were done. That put him squarely in the right, as far as he was concerned.

Ellie folded her arms. "Let me guess. You're one of those contractors."

No point denying it. "Guilty as charged."

She gave him a long, slow once-over—the kind of assessment that walked the line between appreciation and judgment. Oddly, it didn't bother him. He'd take that sort of look any day over the looks he got in bars from time to time. The kind that invited flirtation but mostly sent him running in the other direction. Ellie lifted her chin. "Let me guess. Carpenter."

"Electrician."

She nodded slowly. "You've got your work cut out for you."

He bristled, though her comment most likely had more to do with the state of the house than his skill set. "Looks like you do, too."

Ellie grinned. "I wouldn't have it any other way."

Jack scrambled for something clever to say in return and came up blank. They were teetering on the edge of banter, and he didn't do banter. He sure as hell didn't do it with pretty women on job sites. The oddly unbothered feeling evaporated, leaving him wishing for the buffer of one of his sisters.

"I take it you don't agree."

She'd read his awkward silence as disagreement. Great. He coughed. "I mean, I don't mind a challenge."

Her eyes narrowed, like she was searching for subtext.

Jack resisted rolling his. Why were women always looking for everything to mean something? "Do you know where Pablo is?"

Ellie's body language changed. Subtle, but somehow glaringly obvious. A closing off. A step back without actually moving. Jack didn't find himself on the receiving end of that very often. If anything, he was the one who backed away in social situations. It struck him—too late to do him any good—that his attempt to change the subject came off as rude or, worse, dismissive.

"I have a meeting with him." He glanced at his watch. "Now."

"I think he took a call in the study." Ellie pointed to a set of French doors to the right of the main entry.

Jack nodded, annoyed with the situation and with himself. "Thanks."

Before he could decide his next move, the study doors swung open. A man in skinny gray pants and a snug black sweater emerged. He thrust a well-manicured hand in Jack's direction. "You must be Jack. Sorry to keep you waiting."

Jack accepted the handshake and mustered a smile. "No worries. I got here just a few minutes ago."

Pablo waved a hand back toward the kitchen. "Let's head to the basement. No point going over the fine details until you confirm the overall assessment and plan is accurate."

He nodded again, glad for the efficient, straightforward approach. "Works for me."

Pablo led the way. Jack followed but not without a final glance at Ellie. She regarded him with an arched brow and a smirk playful enough to make him wonder if he'd imagined the tension a moment before. "Good luck," she said, barely above a whisper.

He could feel his face morph into a bewildered expression. What was that supposed to mean? Was she insulting him? Giving him some kind of warning? Or was she trying to get under his skin? Ugh. Women. "Thanks," he mumbled, figuring he could get the last word if nothing else, before striding after Pablo.

Ellie waited for the sound of Pablo and Jack on the basement stairs before stepping back into the closet. She stood still for a second, then leapt out and thrust her arms wide. Because even a happily out gay girl could appreciate the symbolism. After chuckling at her own silent declaration, she went back in for real and positioned her mask back in place. She adjusted the work light, angling her head this way and that to assess what she'd uncovered so far.

All in all, it wasn't as bad as she'd expected. Despite the temperature and humidity fluctuations throughout the years the house sat vacant, the insulation in the outer walls had been upgraded at some point in the twentieth century, which prevented the plaster from disintegrating completely. If the state of the foyer was anything to go on, she'd be able to patch and reinforce the murals from behind and keep most of them intact.

She stuck her head back into the hole, along with her arm and trusty moisture meter, taking readings that would confirm whether her instincts were correct. It all went swimmingly until she got within a foot of the ancient radiator pipe that ran from the basement to the second floor, directly behind the far left side of the wall. She barely touched it, and the plaster crumbled in her hand.

Ellie walked her fingers up the back of the lathe as far as her arm could go before extricating herself from the spot. At least the radiator wasn't—and wouldn't be—on. As much as she didn't love what forced air heat did to plaster in the long term, the prospect of working next to pipes full of scalding water was even worse. Especially in close quarters.

Wouldn't mind being in close quarters with Jack.

The thought snuck up on her—hot, heavy, and completely unbidden. It also included a shockingly clear visual for a guy she'd spent all of three minutes with.

Maybe it was time to get some air. Or water. Hydration was important. And distracting.

She stepped out of the closet just in time to run into Pablo and Jack coming down the stairs and immediately regretted her choices.

"You look like an albino chimney sweep," Pablo said after one look at her.

Jack made that face people did when they were trying to suppress a laugh.

Ellie resisted the urge to cringe and lifted a shoulder. "Occupational hazard."

"Do I want to know what you've found?" he asked.

Knowing full well he didn't want a detailed analysis, especially in the middle of his walk-through with Jack, she nodded. "Not bad, considering. Moderate damage that would be expected with the age of the house. Nothing I can't handle."

Pablo chuckled and canted his head in Jack's direction. "Are you two sharing notes? He basically said the same thing."

It should have been a moment for the two of them to bond—skilled professionals taking on a big project, realistic but undaunted by the scope of work. Only instead of mirroring her knowing smile, Jack merely looked uncomfortable. "Two peas in a pod," Ellie said, since Jack clearly wasn't going to respond.

Pablo either didn't pick up on Jack's body language or didn't care. He made a sweeping gesture with the hand not clutching the iPad. "Ms. Lancaster will be staying in the servant's quarters for the duration of the project, so you'll have to give her warning if you need to cut the main power supply."

Jack regarded her with a raised brow. "You are?"

"I'm in the process of relocating and this project is out of the way from both my previous home base and where I plan to land." That sounded more mature than nowhere else to go.

Jack nodded, either unimpressed by or uninterested in her explanation. Or perhaps both. "It'll only be during the day, I promise. And only a couple of times during the work."

At least he managed to be considerate. "Thanks."

"Jack, let's go to the kitchen to review the timeline and budget. We'll let you get back to your dust." Pablo wiggled his fingers in the direction of the closet, making Ellie laugh.

Jack cleared his throat. "It was nice to meet you."

Ellie looked at Jack, not entirely sure he was talking to her. But his gaze was fixed intensely on her, leaving no doubt. Her stomach flipped a couple of times, making it clear she had more interest in his hotness than the fact that he was awkward and possibly even rude. She swallowed, shoving the flare of attraction to the side. "You, too."

Satisfied with the pleasantries, Pablo and Jack disappeared, leaving Ellie to her own devices. She looked down and, sure enough, her jeans and flannel were coated in plaster dust. She hadn't meant to do more than cut a small hole for an initial assessment. But as was so often the case, it didn't take much for her to get carried away. Fortunately, she had nowhere to be when she left, save the Airbnb she'd booked for the few days before her contract at Hampstead House started. And the only thing waiting for her there was Emily Dickinson, the black cat who'd shown up on her doorstep two years before and never left.

She spared a moment to lament the sorry state of her social life, then got back to the task at hand. Though, truthfully, she'd done all she could do for now, and her puttering had more to do with avoiding another run-in with Jack than it did sussing the salvageability of the plaster. She kept an ear open, noting the sound of voices and Jack's obvious departure.

"You about done in there?" Pablo called.

"Just wrapping up." She joined him in the hall.

"And?" He looked at her expectantly.

"And it's just as I said. There will be spots needing work, but if this wall is anything to go on, they can all be saved."

He gave her a wry smile. "From the looks of you, I'd have to say you could have fooled me."

Since oh-so-serious Jack was not there to see, Ellie struck a pose. "Full-body powder is hot right now. You should try it."

Pablo grimaced. "No, thank you."

He seemed to be joking back, but she couldn't be sure. "I promise to keep my messes as contained as possible. I might not look the part at the moment, but I'm a total professional."

He humored her with a laugh. "I have no doubt."

Phew. "I think we can do a restoration without breaking the bank."

"Music to my ears." He glanced at his watch. "I'm heading out for the night. I feel strange leaving you alone."

"It's okay, I'm just about ready myself." She gathered her things while Pablo hovered. She wanted to ask about Jack but couldn't find a way to without being obvious about it.

"Though you are going to be living here. I suppose I should get used to it," Pablo said, clearly oblivious to where her thoughts were.

He had a point. But that would be different. She'd have her things and her own space. And Emily Dickinson. All she had to do was remember she'd decided it wouldn't be creepy. "I'm a big girl. It'll be fine."

They walked out together, and Pablo locked up, but not before handing over a set of keys that would allow her to come and go as she pleased. Despite his allusion to chivalry, he didn't waste any time sliding into his BMW and pulling away. Something told her Jack, for all his reluctance to be friendly, would have waited.

Ellie shook her head before slipping into her own car. She started the engine and cranked the heat, replaying parts of the day while the dusting of snow melted from the windshield. Jack, of course, took center stage. She let her head fall back. *Well, this is inconvenient.*

It wasn't the first time she had the hots for someone she worked with. It likely wouldn't be the last. Usually, she took it in stride. Hell, sometimes she even looked forward to it. Giving her imagination something to do while she spent hour after hour on the fine detail her work required was a must. And given her current lack of a sex life, a little friendly flirtation could be welcome.

There was just one problem. The hottie in question seemed about as interested in talking to her as he might a hole in the wall.

Sure, she probably looked like some kind of plaster urchin when he snuck up on her. Still. How hard was it to make a little friendly conversation?

It sucked extra because, while she couldn't be entirely sure, she had a sneaking suspicion Jack was trans. Which meant he had the potential to be legit flirtation material and not just fodder for passing the time. She sighed again. Maybe he was having a bad day. Or nervous about meeting Pablo. Maybe he'd warm up. Or, just maybe, she'd work her charm and wear him down.

Chapter Three

Jack sat on the couch while Logan packed yet another box of books. "I can't believe you're leaving me."

"I'm literally moving three minutes away."

"Yeah, but still." Jack pouted.

"You can visit me anytime, you know. And I'll come drink your beer anytime you invite me." Logan taped the box closed and added it to the growing stack.

"You're not going to be next door, though. And you're taking my buddy." He gave Kiwi, who'd fallen asleep paws up on his lap, a belly rub. "She's spent more nights with me than you lately."

Logan's expression changed to one of worry, laced with more than a hint of guilt. "That has been super selfish of me. Do you want me to leave her with you?"

The fact that Logan would even entertain it was a testament to how much she loved him. And probably her guilt over ending the shared bachelor existence that had been their duplex over the last seven or so years. "She's your baby. Just because I've grown attached doesn't change that."

Logan abandoned her packing to scoop the sixteen pounds of poodle mutt fluff into her arms. "She is. And I'm not going to lie, I've missed the crap out of her."

As Logan started spending more and more time at Kathleen's, Kiwi's time at Jack's had increased. Mostly because she was fourteen and hated going in the car. But now that Logan was moving in with

Kathleen, he had no doubts that Kiwi belonged there. "She's going to love that big yard."

Logan laughed. "At least after the snow melts."

Truth. Kiwi hated the cold almost as much as she hated the car. Little old dog prerogative. "Maybe it's time I take a trip to the shelter myself."

"Yeah?" Logan looked pleased at the idea.

He'd been thinking about it more and more. He'd wanted some time after his old beagle mix passed, and then Kiwi was around enough to take the edge off. Now, with both Logan and Kiwi moving out, the prospect of endless quiet left him with a sort of restless, empty nest feeling. And Lord knew he was better suited to a canine companion than a human relationship, at least of the romantic kind. "I'm sure there's some sweet girl who's a little sad and a little scruffy who wouldn't mind hitching her wagon to me."

Logan raised a brow. "So you can be sad and scruffy together?"

"Exactly." The description suited him more than the alternative—a chick magnet.

"Even if I don't approve that message, I'm a fan of the plan. If you want me to go with you so you don't come home with six, I'm all in."

He laughed, mostly because it tracked very close to legitimate possibility. "I hereby name you my adoption chaperone and voice of reason."

Logan offered a salute. "Position accepted." She returned Kiwi to his lap and surveyed the room.

"Ready to call it quits for the day?" He gave her the out since he already knew the answer.

She nodded. "I need beer and food."

"I made chili last night," he said.

"And jalapeño cornbread?"

He feigned offense. "Your question implies I might not."

Logan feigned remorse. "Sorry."

"Finish packing this room and we'll eat."

Logan made a face but didn't argue, shoving a dozen paperbacks into a copy paper box she'd pilfered from the Barrow Brothers office. "Tell me about Hampstead House."

He sucked in a breath and blew it out, debating where to start. "It's a big job, but I'm excited for it. I've never seen so much knob and tube in my life."

Logan laughed. "Heaven."

"It is. So much easier to be working from the original and not decades of patchwork replacements. The only part of the house with cobbled upgrades is the kitchen and the back rooms where the caretaker used to live."

"I'm with you. I understand why people do work piecemeal, but what a mess."

Jack nodded. The work itself would be the easy part. Well, not easy, but squarely in his wheelhouse. Work he could happily do for weeks on end without getting bored. It wasn't the work he was worried about.

"Why are you frowning?"

Ellie Lancaster's chipper smile popped into his mind, front and center. "I'm not thrilled to be working with a bunch of people I don't know."

"Poor curmudgeon. Are you going to have to socialize?"

Rather than resist a lip curl, he indulged in an exaggerated one. "Some of us aren't born with the gift of gab."

Logan pressed a hand to her chest in mock offense. Probably because their mother had used the phrase to describe Logan from the age of five. "I don't think you mean that in a nice way."

"Maybe you should come to the site with me. You can talk to people while I work." Though, he realized grimly, he didn't love the idea of Logan turning on her flirty charm with Ellie. Not that anything would come of it. Logan was smitten as a kitten when it came to Kathleen. But still. "Never mind."

Logan, who'd picked up another box but had yet to put anything in it, set it on the coffee table. She pointed at Jack and made accusatory little circles with her finger. "There's a story you haven't told me. Spill."

Jack groaned even though he'd walked right into it. "The project manager looks and acts like he belongs on *Queer Eye*."

Logan pursed her lips. "As a queer eye or a straight guy?"

The show had moved beyond hapless straight guys, but the sentiment held. "Queer eye."

"You say that like it's a bad thing. Need I remind you that you, too, are queer?"

He was. Between the decade on T and top surgery, he passed, and his attractions leaned exclusively to the female identified. But he waved the rainbow flag with pride, literally and figuratively—a fact that had earned him more than a few curious stares in the tiny towns he frequented in their corner of Vermont. And he always cringed when someone said something they'd only say in front of a cis guy. "You know what I mean."

Logan smirked. "He didn't threaten to make you over, did he?"

"No, but I bet he was thinking about it." Jack shuddered at the image of himself in Pablo's tight pants and form-fitting sweater.

Logan grabbed another stack of books but hovered over the box. "Okay, but surely you'll find some bros once the whole crew starts work. Grab your crotch and talk about fixing stuff. You'll fit right in."

Ellie hadn't exactly left his thoughts, but she swooped back into prominence. "I did meet one of them."

Logan abandoned all pretenses of packing and flopped onto the sofa, turning to face Jack with rapt attention. "Do tell."

"She's an artist, I think. Specializes in plaster restoration and stuff. She's been hired to save the murals."

"Oh, that's so cool." Logan's eyes lit up. "I always wished I had more tactile artistic talent. Did you talk to her? Is she nice?"

Nice wasn't an inaccurate word to describe Ellie. Yet it didn't convey the chipper vibe that radiated from her like some sort of homing beacon. "She's…perky."

"Perky?" Logan seemed genuinely confused by the descriptor.

The incredulousness only made Jack double down. "Perky."

"Huh."

"Like a bohemian." Jack rummaged for other adjectives. "But, like, full of mirth."

"Full of mirth?" Logan folded her arms.

He regretted the word choice even before Logan's response. "Is this where I remind you that even though I didn't end up using it, I scored higher on the SAT than you did?"

"Low blow, dude."

"Deserved." He let out a hmph on principle, even though he couldn't remember another time he'd used the word. "Anyway, I stand by it. She's—"

"Sunshine," Logan said before he could finish.

"Excuse me?"

Logan got excited then, like she'd solved a puzzle. "This woman is the sunshine to your grumpy."

"Is that a thing?" He leaned into his family calling him a grump, since it got him out of at least a few inane social obligations, but Logan's juxtaposition of the terms didn't make sense.

"It's a trope, like in a book or a movie. When we started dating, Kathleen said her friend teased her about being the grumpy to my sunshine before deciding Kathleen was acting more ice queen than grump."

"I am so confused right now." At this rate, he was going to have to start reading Kathleen's books just so he could keep up with the lingo.

Logan let out an exasperated sigh. "If you and this woman—what's her name?"

"Ellie," he said with a grumble, not liking at all where this was going.

"Okay, so if you and Ellie were in a romance novel—"

"We are not in a romance novel." Which was obvious, but he felt compelled to say so anyway.

"I'm just saying. If you were, that would be your trope. Grumpy-sunshine."

Jack stood, more irritated than the situation warranted. "I'm going to my house, and I'm taking your dog with me."

Logan pouted. "Are you rescinding your dinner invite?"

He had half a mind to. But Logan wouldn't be a front porch away for much longer. "It stands. As long as you don't try to write me into anymore smutty stories."

"Who said anything about smut?" Logan asked. "Some of the best romcom movies of all time are grumpy-sunshine, and they're barely PG."

He'd totally walked into that and only had himself to blame. "But there's always kissing and all that happily ever after nonsense. I guarantee there won't be any of that here."

Logan's smirk returned. "If you say so."

Ellie lugged in the final duffel bag from the mismatched assortment she'd managed to cram into the back of her Subaru. She'd probably need to retrieve a few things from storage before her six-week stint at Hampstead House was complete, but she had the essentials. And living with the essentials would let her know what of the non-essentials she really missed. All of which would help her decide just how much space—and how much stuff—she'd need when it came time to look for a place of her own.

While the idea of her own place thrilled her, knowing she'd have to make so many and such big decisions made her head hurt. Buy or rent? In town or out in the country? How close to her mom's new place? And that said nothing about how big, how expensive, and what style. Or how much consideration she should give to where her next job might be.

See? This was why she hadn't made any headway. Too much to think about. And she'd used up all her executive functioning—aka big girl panty—reserves getting her mom situated. Even if she could only afford to kick the can for a couple of weeks, she needed the break.

With a decisive nod for no one but herself and Emily Dickinson, she started the process of unpacking and settling in. Despite Pablo's assessment, and for being servant's quarters, the space was quite nice. A single room comprised the living and sleeping area, with a tiny kitchenette in one corner and a bathroom in another. There was only one window, but it faced east, which would make for lovely light in the morning. And she'd bought one of those enclosed litter boxes, which would make having it in her main living area less icky.

It would certainly do for the short term, giving her the flexibility to work odd hours as the plaster patches and layers of paint dried. That was the case she'd made to Pablo, who'd been dubious about her request to live onsite. It was a legit one, too, even if only part of the story.

No matter. It was all set and sorted now. She had a reprieve from major life decisions and a cozy place to hunker and rest.

What she didn't have was a working refrigerator.

She'd seen one in the pictures Pablo sent and made the mistake of assuming it worked. And she'd assumed she could sweet-talk the kitchen contractors into dragging it into her space rather than to the dump when they did demolition. Fat lot of good all that assuming did her. For all her thirty-three years, she should know better.

It was fine. She'd pick up a mini fridge in town, and that would get her through. Since she only had an induction burner and a toaster oven for cooking, she'd be keeping things simple anyway. "Right, Emily Dickinson?" she asked with a nod.

Emily Dickinson yawned.

"Right." She pulled her phone from her pocket to start a list and found a text from Rhett, her bestie since they'd shared a room freshman year at Smith.

OMG. You're not going to believe it. I found a place and it's not that far from you.

After a bad breakup with her wife of more than a decade, Rhett had attempted to spend some time in Mississippi with her family. She'd only been down there for a month, but it hadn't gone well. Despite bestowing her only daughter with a gender-bending name, Rhett's mother was as traditional, strait-laced, and conservative as Southern women came. Rather than providing a safe place to lick her wounds, the time at home had merely inflicted new ones. The prospect of having Rhett back in New England felt like a gift, not to mention giving Ellie a hell of a lot less to worry about. *Tell me everything*, she texted back.

A string of texts followed, but after the fifth one, Rhett simply called. "Hey," she said with a drawl that would rival Rhett Butler himself.

"Hi." Ellie flopped into the dated but ridiculously comfortable armchair in the corner. "God, it's good to hear your voice."

"Darlin', same. I'm dyin' down here."

Her heart ached for the strained relationships Rhett had with her family. They hadn't disowned her, but they also did that thing where they were sugary nice to her face but said mean things behind her back. Ellie might not have the closest relationship with her own mother, but at least she never had to worry about insincerity. "When are you coming and where are you going?"

"Have you heard of a town called Bedlington?"

"Uh. Yeah. It's like an hour from here. It's where Grumpy Old Goat is made." It also happened to be the home of Barrow Brothers Construction, if the decal on the side of Jack's truck was anything to go on.

"Exactly. So boonies, but with good cheese. And at least one queer person."

A good-looking one, too. She followed GOG on social media and the cheesemaker definitely qualified as a thirst trap. "I'm glad to know those are your standards for choosing where to live."

"I mean, let's keep in mind where I'm coming from."

"Point taken. So, is it a house?" Ellie asked. Rhett was a potter and needed space for both a wheel and her small, but nothing to sneeze at, kiln.

"It's half of a duplex. Owned by this total hottie ginger guy who I think might be trans. What are the odds?"

Probably higher than the possibility of two such guys existing in a hundred-mile radius. "Is his name Jack?"

A beat of silence before Rhett asked, "How did you know?"

"I think your new landlord is also the electrician on this project." Seriously, what were the chances?

"No way. That's wild."

"Wild," Ellie said, not sure what her other thoughts might be yet.

"Though, I'm telling you. There's some sort of queer frequency. We might not be able to detect it, but it pulls us together." Rhett spoke with all the seriousness of someone who fully believed the cosmos worked like that.

Ellie had experienced her own share of Small Gay World, especially since graduating from Smith more than a decade ago. "Either way, it sounds nicer than freak coincidence, so I'll take it."

"Damn right you will. So, you've met Jack? Do you like him?"

"Sure," she said with a marked lack of conviction.

"You don't? But you like everyone," Rhett said.

"I do not."

"Okay. You like every queer person you've ever met who hasn't done something actively mean to you or to the world at large."

Rhett had a point. Ellie sighed. "I do like him. I like that he's queer and, I presume, competent at his job. I like that he likely won't turn out to be some mansplaining libertarian hell-bent on convincing me small government is the answer to all my problems."

"But?"

Since she'd done little more than outline baseline decent human, the question shouldn't surprise her. "But he seems kind of surly. Like, small talk is an anathema. He probably uses people as a verb and never in a nice way."

"Is he wrong, though?" Rhett asked.

Ellie laughed. "God, you're such an introvert."

"Yes," Rhett said without missing a beat. "And you adopted me so I didn't become an antisocial hermit. Maybe Jack just needs someone to adopt him."

"Are you volunteering me for the job?" She could think of worse ways to pass her time. Assuming, of course, Jack didn't turn out to be a full-on grumpy jerk.

"I mean, you're going to be spending time with him, right? At work obviously, but maybe when you come hang at my new place, too."

The thought of all that close proximity sent a tingling sensation along her spine. Not that she had any intention of admitting as much. "I'm sorry, are you predicting that you're going to make a friend? All by yourself?"

"No, silly. I'm predicting you'll orchestrate something and rope us both into it. Then we'll bond over being forced to socialize."

She rolled her eyes. "And you'll both complain to me but secretly like having a new introverted friend to hang out with."

"Obviously."

Like so many college freshmen, she and Rhett had been randomly assigned to share a room. Only after getting on each other's nerves to the point of needing a mediation with their RA had they settled into a groove and, eventually, become inseparable. And while they'd each been the other's type when it came to sexual attraction, a single drunken make-out session during a particularly stressful finals week had put a quick and complete kibosh on any inklings they might be more than friends. "So, when do you get here?"

"I'm driving up day after tomorrow and coordinating with movers on Friday."

When Rhett made a decision, she didn't waste time. "Can I help?"

"I'd love unpacking help over the weekend if you're not busy. I can offer cheese and wine."

Ellie smiled. She'd already been in a decent mood, but now it bordered on giddy. "Can't wait."

Chapter Four

Jack stood on his side of the front porch, watching a swarm of movers make trip after trip into Logan's half of the house. Well, not Logan's half. It didn't belong to her anymore. She'd even gone so far as to sell her half to him, not so much to be rid of it but because he had at least a vague interest in owning income properties, and this would be a good test. He had a feeling she was saving up for an engagement ring, too, even though she hadn't admitted as much.

He hadn't planned to be home when the new tenant moved in, but the movers had been delayed a day and here they were, at quarter after ten on a Saturday morning. Since it seemed rude not to at least say hello, he'd stepped out with his coffee, prepared to offer a welcome then disappear. Only, he'd yet to see his new tenant in the flurry of furniture and boxes filing by. Though they'd spoken only briefly over FaceTime, he was pretty sure he'd recognize her.

While he debated waiting around, he studied the items that streamed past. They were nice. Really nice. An eclectic mix of antiques and newer pieces—all high quality and all in excellent condition. Why was someone who could afford all that renting half a duplex in Bedlington?

"You must be Jack." The assertion came from a masc woman with the sort of Southern drawl that had faded after years living elsewhere but never gone away entirely.

"And you must be Rhett." He jogged down the steps after two guys hefting a mattress went past.

Rhett extended a hand and Jack shook it. "Great to meet you," she said with a level of sincerity he couldn't help but notice.

"Welcome to Bedlington." He tamped down the curiosity that could lead to protracted conversation and focused on his responsibilities. "Need anything?"

"Not yet, but I'll let you know. The place is great."

He knew it was, especially for its age and the price point. He and Logan, with a little family help, had done a lot to it when they bought it, and it showed. Still, renters were few and far between in their neck of the woods, so he appreciated finding someone—someone queer no less—so quickly. "Let me know if the wiring in the basement is what you need. I've done my share of two-forties, but never for a kiln."

Rhett waved a hand. "They're all the same I think."

As though summoned by the comment, two of the movers wheeled said kiln from the truck. Jack pointed to the path that ran along the side of the house. "There's a door that goes directly down cellar there. It'll save you having to navigate doorways and a few stairs."

They nodded their appreciation and headed that way.

"Down cellar." Rhett chuckled as though the phrase itself was funny. "If you'll excuse me, I'm going to go supervise."

"Of course." Jack went back into his side, wanting to avoid any semblance of nosy neighbor vibes. He poured a second cup of coffee and threw a bagel in the toaster.

With no formal agenda for the day, he planned to do some puttering in his shop. Logan had dropped off an old console stereo for them to refurb together. He needed to make sure the wiring was salvageable before Logan spent any time trying to make it pretty. It was a beauty, even in its current state. The mid-century modern vibe wasn't his style, but it remained popular, and he had no doubt they'd make a pretty penny if he could get the original guts in good working order.

A knock came at the front door just as the toaster sprung his perfectly toasted bagel. He grumbled slightly at the thought of it getting cold. Hopefully, whatever his new tenant needed wouldn't take long. He opened the door, expecting to see Rhett and staring at Ellie instead.

"Hi," she said in that chipper way he expected would get on his nerves before they finished working together. She seemed not at all surprised to see him.

"Hi," he returned, certain surprise was written all over his face.

"I'm guessing I knocked on the wrong door."

Wrong door, wrong house, wrong town. What the hell was she doing here? "I'm guessing you did." He shouldn't, but he couldn't help but ask, "Who are you looking for?"

"My friend—"

"Ellie!"

The decibels and delight of Rhett's exclamation answered Jack's question even as it spun off several more. "You two know each other?"

Rhett released Ellie from the hug but kept an arm slung around her shoulder. "Best friends for more than a decade."

Jack groaned, but he managed to keep it on the inside. At least he hoped he did. "Seriously?"

"Yeah." Rhett angled her head toward Ellie. "I told this one I'd found a new place, and she was all, I think I know that guy. How wild is that?"

"Wild." He'd have gone with weird or inconvenient or irritating, but he'd been trained well enough by Logan and Maddie to keep observations like that to himself.

"Hope you're not sick of me yet," Ellie said with a grin.

He wasn't that much of a curmudgeon. Still. Finding Ellie as attractive as he did meant having to run into her—both at work and at home—would wear on him sooner rather than later.

"I promise I'll keep her on my side." Rhett winked, though Jack couldn't be sure whether it was intended for Ellie or for him.

"I'm pretty sure the two of you are going to hit it off," Ellie said.

Great. Platonic fix-ups came a close second to romantic matchmaking on the list of things he disliked most.

"It's only because we're both introverts," Rhett said. "She imagines us sitting in companionable silence drinking beers."

The irritation of Ellie trying to make him a friend gave way to irritation that she apparently knew him that well already. "I can think of worse things."

Rhett laughed. "Same."

Ellie waved a hand between them. "See?"

Jack nodded, his way of admitting she was right without liking it.

"We'll get out of your hair," Rhett said, as though sensing Jack's discomfort.

"I'll be in the basement if you need anything." He might not like this development, but he was pretty sure he'd at least wind up liking Rhett.

"Enjoy your Saturday," Ellie said with genuine warmth.

"You, too." He offered an awkward wave and went inside, slightly exasperated by the situation and annoyed that he was.

His aggravation intensified when he discovered his bagel had gone hard and his coffee cold during his absence. He put the coffee in the microwave and got out a fresh bagel, deciding the waste was better than the disappointing texture of a re-toast. He smeared it with extra cream cheese and took both his mug and saucer down to the basement. He connected his phone to the speaker system and willed himself to relax. One, because he didn't want to be one of those dudes who had a heart attack at forty because he was wound up all the time. Two, because he had better things to do.

His preferred coping strategy—out of sight, out of mind—did the trick. By the time he'd finished his breakfast and pulled out his tools, his mood was mellow enough to hum along with Billie Holiday. It was fine. He might wind up crossing paths with Ellie more than he bargained for, but his work and his free time would remain what he loved most: blissful solitude.

Since she'd spent most of the weekend with Rhett, Ellie blocked her Sunday afternoon for a trek to Riverdale Estates, the assisted living slash retirement community her mother now called home. The parking lot was nearly full when she pulled in, which made her smile. Everyone deserved visitors, even if it meant she had to do a couple of laps to find a spot.

She walked up the wide concrete path to the main entrance. None of the landscaping was in bloom now, but the brochures and photos on the website promised a riot of lush color come spring. It was one of the things that had sold her on Riverdale. Her mom wasn't much of a gardener, but she could sit outside with a cup of tea like a boss. Well-maintained grounds counted almost as much as the state of the residents' rooms and common areas.

Ellie signed in at the front desk, delighted that the woman who sat behind it already knew her and greeted her by name. "How are you this afternoon, Laura?" she asked in return.

"Oh, fit as a fiddle. Mrs. Lancaster is finishing up a bingo game, I think. She'll be so happy to see you."

"But not happy enough to abandon the blackout." Ellie laughed.

Laura laughed in return. "Well, a woman has to have her priorities."

"Don't we all?" She didn't begrudge her mom's borderline obsession with bingo or her occasional outings to the casino for an afternoon of penny slots. The truth was that Donna's inclination to be a joiner meant she was well suited for the assisted living lifestyle. Enjoying the activities and no longer having to worry about things like cooking or laundry balanced any sadness over leaving the familiarity and independence of home.

The desk phone rang, and Ellie took that as her cue to offer a friendly wave and go find her mom. As expected, Donna sat in the dining room with twenty or so other residents, eyes trained on the three bingo cards lined up in front of her.

"I-thirty," called a woman in bright pink scrubs. "I. Thirty."

Donna slid a marker into place on one of her cards, just as the woman across the table from her hollered, "Bingo!"

Mumbles of disappointment rippled through the room. An aide came over to check the winner's card and Ellie used the lull to slide into the empty seat next to her mom. "Have you won any?"

Mom pointed to a stack of four quarters above her cards. "One game."

"Well, a win is a win, right?"

"It sure is." Donna moved the markers to the side once her companion's win was confirmed. "Do you mind if we stay for the blackout?"

"I'd never pull you away," Ellie said with sincerity.

"Do you want me to ask if you can play?"

Ellie did a little wave with both hands. The mere chance she could deprive one of the residents of the five-dollar jackpot was deterrent enough. "Oh, no. I'll just watch you."

That got her a suit-yourself shake of the head but no argument. The blackout game started, and her mom's attention went to her cards. Ellie used the time to study the other residents. More women than men, which was to be expected. Several sat in wheelchairs, and a number of others had various styles of walkers parked next to them.

Her mother was definitely one of the younger people there, and probably more ambulatory than most. Other than the tremble in her hand—a side effect of the Seroquel her doctor had added to her list of prescriptions a few years prior—she had every appearance of good health. That was the thing with mental illnesses, though. They could be invisible. Until they weren't.

The truth of it was that Ellie still struggled sometimes with the exact ways her mother's schizophrenia manifested. On one hand, she had profound gratitude that the pharmaceutical cocktail her mom's psychiatrist constantly fine-tuned kept her mother calm and lucid and able to live with some degree of normalcy. On the other, the less sophisticated treatment methods Donna had endured during her teenage years—including some of the first wave antipsychotics and electroshock therapy without anesthesia—had blunted her emotional development and left Ellie feeling she lived with a peer more than a parent for much of her childhood.

Her own time in therapy had helped on that front. Ellie had made peace with the things she'd missed. Now, she could appreciate that her mom was physically well and never made Ellie question whether she was loved. It was more than a lot of people had.

The game ended when a gentleman with Down's syndrome edged out the competition with a fully covered bingo card. "Can't win them all," her mom said after an initial "phooey."

They headed back to Donna's room. "How's your week been?" Ellie asked.

"Good, I suppose. We had a visit from a group of Girl Scouts and did a craft project with them." Mom smiled softly. "It's good to be around kids since God only knows if you'll ever give me grandchildren."

Ellie nodded. Her mom didn't mean it as a dig, or at least not really. Her illness made her self-absorbed in ways that might feel toxic with another person. But Donna always had the best of intentions. In addition to making peace with things, Ellie's years in therapy allowed her to hold space for both the good intentions and the hurt that such comments caused regardless of intentions. "What did you make?"

Donna pointed to the riot of red, pink, and white hearts masquerading as a wreath. "Valentine's decorations."

It looked a little bit like a Party City store had vomited its Valentine aisle all over the otherwise defenseless door. But Donna loved color, so if it brightened her day, who was Ellie to rain on that parade? "It's so cute."

"I let one with pigtails and glasses decide what we should put on it."

Well, that explained that. "I'm sure she had a blast."

"I think so." Donna nodded. "She said her mommy told her 'more is more' and not to worry about going overboard."

Ellie chuckled at the advice. Better than the alternative, especially when it came to little girls navigating a world that wanted them to do and be the exact opposite. "Looks like you succeeded."

"I was hoping you could take me shopping for a few things."

Ellie was accustomed to abrupt conversational shifts, just as she was used to her mom's love of running errands for odds and ends she could easily ask Ellie to bring over. "Of course. I thought we might go out to dinner, too."

"That would be nice. I just need to get my purse."

For Donna, "getting her purse" would be a twenty-minute affair of sorting money, organizing tissues and hand sanitizer, and a trip to the bathroom. Oh, and the protracted process of switching house shoes for winter boots. She didn't mind, though. Her mother's fastidiousness around routines served as a proxy for her feeling in control. Even without experiencing schizophrenia firsthand, Ellie could appreciate her mother's needing that after being denied it in so many areas of her life.

While Donna puttered, Ellie took stock of the space. They'd decided to hold onto one of the wing chairs from the living room, along with Donna's dresser and nightstand. She'd worried the room might look crowded, but Donna kept it neat as a pin, so it felt both purposeful and personal.

Tidiness was a trait Ellie hadn't inherited, unfortunately. And without her mom's constant nudging, one she struggled with even more as an adult. She chalked it up to being an artist and free spirit, so she didn't lose sleep over it. There were plenty other things to worry about.

When Donna finally declared she was ready to go, Ellie headed to the front desk to sign her out, then pulled the car around to the front door. She checked her phone as her mom got settled in the passenger seat and found a text from Rhett about bonding with Jack over time spent in basements with projects. She smiled but tucked her phone away without responding. She'd text later when she was back home at Hampstead House. Now was the time for daughter mode, and while she was happy to do it, it always felt better to keep it separate from everything else.

Chapter Five

D o you have to be right here?" Ellie asked with a huff.
"Half the wiring to the second floor runs through this wall,
so yeah, I do." Under normal circumstances, Jack would respond with
a simple yes, claim his space, and go about his business. But nothing
about being around Ellie was normal. She bugged him, got under his
skin. Not an entirely unusual phenomenon—his family didn't call
him a curmudgeon for nothing. But when it came to Ellie, he couldn't
tell if she set him off because he didn't like her, or because he did.

Ellie's eyes narrowed with suspicion and had him worrying she
could read his thoughts. "Do you have to do it right now?"

Technically, no. But shifting to another part of the house would
mean upending the order of tasks he'd created for himself. He didn't
like changing his plans under the best of circumstances. Doing so
to appease Ellie? Not a chance in hell. "Yes. I'm pretty sure the
homeowner would say safe and functioning electric is more pressing
than making the walls pretty."

Suspicion gave way to disdain. To be fair, he'd managed to
insult her in addition to getting in her way. "Have you even met the
homeowner?"

He hadn't. Honestly, he didn't need to. He knew his scope of
work, the timeline, and the budget. Pablo signed checks and proved
competent enough to field any questions or snags he ran into along
the way. He'd simply been making a point. He lifted his chin. "Have
you?"

Something in her demeanor shifted. "No, and it's driving me crazy. I'm going to have to take some artistic license with some of these murals, and I'd really like her to weigh in on her preferences for color and tone. I've never taken on a commission without understanding who the client was and what they wanted."

If he weren't so busy proving his own point, he would have laughed at the vociferating. Not to make fun of Ellie, but because he finally got her. Or, rather, at least part of her. A shared passion for doing a job well and to the client's specifications officially gave them one thing in common.

He was spared having to say as much when Pablo swept in. "Darlings, I just got a call from Bea. She's on her way over to tour the progress so far."

Jack did laugh then—at the cosmic timing but also because Ellie looked like she was trying to decide who punked her.

"For real?" she asked.

Pablo shrugged. "Apparently. She's going to Montreal for the week and decided to take a detour."

Ellie nodded, all eager enthusiasm now. "That's great. I wanted to ask her a few things before I get too far into painting."

"You didn't want to ask me?" Pablo pressed a hand to his chest, feigning offense. Or at least Jack thought he was feigning.

Ellie put a hand on his arm in that easy confident way she had. "Of course I want your opinion. But art is so subjective. There's no way of knowing that what I like or you like would be at all what Ms. Castleton likes."

"That, my dear, is truth." Pablo laughed and put his hand on top of Ellie's.

Jack studied the gesture. With people like Logan and Clover in his life, it wasn't foreign. Still. It struck him just how different some people were from, well, people like him.

For all that people liked to say opposites attract, he spent most of his life presuming the opposite. Like the way Maddie and Sy butted heads at first but were two peas in a pod when it came down to it, and as a result perfect for each other. Yet, people like Logan—gregarious almost to a fault—wound up in love with someone as reserved as Kathleen.

What did that say about him? And when had he started contemplating the laws of attraction and compatibility? He chuckled at the out of character rumination. Logan would have such a field day.

"Care to share, sir?" Pablo regarded him with a raised brow and amused expression.

"Just lost in my own thoughts." He turned to Ellie. "You do your thing here. I'll go up to the attic and work on stripping out the old wires there."

If she didn't trust the magnanimity of his offer, she didn't let on. At least not out loud. "Thanks."

Jack went for a curt nod, suddenly wanting nothing more than a moment to himself. He started up the stairs, then realized he didn't have the tools or the supplies for the job he'd just announced he was going to do. He turned around and went back the way he'd come before getting into it with Ellie in the first place.

He gathered what he needed from his truck and was about to head in when a vintage Land Rover pulled into the small lot. Normally, he didn't go for showy cars or obvious displays of money, but damn. She was a beaut.

When the woman behind the wheel got out, he had a similar experience—a bit showy for his tastes but damn. She was gorgeous. He hung back, not wanting to fling himself into a social situation unnecessarily, especially with someone he'd never met.

He busied himself with every intention of waiting until she'd gone in, but it was not meant to be. He made the mistake of looking up too soon. She homed in on him, made eye contact, and he was stuck. He lifted a hand and tried for a friendly smile. "Good morning."

"And a very good morning to you." She strode over with all the confidence of a woman who owned the place.

Jack froze. Did she own the place? Was this Beatrice Castleton? The eccentric heiress who'd bought Hampstead for who knew what reason and was bankrolling what had to be a several-million-dollar renovation? Context clues told him it must be, though he'd expected someone older, starchier.

"I'm Bea." She extended a hand. "I'm the one with the bright idea to fix up this place."

Jack shuffled the supplies he held to accept the handshake, surprised by its firmness and vigor. With the proximity, he realized his initial assessment might have been off by a decade or so. Threads of silver streaked through Bea's hair and the lines around her eyes hinted at mid-forties rather than thirties. "I'm Jack, your electrician."

"Delightful. How's it going?"

He nodded, unsure whether she really wanted to know or if it was a rhetorical question. "It's progressing. I've never seen so much knob and tube in my life."

She quirked a brow. "I'm going to assume that's old wiring lingo."

He laughed in spite of himself. "Yes. Sorry."

"No need to apologize. I should probably know at least a little, right, as the person who bought it?"

He certainly thought so, but Maddie had trained him not to voice it to homeowners who had no interest in understanding the guts of their houses. "Just know that, by the time you move in, it will be fully upgraded, safe, and good to go for the next hundred years."

"That's good enough for me." Despite the fact that Jack's hands were full, she hooked her arm through his. "Walk me inside."

He awkwardly set down his tools and the roll of wire he'd planned to take up to the attic, knowing better than to say no. "So, what inspired you to buy this place?" he asked, figuring that was a safe enough topic of conversation to get them through the door.

"Oh, just your standard midlife crisis."

She'd said it casually, but Jack had the feeling he'd stepped on a landmine. "In a good way, I hope," he added, not sure how else to cover his tracks.

"Absolutely. My parents died, and I inherited a company I didn't really want to run. I decided to sell and be that weird lesbian who lives in a big house in the middle of nowhere, entertaining my equally weird friends and pretending the real world doesn't exist."

Jack scrambled for an appropriate response. It sounded sort of ideal—especially the part about hiding away from the real world. And yet everything about it sat so wholly outside his lived experience, he wasn't sure he should pretend to relate. He settled on, "That's quite a plan."

When they got to the back door, Bea released his arm and stepped to the side, clearly waiting for him to open it for her. He did, and she gave him a slow once-over and a knowing smile. "Perhaps you can be one of those friends."

She swept past him and into the house, not waiting for a reply. Pablo was waiting for her, and effusive greetings and hugs ensued. Jack stood in the doorway for a moment, not sure if he should follow or if he'd been dismissed. When Pablo gestured in the direction of the foyer, she headed that way without a backward glance.

It was enough of an answer for him. Unfortunately, Pablo caught his eye and waved him in. Jack sighed and spared a longing glance at the supplies he'd set down. They wouldn't take a walk in his absence, but at the rate he was going, he was going to spend more of his day making trips back and forth than getting anything done.

Ellie heard Bea before she saw her. She had a loud laugh and the kind of voice that came with being the center of attention. Ellie hovered in the foyer while Pablo rounded up the rest of the crew and made introductions. She reminded herself not to be intimidated.

Bea turned out to be charming and enthusiastic, if a little extra. Well, extra in the attention she showered on Jack. It wasn't even remotely subtle and left her struggling to keep a straight face. It did make her a hell of a lot less intimidating.

Pablo dismissed everyone back to their work so he and Bea could do a walkthrough of the house. Despite her vague discomfort, Ellie asked if she might beg a few minutes to go over some stylistic decisions that would affect the final look and feel of the downstairs murals. Bea agreed, and Pablo disappeared into the study to make a call.

Ellie did her best to explain the options in laymen's terms. Bea listened—intently for about a minute and then impatiently for another thirty seconds—before making a face.

"Am I overwhelming you?" Ellie asked.

Bea laughed. "Maybe."

"I just want you to be satisfied with the result." She resisted saying pleased, but barely.

Bea looked at Ellie, then the mural, and frowned. "I'm sure I will be. I want you using your talent to do whatever you think will look best."

It was a pastoral scene, probably meant to evoke rural Vermont, but it could just as easily have been England or France—the style and influence were that obvious. It had been painted in the 1830s, but the dress of the figures felt like a bit of a mashup. The original artist was unknown, but they seemed to have an eye on aesthetics more than authenticity. It probably would have maddened her professors, but Ellie kind of liked it.

"But?" Ellie asked when Bea continued to frown.

"But I want you to give it some character."

Ellie's mind raced but came up with nothing she could put a finger on. "Character?"

"Touch it up. Keep the overall look. But, like, make it gay."

She knew she hadn't misheard, but meaning escaped her. As did an appropriate response. "How so?"

Bea angled her head one way, then the other, before pointing to the picnicking couple in the bottom left corner. "What if you tweaked them just a little, made the man look like a butch woman."

It actually wouldn't be a stretch. The stylized nature of the painting made the figure borderline androgynous to begin with. A few adjustments to the face, a slight swell to the chest—and boom. "I could do that."

"And these two." She pointed to a pair of men standing with their horses. "Could you make them hold hands?"

That would be a bit more involved, but certainly doable with her skillset. "Yes."

"Does it bother you that I'm asking you to do that?" Bea asked.

"No. Of course not. I mean, I'm queer, actually." And not usually that awkward about coming out to someone.

Bea smiled. "I know."

Ellie blinked. Even most people with solid gaydar misread her if she wasn't with another queer person. "You do?"

"Not to sound creepy, but I had Pablo track down as many queer craftspeople and queer-owned businesses as he could find in a reasonable radius." Bea shrugged. "It's where I prefer to spend my money if I can."

Ellie loved the intentionality of that, even if it felt weirdly personal. "Oh."

"I wanted to know if doing that to the painting would be an affront to your artistic sensibilities."

"It's your house, your money," Ellie said reflexively. But then she did a gut check and added, "I think it's a great idea. Queer people obviously existed in this world. I feel more of an allegiance to them than to whoever painted this mural in the first place."

Bea's whole face lit up. "Exactly."

It struck her how much stock people in her line of work put into ideas of authenticity and accuracy. But holding true to the artist's intent wasn't the only way of accomplishing that. How funny that she'd never really thought of it that way before. "Are you hoping to have me do that with all the murals?"

"Yes. Absolutely." Bea gave a decisive nod.

Ellie's mind began to spin with possibilities.

"Wait," Bea said. "What if you went over-the-top with the one in the bathroom?"

"Over-the-top?" Ellie asked.

"Leave the composition of the painting as it is, but add things like feather boas to the men, five o'clock shadow to the women." Bea made circles with both hands, picking up speed with each embellishment. "Give them full drag makeup."

It was almost too easy to imagine. Irreverent in the best possible way. "Pastoral meets pride parade?"

"Yes!" Bea flung both arms skyward, like she'd won a prize. "You get it."

She did, and she was weirdly excited about it. "Do you want me to do some mockups of the design for you to approve?"

Bea waved her off. "I've seen your work. I trust you."

The thrill of that lasted all of three seconds before having a head-on collision with reality. "We can probably pass off the subtle changes without drawing attention to them, but I don't think the Historic Preservation folks are going to go for anything drastic."

For all her delight a moment before, Bea's expression darkened, like a summer storm cloud that appeared out of nowhere. "Pablo didn't tell you?"

Ellie's gaze flicked around the room, but he was nowhere in sight. "Tell me what?"

"We decided to sever our arrangement with them." Bea's eyes turned as frosty as her tone. "There were, let's say, irreconcilable differences."

Ellie had worked on some houses where the owner had wanted to do that and not been given the option. It made her wonder whether the house fell out of any formal jurisdiction for that level of oversight, or if Bea had somehow bought her way out of any contractual obligations. Either way, the result left her torn. On one hand, she loved the freedom it would afford—to make her own mark, to introduce queer themes, to take a few liberties when it came to color. On the other, she'd just lost a huge feather in her professional cap. This project would have been her first historic preservation as lead, an accomplishment that had the potential to open all sorts of other doors.

"You're not going to quit, are you?" Bea asked.

"No. No, of course not."

"Good. I'm not too worried about the rest of the contractors being purists, but I worried you might be." Bea let out a sniff of disdain.

Ellie was a lot of things. Purist was not one of them. But rather than take offense, she simply shrugged. "Pure preservation has its place. I don't think a person's home needs to be one of them."

"Tell that to the stick up their ass people at the Historic Preservation Trust." Bea rolled her eyes.

She'd pass on that, since several of those people were friends and—hopefully—future colleagues. But Bea didn't need to know those details. "I'm glad you're doing this project on your terms."

"Damn right I am. What's the point of a midlife crisis if you can't do what you want for once?"

Pablo appeared and summoned Bea for a consult in the kitchen about appliances. Ellie offered a smile and watched her go, more than a little relieved to have the conversation over and done. She wanted to like Bea, but something about her gave Ellie pause. The phrase loose cannon came to mind.

For better or worse, Ellie could sense emotional volatility from a mile away. Fortunately, she could handle it better than most. In this case, she'd avoid any personal fallout by steering clear and staying on Bea's good side. Hopefully, Bea was merely mercurial. Not her favorite thing in the world, but she'd certainly handled worse.

Chapter Six

"Thanks for coming with me." Jack glanced at Logan. "I have this irrational fear of adopting ten instead of one."

"That's the thing. It's not an entirely irrational fear." Logan chuckled with the wisdom of lessons learned the hard way. "Because they all deserve it."

"Then I'm doubly glad you're with me." Because as much as he might like to take them all home, he had limited space and not a whole lot of yard.

"For the record, sometimes two are genuinely better. They can keep each other company while you're at work."

Jack narrowed his eyes, losing confidence Logan would be able to maintain her Voice of Reason role. "You're supposed to talk me out of that sort of thing."

Logan wagged a finger, looking every part their parents' octogenarian neighbor. "No, I'm supposed to make sure you don't leave with more than you can handle. That's not the same thing."

Those were the words he'd used. Only now did he realize lack of specificity had the potential to get him into trouble. "You damn well better hold me to at least that."

Inside, a single woman worked the reception desk. Other than a few chairs and a box for donations, the waiting room sat empty. "Good afternoon," the woman said. "How can I help you today?"

"My brother here is looking to add a new member to his family," Logan said before Jack could decide on the right phrasing.

"Well, you're in the right place." The woman—her name tag said Susan—beamed and shifted her attention to Jack. "Have you looked at our website? Is there someone in mind you'd like to meet?"

Jack cringed. He totally should have done that beforehand. "No, actually. I, um, just thought I'd show up. It's my first time."

Susan's eyes narrowed slightly. "First time at this shelter or first time adopting a pet?"

He froze, gripped with the sort of performance anxiety that used to come with having to give presentations in school. Was there a test? Should he have studied?

"First time adopting solo. We grew up with animals and he's spent more time with my senior poodle mix than I have over the last couple of months." Logan gave a casual flick of the wrist. "He's realized what an empty nest he has now that she's back with me full-time, so he's finally going to bite the bullet and become a daddy. And since he looks tough but is really a tender heart, I'm here to make sure he doesn't take everyone home."

"I'm standing right here," he said, exasperation chasing away the misgivings.

Susan offered him a sympathetic smile. "We actually wouldn't let you take them all home."

Jack cleared his throat. "Thank you. I promise I wouldn't actually try."

"Oh, good."

Between Susan's reassuring tone and Logan's playful elbow to his ribs, Jack relaxed. "So, yes. Looking to adopt. Probably older and on the smaller side since that's what I'm used to, and I don't have a huge yard or hiking habit."

Susan nodded. "It's good to know what you offer and not just what you want. Let's go take a look at our small dog space."

He expected something cold and sterile, all concrete and chain-link fence. That's what the tear-jerker commercials had planted in his mind. This area had the requisite concrete floors, but soothing paint colors and plexiglass partitions made it feel at least a little homey.

"We've only got five in our under-forty suite right now, including a bonded pair that came in last week when their owner passed away unexpectedly. Their bios are on each door, but I'm also happy to share what I know. Take some time to look around and let me know who you might want to do a meet and greet with." Susan stepped off to the side, sending the message that she wouldn't hover but had no intention of leaving them with the animals unattended.

Jack, as overwhelmed as he expected to be, turned his attention to the dogs. A quick survey assured him they were all cute and deserving of infinite treats and belly rubs. He read each bio, chuckling at how cleverly they conveyed shyness, a penchant for underwear stealing, and a variety of other traits. When he got to the bonded pair, he tried to skim the sheet since falling in love with one meant committing to both.

It worked for about fifteen seconds. Dorothy, the beagle mix, had soulful eyes and floppy ears. Sophia was—best guess—a terrier of some kind mixed with a pug. She had a curly tail, ears that stuck out to the side, and wiry brown and black fur that stuck out at jaunty angles. They sat curled together on the platform bed in their room and regarded him with what he could only describe as a world-weary curiosity. "Hi, you two."

"Uh-oh," Logan said, looking from Jack to the dogs and back.

"They seem so sad." Jack clicked his tongue. Their ears perked, but they didn't get up.

"They're both ten. Their owner had them since they were puppies." Logan let out a sigh. "They must be so confused."

He knew this sort of thing happened all the time. And really, it wasn't the saddest of the circumstances that landed animals in shelters. Still. Something about this pair spoke to him. "You did say two could be better."

"I did." Logan nodded slowly. "I could warn you about the challenges of caring for a senior, but I feel like you already know."

He did. He adored Kiwi, even as her sight and hearing started to fade and her accidents in the house grew more common. More than anything, he loved the mellow way she showed affection and made her way in the world. "I think my mind is made up."

Logan clamped a hand on his shoulder. "Congratulations, Pops."

An hour and a crap ton of paperwork later, the four of them emerged with all the eagerness and speed of a toddler in a snowsuit.

After a lengthy stop at the pet store—during which Dot and Sophia rode in the cart like the princesses they were—they headed home. Back at Jack's, Logan offered to unload while Jack took the dogs for a walk.

They made it to the stop sign, but he resisted taking them around the block since the temps remained well below freezing. "We'll work up to it, girls. Spring and summer are for nice long walks."

He explained this, and a number of other things, as they made their way up the short brick path from the sidewalk to the house. He also inquired about whether they liked their new coats and if they might be interested in trying booties to keep the salt from their paws. He was so focused on the two of them, he didn't notice Rhett and Ellie until they both let out gasps.

"Well, who do we have here?" Rhett asked.

Jack did introductions, both canine and human, since neither Ellie nor Rhett had met Logan. It made him realize that perhaps the one downside of getting dogs was the increased likelihood people would want to talk to him when they were out and about. Rhett bent and extended a hand for inspection—clearly practiced in the ways of dogs. Ellie, on the other hand, was on the ground, beyond enamored. She didn't cross any of the lines that people sometimes did, which would have really bugged him, but she did talk to them like they were the cutest and most remarkable creatures she'd ever encountered. The whole thing left Logan grinning and him standing there awkwardly, wishing for a graceful exit strategy.

Fortunately, Rhett came to the rescue, reminding Ellie they had somewhere to be and venturing that Jack and his new pups might like to go inside and start settling in. Ellie blushed and apologized, and Jack pretended hardcore that her blushing didn't affect him. Everyone went their separate ways.

But of course, that couldn't be the end of it. He'd no sooner closed the door behind them and unhooked the leashes when Logan started in.

"You didn't tell me the artist you have the hots for is friends with the potter who's your new tenant," Logan said as she set down the bags of food, treats, and other supplies they'd picked up,

"I don't have the hots for her, which makes who her friends are irrelevant." He contemplated washing the new beds before setting them out, but since he wanted to give the dogs a nice bath after they'd rested from the day's adventure, he figured all that could be done together. He set them on the floor next to the fireplace. Dorothy climbed into one and Sophia promptly joined her. Jack smiled at them before grabbing the bag of food and heading to the kitchen.

Logan followed. "You don't have to like having the hots for her, but don't pretend you don't. It insults my intelligence."

Jack dumped kibble into the bin he'd used for Kiwi's food. "Maybe I like insulting your intelligence."

"Weak."

It was, and he knew it. "They're best friends from college, apparently."

"Oh, that's fun. Where did they go?"

Jack rolled his eyes. "Smith."

Logan laughed. "Of course they did."

The queer world was a small one. As was New England. Put the two together and it felt like a novelty to meet someone who wasn't connected somehow. One of the reasons he didn't fling himself into the dating pool very often. One of many, but one. "So, yes. Even if I'd been inclined to have—or act on having—the hots for Ellie, now that I know she's all up in my worlds, I'm not going to touch that with a ten-foot pole."

Logan lifted her chin. "You keep talking about her like that and I don't think she'd have you."

He preferred avoiding to alienating women, but Logan would consider that splitting hairs. "If that's the case, then maybe I will."

"You're the worst sometimes. You know that, right?"

Instead of arguing, Jack turned his attention to the dogs, who remained settled together on one of the two beds. They looked perfectly content and about two seconds from falling asleep. He smiled at their uncomplicated approach to life. These were the women he understood.

❖

After a day of shopping and dinner in Bennington, complete with loads of teasing about Jack, Ellie decided to accept Rhett's offer to crash at her place.

"Wine?" Rhett asked.

"Yes, please." Ellie pulled the slippers from her just-in-case duffel bag and slid her socked feet into them.

"Let me see what I have." Rhett went to the wine rack and pulled out a bottle. "Syrah?"

"Yum." She leaned against the doorframe while Rhett got out a corkscrew and a pair of glasses. "Oh. I didn't tell you about meeting Bea."

"Bea Castleton, the pickle heiress who hired you as part of her multi-million dollar renovation of the historic mansion she bought as her private residence?"

Ellie laughed. "Yes, that one."

"How did it go?"

"Eh?" She tipped her head back and forth. "It was okay. She's…a character."

"What do you mean, she's a character?" Rhett popped the cork and eyed Ellie with curiosity.

Ellie wagged a finger. "Don't pretend you don't know what that means. You're from the South."

Rhett poured wine into the waiting glasses and handed Ellie one. "Oh, no. That's an umbrella term that covers all manner of sins. Calling her a character might mean she's a hoot, and it might mean she's a raging asshole."

She let her shoulders slump. "What do you call someone who's a hoot one minute and a raging asshole the next?"

"My mother."

Ellie snorted. They'd been friends long enough for her to know Rhett was only partially kidding, but she didn't apologize or prod. They'd also been friends long enough that Rhett would tell her if something new happened and she needed to vent.

"Sorry. Couldn't resist." Rhett lifted her glass in playful resignation and took a sip. "Seriously, though. Was she an asshole to you?"

"No, no. Nothing like that." Ellie took a sip of her own wine while she decided what to say. "It's just, I get the feeling she could be, you know? Like cross a line with her and look the fuck out."

Rhett nodded slowly. "I'm familiar."

"It makes me sad because she's queer and what she wants me to do with the murals is so cool. But I don't feel like I can let my guard down."

"You should trust your gut, though. You're so good at reading people. If that's the vibe you're picking up, that's the vibe she's putting out. Whether she intends to or not." Rhett tipped her head and stared at seemingly nothing in particular. "It's a shame."

"Yeah." Fortunately, Ellie didn't anticipate seeing much, if any, more of her.

"Did Jack share your read?"

She flinched, sending her wine sloshing over the rim of her glass. Just enough to leave a dark, purplish-red splotch on her light pink T-shirt. "Shit."

"You okay? What did I say?"

Ellie rolled her eyes. "Nothing."

"Obviously not."

How could she describe the icky feeling she got when Bea practically draped herself on Jack without sounding idiotic or, worse, jealous? "I didn't talk to him after she left."

"Okay. Reasonable. But that doesn't explain your Miss Butterfingers moment."

Ellie groaned. If she couldn't be an idiot in front of her best friend, what was the point? "Bea was all over him. Like, all over. It was gross. You just reminded me of it is all."

Rhett leaned forward, propping her chin on her fist. "Is the nature of your ew rooted in her behavior in general or the person on the receiving end?"

"The nature of my ew?" God, she loved this woman.

"Don't evade with a critique of my rhetorical choices."

"I'm not evading." She huffed. "Okay, I am. Mostly the behavior in general. But a little the fact it was Jack."

"Because?" Rhett asked, all innocence.

Ellie laughed. "You know, I can't decide whether I'm irritated that he would lap that up or worried that he doesn't know better and might get himself into trouble."

"Fascinating."

It so didn't help that Rhett now lived next door to Jack. "I mean, I find him attractive. Obviously."

"Obviously."

"But he's so damn aloof, I'm not sure I want to be in the same room as him." Which was painful to admit as a girl whose identity had a lot tied up in being able to bring out the best in people.

"Oh, you've got it bad, don't you?" Rhett's expression was equal parts teasing and pity.

"Yep." She gulped her wine, oddly relieved to have admitted it.

"What are you going to do about it?" Rhett asked.

"Nothing." She lifted a finger. "Well, not nothing. I'm going to be my usual charming self, and it's either going to wear him down or drive him bananas. And I'm going to be okay with either."

Rhett laughed so hard she had to set down her glass and wipe her eyes. "Yeah you are."

She shrugged, resolved as much as relieved now. "Ball's in his court. We'll see."

"You know how badly I want to make a balls joke, right?"

Rhett might be the wisest and most insightful person in her life, but it didn't mean she didn't also have the mentality of a thirteen-year-old boy at times. "I do know. Does that mean you're going to exercise restraint?"

Rhett sighed. "Restraint is overrated."

They both joked about that, but when push came to shove, neither of them made a habit of being reckless or impulsive. Not in life and not in love. Rhett had stayed in a crappy marriage a lot longer than she should have, and Ellie had fallen in love but managed to steer clear of the kind that might truly break her heart. "Hey, you got me to admit I have the hots for him. That has to count for something."

"A doorknob would have the hots for him," Rhett said. "At least one whose general attractions included trans guys."

Rhett did not fall into that category, but Ellie loved that she made a point of appreciating things outside her own scope of desire. So many people—queer or otherwise—went out of their way to put on blinders in that regard. It was so pedestrian. "Well, this doorknob loves her a trans guy."

"Even if he's cranky?"

Ugh. So ridiculous. "Even if he's cranky."

Chapter Seven

Jack was not one to obsess. He reminded himself of that fact as he obsessed over Ellie's car in the driveway for the entire weekend. Well, obsessed might be an overstatement. But he noticed it each and every time he passed the front window, each and every time he took the dogs for a walk.

It didn't help that he'd made a point of spending most of the weekend at home to make sure Dot and Sophia were getting acclimated to their new home. Which also meant minimal time puttering in the basement on one project or another. Even curling up on the sofa with one of Kathleen's romance novels failed to hold his attention.

Again and again, his thoughts drifted to Ellie. Her cheerful smile, her way of teasing him about one thing or another. And, if he was being honest, the look of irritation in her eyes when she saw Bea fawning all over him. Which was the sort of thing that should have made him chuckle if not roll his eyes.

And yet.

He'd also had more than a passing thought about kissing her. Wondering if her mouth would yield under his, what she would taste like. Imagining what those quick and agile fingers would feel like playing across his skin.

It was all the more annoying since he had no intention or opportunity to act on it. They worked together for Pete's sake. Not that such a trivial detail had stopped either of his siblings from falling in love with a client. But Ellie wasn't even that. She was a colleague. Sort of. Fellow contractor. He had a code.

A lot of good his code did him on Monday morning when Ellie's SUV still sat behind Rhett's. Taunting him. Making him wonder if Ellie and Rhett were the sort of best friends that came with benefits. Not that it was any of his goddamn business.

Gah.

And now he had to get dressed and go to work and bump into her. On top of which, it was snowing, which would make his drive notably less relaxing. And his dogs were giving him do-you-have-to eyes. He ate his oatmeal grumbling, wondering if he should try to beat Ellie in leaving or wait her out. He settled on the former, always preferring to be early than risk being late.

"I know. I wish I didn't have to go either." Jack arranged the throw blankets on the couch so Dot and Sophia could each have their own, either to dig up as a bed or to burrow under like the filling of a doggie burrito. "At least on days like this. Snowy winter days should be for good books and big snuggles."

They snuffled their agreement, but didn't waste time waiting on him to make themselves comfortable. He tugged on his boots and coat and spared one final look out the front door. Ellie's car remained, covered with the same three inches of snow as his truck, but there was no sign of her. Perfect. He grabbed his things and stepped onto the front porch the exact moment Ellie did. Because of course.

"Good morning," Ellie said, in all her perky glory.

He tried to ignore the way her periwinkle puffer jacket made her eyes seem even bluer and gave what he hoped was a friendly nod. "Morning."

"How are your girls settling in? Were they sad to see you leave?" That playful smile—that had visited more than one of his dreams—spread across Ellie's lips.

Jack cleared his throat, annoyed that she asked such a perfect question and annoyed that he noticed the way her jeans hugged her thighs. "Logan is going to check on them around lunchtime."

Her features softened, even though his answer had been both evasive and impersonal. "Maybe it's harder for you to leave them than the other way around."

He couldn't help but laugh at that. Because for all his preference for solitude when it came to people, he was a total softie for animals, and Sophia and Dot had already taken prime real estate in his cold, curmudgeonly heart. "Something like that."

"It's always the way. I've been gone one night, and I fully expect Emily Dickinson to have me scrambling to make it up to her with nothing more than a tail flick and a look."

Jack opened his mouth, then closed it, not sure context clues got him all the way to knowing what the hell she was talking about.

"Oh. My cat. Emily Dickinson is my cat."

"Ah." Why had he even doubted himself?

"Anyway." She tipped her head toward the shared driveway. "We should probably get going."

Seriously? She was telling him to stop chitchatting? "Do you, uh, need help brushing off your car?"

Ellie smirked. "I think I'm good, but thanks."

She sashayed down the steps, and it hit him she probably took his offer as a come-on. A clumsy one at that. He let out a low growl and strode to his truck. After getting the defrost going, he made quick work of the windshield and windows. Between his hurrying and Ellie's surprising meticulousness, he finished before she'd made it halfway around her vehicle. He had another pang of feeling like he should offer to help before kicking himself and going on his way.

He beat her to Hampstead House, obviously, and used the few minutes lead time to haul more coils of wire inside and down to the basement. Other contractors had arrived and were already at work. Pablo swept from room to room, making sure people who needed to consult with each other were introduced. Jack made a point of connecting with the foreman of the main crew, since she'd be overseeing the rearranging of walls and other things that affected him. All the while, he had to resist the urge to peek out the window for proof Ellie had arrived safely.

It became a moot point when he practically ran into her in the main hall where they'd first met. He'd come up to confirm the configuration of the appliances slated to go in the kitchen, and Ellie was heading to the study, all but swaddled in a drop cloth.

"Sorry," she said around the tangled mass of canvas.

"Need a hand?"

"What makes you ask?" Ellie laughed, then gave the end dragging on the floor a kick. "I think I've got it."

"Do you always turn down offers of help?" he asked, then immediately wished he hadn't.

Her eyes narrowed for the briefest of moments, but that playful smile slid almost instantly into place. "Depends on who you ask."

The coy answer irritated him, perhaps because he'd asked her. Literally. "I guess I'll stop offering, then."

"Oh, no. I didn't mean it like that. I just…" Ellie adjusted the drop cloth in her arms, then attempted to blow a wisp of hair from in front of her eyes. "Bad habit. Thank you for offering."

Was that a yes or a no? And perhaps more importantly, how did he keep getting into these pseudo-conversations with her? For someone who prided himself on keeping to himself, he wound up talking to Ellie at every turn. "How about I get the door?"

"Perfect. Thank you."

He swung the door wide and she swept past, trailing a corner of the drop cloth behind her. "Any time."

She glanced at him over her shoulder, complete with a smirk and wink Logan would insist was flirtatious. "I'll keep that in mind."

The days marched on. Ellie tried to flirt with Jack. Jack stubbornly resisted. It had become a game, almost, seeing how long she could hold him in conversation before he gruffly excused himself and disappeared into another part of the house. She tried to tell herself it was all in good fun, but the truth of the matter was that she'd started to get on her own nerves.

Like this morning. Ellie had barely finished her coffee when the banging started. She generally prided herself on being a morning person, but sleep had been elusive for going on a week now. Not that she didn't sleep at all. More that she woke at every unfamiliar sound, often from the sort of dream that didn't count as a nightmare but left her mind spinning.

"Sexual frustration," Rhett had said knowingly when they'd met for dinner the night before.

She'd rolled her eyes but couldn't bring herself to argue. Mostly because it was true, and she'd never been big on lying. "I just can't figure him out. He's cranky one minute and disarmingly considerate the next. Some days I feel like he's avoiding me like the plague and others we're practically tripping over each other at every turn."

"Sounds like he's into you but doesn't know what to do about it."

She'd considered the possibility. "He's not awkward, though, you know? It's more like we're talking and it's nice and maybe even bordering on flirty, and then he suddenly catches himself and gets annoyed and sulks off to pout by himself for a few hours."

Rhett had laughed at the assessment. "Oh, so he likes you but doesn't want to."

That was the bit that had stayed with her the last few days, had laced her own interactions with Jack and made them even more stilted. She had half a mind to start avoiding him. It wasn't how she worked, though. Not with people in general and certainly not with someone she felt drawn to. Okay, fine. Attracted to.

Reading people—sussing out in an instant what would make them smile or simply feel more at ease—was her superpower. She wasn't about to hang up her cape because Jack Barrow remained an enigma. Who pouted.

With the satisfaction of a woman who'd settled something hanging over her head, she finished getting ready for the day. Since she planned to spend it starting the paint work in the study, she donned her favorite overalls and the Chuck Taylors that bore the drips and splats of dozens, if not hundreds, of projects.

She opened the door to the main house, debating whether to seek Jack out or simply make a point of running into him over the course of the day. A notification ping on her phone stopped her in her tracks. She looked at the screen and frowned. The moderate snowfall predicted yesterday had turned into a blizzard warning, with heavy accumulations starting midafternoon. Dammit.

Ellie took a deep breath and considered her options. Work a half day and go hunker with Rhett? Go forage for provisions now and be prepared to ride things out here? Since she had a crap ton of work to do, and since she'd lived through more than one blizzard warning that fizzled into a few inches of snow, she settled on the latter. Running into Jack would just have to wait.

At the store, she bought the basic snowstorm fare—coffee and creamer, a loaf of sandwich bread, peanut butter, some canned soup and crackers, and jarred pasta sauce. Funny how similar that was to her standard grocery list right now given her limited kitchen facilities. But since it was blizzard preparation, she rocked a little bit of the unsupervised child in a convenience store vibe, too. Jalapeño popper flavored cheese puffs, peanut butter cups, and a giant bag of gummy bears. If she might wind up stuck by herself for a couple of days, she wanted it to feel like a party, not a prison.

After loading up her groceries, she made a detour to the wine store. She indulged in a mixed case of red, more because the ten percent discount equated to a free bottle than any intentions of drinking herself into a stupor. Though she considered wine on par with chocolate in situations like this—always better to be prepared. She stopped by the pet store to grab an extra bag of Emily Dickinson's preferred food and headed home.

By the time she got back to the house, it was just after noon, and the snow had started to fall. She found Pablo in the kitchen, encouraging people to head home within the hour and hunker safely. He turned to her with a look of concern. "And you, my little chickadee. Will you be okay?"

"Well, I've got blankets, junk food, and twelve bottles of wine to keep me company."

He laughed. "Forget going home to my husband. I'm staying here with you."

Ellie grinned. There were certainly worse people to be stuck with. "You're welcome, though it would require sharing a bed with a girl."

"And that's my cue to go," he said.

"I thought so. Drive safe and I'll see you in a couple of days if we get hit as hard as they're saying."

Pablo's expression turned serious. "I'm prepared to call a snow day. If that happens, don't feel like you have to be the only one working."

She appreciated that he'd extend the pass to her, even though she and most of the crew were paid by the project and not the hour. "I'll play it by ear. Depends on how well the heat holds."

Pablo rolled his eyes. "If the new furnace fails its first blizzard, just shoot me."

She wasn't really worried about that and doubted he was, either. Still, she knocked on a piece of door trim. No point jinxing things when she'd be the only one here to deal with it.

The house emptied quickly. She'd spent enough nights and weekends alone not to find the quiet eerie. If anything, the way the snow muffled sounds from the outside lent a peaceful quality. Like a greeting card, or a snow globe.

Too bad the chimney work hadn't been completed yet. It was easy to imagine building a big fire and curling up in the study with a good book and a glass of cabernet, pretending she was the eccentric recluse, tucked away in her manor house. She'd have to settle for a cozy chair in the corner of her little room. But since the good book and glass of wine came with that scenario as well, she wasn't about to complain.

The only question that remained was whether to put in a reasonable workday first or get right to it.

Chapter Eight

Jack stepped back from the panel, pleased with his work. He'd already installed the new one and had most of the breakers hardwired in. But today had been about pulling a lot of the knob and tube that needed to go, tidying the lines that would run to various parts of the house, and creating the schematic that would tell the new owner exactly which breaker controlled what. A painfully tedious job, but so damn satisfying, he couldn't bring himself to mind.

He rolled his neck and shoulders a few times, working out the knots that settled when he stayed in one position too long. Then he pressed his palms to one of the floor joists overhead and stretched. As he did, his eye caught a blanket of white covering the small window at the far end of the basement. "Huh."

Must be snowing harder than he realized. Which he'd honestly take over the sleety slushy mess they often got as winter slogged its way toward spring. Even if he didn't love driving in it.

He gathered his tools and checked his watch. Just after four. He'd check in with Pablo and see what rooms upstairs were ready to have light fixtures installed. That should keep him busy until quitting time.

Jack climbed the stairs, pausing halfway. The house was eerily quiet. Odd. Maybe some of the crew knocked off early. Hopefully it was that and not some major snag that ground work to a halt. Those were the worst. He opened the basement door to that same eerie quiet, paired with the borderline creepy dimness that came with gray skies and no lights on. Where was everyone?

A sound came from the study, but it wasn't banging or sawing or drilling. Nor was it the sound of work boots striding around, cleaning up a day's work. It was singing, or at least it was trying to be. Someone was butchering Taylor Swift's latest—not loudly, but with feeling.

Jack approached with caution, not out of fear for his safety, but because he had a sneaking suspicion whose voice it was. Ellie wasn't the only female member of the crew, but she was the most obvious. Not to mention the one most likely to be working solo. And, if he was being honest, the one most likely to indulge in a singalong no matter who might be around to suffer through it.

The door was cracked, so he pushed it open slowly. It was Ellie, all right. Clutching a palette in one hand and a paintbrush in the other. And what she lacked in vocal talent, she more than made up for with dance moves. He so never wanted to be that guy, but all he could think was *damn*.

Ellie rolled her hips one way, then the other. She arched her neck and bumped her chest back and forth. Not overtly sexual, but with the rhythm and confidence that announced she was the sort of woman who could do all manner of things with her body. He hated himself for going there, but again. *Damn.*

She spun his way and promptly jumped back, screamed, and dropped her paintbrush. Fortunately, the thumb she had hooked through the palette kept it from falling. Or flying.

"Sorry," he said before realizing she likely couldn't hear a word he said.

She pulled out the earbuds. "What are you still doing here?" Ellie asked, though it sounded more like an accusation than a question.

"Working." Jack matched Ellie's accusatory tone with an exasperated one of his own. "It's not even five."

"But a blizzard is coming,"

Snow had been in the forecast, but no more than four to six inches. As long as roads were being plowed, that was barely enough to bat an eye at. Certainly not enough to warrant panic. Or an admonishing mother tone. "I know. Notice I stopped before dark."

She flung out an arm, pointing at the window. "The forecast changed. It's a fucking blizzard."

Snow fell fast and heavy, and the flakes swirled with the vigor of a nor'easter. That didn't necessarily mean major accumulation, though, much less a blizzard. "How much are they predicting?"

"Two inches an hour overnight with up to three feet total by this time tomorrow."

"Shit."

"No shit, shit. Do you not pay attention to, oh I don't know, the news, the emergency alert system, or what's literally happening outside your window?"

"I was in the basement." It sounded weak even to him. That tiny rectangle covered in white notwithstanding.

Ellie rolled her eyes, the mother hen attitude giving way to that mirth he'd tried to explain to Logan. "Well, you're stuck now."

"I'm not stuck." He had four-wheel drive and a lifetime of experience driving in Vermont winters.

"Pretty sure you are."

Why did she seem so fucking amused? If he was stuck, that meant they were stuck together. "I'm going to go out and see how bad it is."

"Suit yourself."

He put on his coat and went to the back door. He opened it to a gust of wind and a slap of snow to the face. After blinking away what had blown into his eyes, he surveyed the situation. The steps from the small back porch to the parking area were a barely defined mound. He could see the shape of his truck, but the drifts had already risen to the wheel wells. "Shit."

Ellie appeared behind him, her face poking around his shoulder. "Let me guess. You're stuck."

"I can't be stuck." He didn't have clothes or food. Dot and Sophia were waiting for him to get home.

"I think you're confusing 'can't' with 'really don't want to.' It's a common mistake." Despite the sarcasm of her words, her voice kept that infuriatingly chipper tone.

"Could you stop being so fucking clever about everything for a second? I need to think." As in, figure out his options and execute the best one before the situation got any worse.

Ellie didn't leave. She stood there, arms folded, like she was waiting for him to perform. Since going outside would accomplish little more than making him cold and wet, he stalked to the front of the house and pulled out his phone.

He'd missed a flurry of texts on the family group chat—questions about who'd be in charge of plowing and making sure everyone had groceries and adequate emergency supplies. If the Barrows were discussing emergency supplies, the storm was no joke. Fortunately, things weren't so dire yet that anyone was worried about his lack of response. That would have made him feel like an ass on top of feeling like an idiot.

He squeezed his eyes shut, knowing there'd be both ribbing and concern, before typing a reply.

I'm still at the job site. Lost track of time working in the basement and missed the blizzard warning.

Maddie replied immediately with *Dude* and Logan chimed in with *I think the roads are too bad for a rescue mission.*

He assured everyone he could survive for a day or two on the bottled water and snacks he kept in his truck. He had heat and shelter and, though he'd just as soon do without, company. Logan offered to pick up Dot and Sophia when she did a first plow of the family properties before it got dark. All in all, it was nowhere near the end of the world. So why did it feel like it was?

"So?" Ellie asked when Jack finally put his phone away, fully prepared to gloat.

"So, it looks like I'm stuck."

She smirked. "You could be a good sport and say it looks like I was right."

He scowled. "Why would I give you the satisfaction?"

"Goodness of your heart?" She batted her eyelashes in a way that would make Rhett proud. "Or perhaps because I'm the one who lives here, and you've basically invited yourself over for the night."

She'd meant to make a joke, but Jack's scowl turned into this stern, stoic expression that was oddly even more ominous. "The house is big. I'll be sure to stay out of your way."

"That's not what I—"

He lifted a hand, essentially cutting her off. "Look, I don't want to be here any more than you want me here. I'm going to go out to my truck for the supplies I have with me, then I'll go upstairs and stay out of your hair."

Ellie opened her mouth to tell him to take a freaking chill pill already, or that she was a nice person who'd happily share her supplies, but he didn't give her the chance. He stormed off, only to return a minute later with his coat. He tugged a wool hat over his head and strode out into the snow, grabbing the shovel Pablo had put by the door and digging a path in the direction of his truck.

She hovered for a moment, debating whether to offer assistance or watch him slog along by himself. Slog was putting it mildly. She could tell from the crisp lines the shovel made with each scoop that it was the sort of wet, heavy snow that made for fantastic snowmen and backbreaking work.

In the end, she settled on neither. Since there was only one shovel, there was little she could do to help. And something told her half an hour of shoveling snow and freezing his ass off would do little to improve Jack's demeanor. Even if his shoulders and ass looked great doing it.

Ellie retreated to the study, hoping to get her mojo back. She left the earbuds in her pocket, wanting to hear if Jack called her. Oh, and not wanting him to scare the living bejesus out of her again. She cleaned her now dusty paintbrush and stared at the mural, willing herself to remember what she'd been doing before being so rudely interrupted.

She'd meant to lighten the mood, not piss Jack off. But of course, a guy like Jack wouldn't appreciate that. And now she was stuck with him, and instead of his usual grumpy state, she had to contend with him being actively mad at her.

Great.

Knowing she needed a distraction and reset if she had any chance of regaining her focus, she settled cross-legged on the drop cloth on the floor. She called her mom to check in but got voicemail. Probably she was at dinner already, and Donna had strong feelings about phones at the dinner table. It still counted as a dose of daughterly duty, though, so she let herself off the hook and texted Rhett to commiserate.

Being the absolute champ of a best friend that she was, Rhett responded immediately. *I'm sorry. Let me get this straight. You're trapped in that big old house, in a blizzard, with the guy you have the hots for?*

Ellie blew out a breath. *Basically. But he's even grumpier than usual.*

I feel like I should remind you he's never been grumpy with me.

That warranted a groan. *Why? Why do you feel like you should remind me of that?*

Because I think Jack thinks you're pretty.

It wasn't the first time Rhett had said as much. Hell, Rhett insinuated a hell of a lot more than that on a regular basis. And while Ellie didn't mind the teasing, in this instance, it only served to amplify the fact that being around Jack was like trying to get up close and personal with a cactus. *Well, unless you can convince him of that fact, that's a whole lot of no help.*

That got her a shrug emoji followed by *Ask him if he needs me to do anything.*

She wanted to be annoyed on principle, but it was a valid thing to offer, considering Rhett was literally next door. Oh, and his dogs were probably there. Ugh. *Okay. Let me give him a hot minute to get back inside and I'll go look for him.*

Rhett didn't respond, so Ellie hefted herself off the floor and picked up her paintbrush. Focus. She just needed to focus. On her work and not the hot guy grumbling about his poor choices.

It worked, sort of. She managed to add a more structured jaw and some five o'clock shadow to one of the figures lounging with a parasol. And maybe it was Jack's face front and center in her mind, but it wasn't like she turned the person in the painting into a ginger.

The thought made her giggle, which, in turn made her sigh. Not a sigh of relief, exactly, but the kind that came with remembering who she was and what she was about. There was literally zero reason to let Jack get under her skin. If he chilled the fuck out enough to be friendly—or flirt—that would be great. If not, she could be unflappably nice. And if that got under his skin, well, that was his problem.

CHAPTER NINE

The annoying thing about manual labor was that it gave the brain plenty of time to stew. By the time Jack cleared a path to his truck, gathered the random snacks that would constitute both his dinner and breakfast, and trudged back to the house, he was exhausted. Being wrong really took it out of a guy.

"I owe you an apology," Jack said after finding Ellie back at work in the study, reminding himself that a willingness to say sorry counted as a sign of maturity.

"Yeah, you do." Ellie folded her arms, clearly not willing to let him off the hook so easily.

He'd be dead before admitting it, but he liked that about her. Respected it. "I panicked. Now that I have dogs, I make a point of getting home at a reasonable hour. And with Logan not right next door, I don't have a built-in backup."

Admitting the source of his freak-out made him feel foolish, but it was clearly the right card to play. Ellie's features softened. "You're allowed to worry about your babies."

If a tiny part of him wanted to argue that descriptor, the rest of him knew it was one hundred percent true. "It doesn't excuse my behavior, though."

Ellie smiled. "No, but it makes me inclined to give you a pass. Were you able to arrange someone to take care of them? I'm sure Rhett wouldn't mind."

He'd considered that. Would have called her if he hadn't been able to get ahold of Logan. "I got through to my sister. It's not quite as bad up in Bedlington yet, plus she volunteered to do the first round of plowing the family driveways. She's going to pick them up and take them back to her house."

A shadow of what looked like sadness passed through Ellie's eyes, but it disappeared so fast, Jack wasn't sure he hadn't imagined it. "I'm glad."

"Do you have siblings?" he asked before he could help himself. Ellie shook her head. "Just me."

"Are you close with your parents?" Maybe it was remorse loosening his lips, trying to compensate for being an ass with the social niceties normal people exchanged as a matter of politeness.

"My dad passed when I was fifteen. I'm kind of close to my mom, but it's..." Ellie frowned. "It's complicated."

Since he typically went out of his way to avoid engaging in said niceties, the comment left him at a loss. Was that code for "please ask me more" or "I don't want to talk about it"? Clover's face appeared in his mind, like a little fairy of empathy and grace. With it, one of her signature phrases for conundrums like this. "That sounds hard."

Ellie shrugged with a smile that screamed "thanks but I really don't want to talk about it."

"So." He might be able to read the cue, but it didn't mean he knew where to go next.

"So." Her smile became more of a smirk. "Does that mean you're staying with me tonight?"

Jack blew out a breath—his own tell for wanting to change the subject. Even if it would be better to sort it out now instead of bedtime. "I don't want to impose."

"Well, since I have the only furniture, functioning bathroom, and semblance of a usable kitchen, I'm thinking you don't have much of a choice."

He'd barely wrapped his head around not being able to leave. No clean clothes and no toiletries landed hard. Not to mention nowhere to sleep. "Do you have furniture?"

"Only one bed, I'm afraid."

"I can sleep on the floor," he said way too quickly, though a rug would beat bare floor.

Her look told him she knew exactly where his mind had gone. "I have a comfy chair." She lifted a finger. "Not ideal, but definitely better than the floor."

"Beggars can't be choosers, right?" He'd been going for funny but worried it came out snarky. "Kidding. I mean, kind of. I'm definitely a beggar in this situation."

"Does that mean you are or aren't a choosy one?" Ellie's eyes danced with humor now.

Better to have her make fun of him than think he was an asshole. He'd already painted himself into that corner once today. "Not choosy at all. Grateful. I meant to say I'm grateful for anything that's not a drop cloth in the middle of a construction zone."

"That's the spirit." She gave him a friendly punch in the bicep. "Since you're being such a good sport, I'll even share my storm rations with you."

"Storm rations?" When had she had the time to go out for storm rations?

"To be fair, I've been living mostly on low-maintenance nonperishables anyway. Not much of a kitchen. But I did stock up on wine and junk food. It feels mean to keep it all to myself."

Not that every part of this didn't suck, but the offer—and what it signified—might just qualify as a silver lining. "I'd be in your debt."

Ellie made a show of looking him up and down. "I like the sound of that."

Under other circumstances, he'd think Ellie was flirting with him. He wasn't great at reading things like that, but he'd accidentally led enough women on that he'd learned how to tune in and turn down the volume. Because apparently some people were drawn to the strong and silent—or as Maddie so eloquently put it, sullen and surly—type.

But surely that wasn't the case here. If anything, Ellie's incessant cheerfulness seemed designed specifically to antagonize him. Maybe not at first, but certainly by now. And yet here they were, bantering in a way that would have his siblings teasing him had they had the ability to eavesdrop.

Ellie's shoulders fell, but her expression remained playful. "Now I'm kidding. I'm not actually going to lord it over you."

It bugged him that her assumption would be that he couldn't take a joke. But perhaps he'd made that bed for himself. Either way, it was for the best. "You can. A little at least."

"I'll keep that in mind." She angled her head. "Are you going to work more, now that you're stuck here?"

He didn't feel especially compelled to, but if he didn't, it meant an entire evening of hanging out with Ellie. He could barely fathom making dinner conversation, much less enough to pass however many hours they had until he could reasonably call it a night. "Yeah, maybe I will."

"I thought you might." She glanced at her watch. "Want to go until seven or so, then eat?"

He nodded, probably more eagerly than necessary. "That sounds great."

"You get your choice of jarred marinara over angel hair or tomato soup from a carton with a grilled cheese. I'll let you ponder while you work."

Jack chuckled. "No thinking required. If grilled cheese is an option, it's always the right answer."

She gave him one of those looks again—up and down, real slow. Enough to make him fidget. "Look at that, we have something in common."

He swallowed and ignored the very inconvenient way his hormones chose to interpret matters. "Look at that."

Ellie stepped back to assess whether the colors that looked fantastic close up blended with the overall painting. But instead of the perspective she'd been aiming for, she found herself plunged into darkness. "What the?" Since the obvious answer was that it had something to do with Jack, she closed one eye and hollered, "What did you do?"

There was a crash from somewhere in the basement, followed by an expletive. A moment of silence, another crash, then Jack's footsteps on the stairs. Footstomps? Was that a word? The flashlight from his phone appeared in the doorway a moment before his shadowy form.

"I didn't do anything." His emphasis on "I" implied it might have been her fault.

She gave him a withering look before gesturing with both her palette and brush. "Well, I sure as hell didn't."

Jack let out a sound that resembled a growl. "It's probably the generator."

She felt her eyes go wide, hated being the deer in the headlights, but she couldn't seem to help it. "The generator?"

"It's probably out of fuel. I'm sure no one checked it before hightailing it out of here."

She hooked her paintbrush under the thumb poking through her palette and scrubbed her free hand over her face. "Fuck me."

"No, thank you. At least not until we get the power resolved."

Ellie blinked at him. "Did you seriously just say that?"

Jack shrugged. "You started it."

She could get all huffy. But the comment was the closest she and Jack had come to a real moment of connection. And damn it all if it wasn't funny. Like, really funny. So, she laughed. Laughed and laughed and laughed some more, until tears streamed down her face and it was all she could do to remain standing. "I did," she said when she could catch her breath enough to form words.

"I don't feel great about going out in this weather with no light, but I think I should try."

She sure as hell didn't want to. But just about as low on the list was Jack venturing out on his own, because if he didn't come back she'd have to go out looking for him and they'd both die of hypothermia. "Do you know how to restart a generator?"

He gave her a bland look, making her realize the borderline insulting nature of the question for someone in his line of work.

"Sorry."

Jack shrugged. "I can't promise that's the problem, but it's likely. And it's going to get pretty damn cold in here without the furnace running."

A zip of panic swelled in her chest. "Wait, I thought the furnace ran on gas."

"It does. But these new models require electricity for the sensors and thermostat."

Of course they did. "Fuck."

"Me?" Jack arched a brow.

"No, thank you. At least not until we get the power resolved." Not the truth for her, exactly, but it seemed like a better idea to be clever than admit wanting to jump his bones.

Jack smirked. An honest to God smirk. Fear of freezing to death took a back seat to delight, at least momentarily.

"Do you, um, need me to go out with you?" Ellie asked, tone not even a little bit convincing.

The smirk faded, and Jack lifted his chin ever so slightly. "I got it."

Okay, so she might be imagining it, but she'd swear there was a trace of bravado there. But, like, chivalrous tough guy, not cantankerous. She swallowed, not wanting to admit how quickly that could get her into trouble. "I'd argue, but I'm pretty sure I'd be zero help."

Jack nodded, full strong and silent mode engaged. She followed him to the back entry and experienced a moderate twinge of guilt as he pulled on his coat and hat once again.

"Please be careful."

Another nod. He fished a headlamp from one of his pockets and slipped it on over the hat. If he wasn't about to go out there and save her ass, she'd have teased him about hers being bigger. But since she didn't know how he'd take it—plus that whole bit about saving her ass—she kept her mouth shut.

He disappeared into the darkness. Even the beam of light got swallowed up by the swirling snow. Ellie closed the door to keep in the heat but hovered, figuring the least she could to was stand vigil. When the dot of light reappeared a couple of minutes later, swaying back and forth with Jack's stride, relief swept through her. Until she realized how briefly he'd been gone. And how quiet and dark the house remained.

She opened the door and Jack hurried in, stomping the snow from his boots. A blanket of white covered his hat and shoulders, and Ellie had to resist the urge to brush it away. "That was fast," she said, trying to channel optimism.

"There's no fuel."

"What? How is that possible?"

Jack shrugged. "I'm guessing it's someone on the crew's job to take the cans to get filled, and that's what they did."

"And planned to bring them back full the next day." It was a perfectly logical thing to do. With her quarters running off the main power supply, the generator only needed to run when the crew was working. Well, and to provide whatever electricity the furnace needed, but that probably wasn't very much. Ellie shook her head. "What do we do?"

"We hunker and come up with a game plan in the morning. We should have a better sense of just how stuck we are by then, too. And how quickly we can get dug out."

Just how stuck. She'd grown up in New England and still shuddered at the thought. It was one thing to have a snow day because the roads were bad, and you had all the creature comforts of home with no responsibilities for the day. This was definitely not that. And while they probably weren't in any real danger, she didn't like the idea of having limited resources and few options. "Yeah."

Jack blew out a breath. "I guess that means grilled cheese is off the menu."

They wouldn't starve by any stretch of the imagination. But a cold cheese sandwich would certainly feel like roughing it. At least there was wine. "Unless you're building us a fire."

"I wish," he said, rolling his eyes.

Reconstruction of the fireplaces and repointing the chimneys were on the docket, but they involved an expert who hadn't been brought in yet. "Yeah."

He shifted his weight from one foot to the other. "I guess we're done with work for the day."

It was her turn to do the stoic nod.

"Do you need help cleaning anything up? I can hold a light while you wash your brushes or whatever."

Of course he had to go and be thoughtful on top of everything else. "I can manage. You're not the only one with a headlamp."

"Handy little things, aren't they?"

One more thing they had in common. "I'll just be a few minutes. You're welcome to head to my room if you want. There's at least somewhere to sit. Though Emily Dickinson might help herself to your lap."

"I'll, uh, head down to the basement and make sure I left things okay there."

The stilted delivery made her think it had less to do with tidying his work area than the prospect of going into her space alone. It seemed silly to her, but whatever. "Okay. I guess I'll see you there in a little bit."

He nodded and headed for the basement stairs like a man on a mission. Once he'd gone, she shook her head. As much as she might have fantasized about spending the night with Jack, the reality of the situation landed like a fifty-pound sack of plaster. Fantasy or no, something told her it was going to be a long night.

Chapter Ten

Jack hovered outside the door to Ellie's room, more than a little apprehensive about what the next few hours would bring. But since he'd run out of legitimate stall tactics, there wasn't much more to do besides get on with it already. He knocked softly on her door and waited.

"Come in."

He didn't know what he expected to find, but half a dozen candles casting a warm glow over the whole room wasn't it. "Whoa."

Ellie, who was standing at the small stretch of counter in the kitchenette, turned. "Sorry for the romantic vibes. I figured being able to see without blinding each other with headlamps would be preferable."

He chuckled as he flicked his off. "Fair."

"So, no grilled cheese, but I did buy some fancy cheese and salami and stuff, so we can rock a charcuterie board if you're into that."

"I'm never going to say no to aged cheese and cured meat. As long as you're sure you don't mind sharing." Though, now that he knew that was an option, the trail mix and granola bars he'd rustled from his truck seemed extra sad.

"I'm sure. Besides, having company makes it easier to justify a whole spread. And I love a whole spread." She pointed to a bottle of cabernet. "Wine?"

It didn't seem like a great idea, but damn if it didn't sound nice after the day he'd had. "Sure."

She poured two glasses and handed him one. "Here's to the power coming back on soon."

General misgivings about the evening or not, he could drink to that. "Cheers."

Ellie sipped her wine before shifting her attention back to the cutting board. "Make yourself comfortable."

He considered his options. Bed? Nope. Even the chair in the corner felt just a little too casual. And it was currently home to a black cat with bright green eyes he assumed was Emily Dickinson.

Since they'd probably eat at the table, he perched on one of the delicate metal chairs of the vintage bistro set and hoped he didn't send it collapsing beneath him. It proved sturdier than it looked, and he let himself relax. Okay, relax might be an overstatement, but he settled back and crossed his ankle over the opposite knee. "So, um, how are you liking staying in the house?" he asked.

Ellie carried a large plate—practically overflowing with cheeses, salamis, olives, and crackers—to the table. "It's weird but also really great. And I couldn't ask for a better commute."

"There is that." He gestured to the spread. "Looks like enough for a party."

Ellie laughed. "I may have gone overboard. Getting snowed in does that to a girl."

"Despite current evidence to the contrary, I'm all about being prepared." And being caught so ill-prepared still had him on edge.

"A regular Boy Scout." Ellie lifted a hand. "Assuming the Boy Scouts weren't so obnoxious and homophobic."

They hadn't discussed politics or queerness or anything else, at least not explicitly. But the phrasing helped him relax. Again, as relaxed as he could be stranded with a gorgeous woman who seemed hell-bent on getting chummy no matter how much he tried to avoid it. "Obviously."

Despite his comment about there being enough for a party, they put a sizable dent in the food. He hadn't realized how hungry he'd gotten shoveling and freaking the fuck out. When Ellie got up to put away the leftovers, Jack stood as well. He wasn't sure where he was going exactly, but that was hardly the point.

He continued to hover awkwardly while Ellie pulled blankets and another quilt from the small closet, wondering if he should offer to sleep in the study. The reality of no heat loomed, however, and logic won out.

Ellie dropped the armful she'd gathered on the bed. "I'm glad I decided to keep all these here instead of putting them in storage."

"I'm glad, too."

"So." She eyed him expectantly.

"So." He eyed his feet.

"Thoughts?" she asked.

Jack glanced at the armchair, then the bed. He reluctantly returned his gaze to Ellie. "We should probably sleep together," he said.

"Is that so?" Ellie's expression was unreadable.

"I don't mean sleep together, sleep together." He shot her a dubious gaze. "For the record."

She smirked. "Well, as long as it's for the record."

Irritation over being teased gave way to just how ridiculous their situation was. "You know what I meant."

"I did. I do. You're just so fucking easy to tease. I'm sorry." Ellie looked at the floor, but when her gaze returned to Jack's it didn't hold even a trace of reticence.

"I don't think you are," he said, but without any bite.

"Maybe a little." She eyed the bed. "I think you're right. It's only a little chilly now, but it's going to get real cold real quick. Sleeping together means combining body heat but also sharing the blankets I have."

It would certainly get them through the night. And whether they got plowed out the next day or not, he'd use the daylight hours to figure something out. "I promise to be a perfect gentleman."

Ellie clicked her tongue, and her expression made it clear the comment landed as ridiculous as it sounded in his own ears.

He angled his head, took a chance. "For the record."

She laughed then, a lovely and rich sound that had him thinking several ungentlemanly things. "I wasn't going to admit this, but I'm glad you're here."

Jack thought about his house and his bed, his favorite sweatpants. He thought about Dorothy and Sophia curled up in their beds, burritoed in their favorite blankets. Then he thought about Ellie being here alone. He didn't have a hero complex, but even he balked at the prospect. "I am, too."

She gave him a dubious look. "I'm sure you'd rather be home."

"Obviously." He tried for a playful eye roll and hoped it translated. "But no one should be trapped in a blizzard alone. Especially not when the power goes out."

Ellie tsked. "That's awfully gallant of you, Jack Barrow."

"Just don't let it get out, okay?"

"Your secret is safe with me." She made a buttoning gesture over her lips, and it was a hell of a lot cuter than Jack wanted to admit.

After generously giving him her spare toothbrush and insisting he go first, Ellie went to the bathroom to change. Jack sat to pull off his boots. His socked feet hit the cold floor, and he realized how much the temperature in the room had fallen. He hurried to take off his work pants and flannel shirt, grateful the T-shirt underneath had escaped the dirt and dust of the basement. After a moment of hesitation, he slid into the far side of the bed. Better that than to have Ellie find him standing around in his boxers.

Ellie emerged in a pair of flannel pajama bottoms covered in rainbows and a long-sleeved tee. She wasted no time getting in next to him and tugging the blankets up to her chin. "Brr."

"I know." Jack cleared his throat. "I, uh, I'm sorry I don't have anything to sleep in."

Ellie rolled to face him and eyed him with amusement. "I don't suppose I could interest you in a pair of my leggings."

He winced. "If it bothers you, I can. I don't want to be a jerk about it."

"You're not. I think most guys feel the same." She shook her head. "I don't see how they're any different than long johns, though."

He hadn't thought of it that way, and suddenly wished he was wearing some. "Why didn't you say so?"

"Because it's so obvious." She rocked her head side to side. "And because I didn't want you to feel pressured."

Given her lack of qualms when it came to giving him a hard time, he couldn't help but wonder if there was a certain gender sensitivity in her reasoning now. He appreciated that. "I totally would, but now I feel bad about making you get up."

"As long as you're comfortable, that's all that matters."

He actually was. Even in the dead of winter, he never slept in more than what he currently had on. "Then let's stay put and preserve the warmth we have."

Ellie burrowed further under the covers. "Deal."

"If I snore, just smack me."

She quirked a brow. "How likely is that?"

"Eh? Depends on who you ask." Only after saying it did the implications register. "I mean, my sister swears I do, but she might be lying."

"Well, I guess same here. Though I've never had any complaints." Ellie winked.

"It's your bed," Jack said. "You're entitled."

"Then I'll admit I'll likely put up with snoring to keep your body heat."

Jack coughed. They'd officially strayed much deeper into banter territory than he was comfortable with. Though talking about sharing body heat perhaps strayed into flirting territory. Either way, it was not where he needed his thoughts going.

"Sorry. I promise I'll be a proper lady to your perfect gentleman."

Even with only a lone candle still burning, he could make out the gleam in her eye that in no way matched her words. "I'll, uh, see you in the morning."

Ellie grinned, making him feel like a complete oaf. "Good night, Jack."

She rolled away to blow out the candle, plunging them into complete darkness. She settled back in beside him, letting out this little sigh that made him think of other ways he might get her to make such a satisfied sound. He squeezed his eyes shut, hating the way T made him feel like a horny teenager sometimes. Much of the time. All the time. Even when the rest of him knew better. "Good night, Ellie."

Ellie woke with her back pressed against Jack's front, Jack's arm draped around her middle. It was impossible to know whether she'd wiggled herself into that position or if he'd curled around her in the night. Perhaps it was mutual, even if unconsciously done. What she did know was that he felt fucking fantastic. Strong and solid and—though it seemed like a strange descriptor to use—peaceful. She'd slept better than she had in weeks.

She resisted the urge to stretch or roll around, not wanting to wake him and break the spell. Because surely he wouldn't cuddle her like this on purpose. She wouldn't either. Even if she could admit wanting to.

Jack stirred, as though her thoughts had penetrated his and roused him. He nuzzled into her hair for about two seconds before his entire body tensed.

"It's okay," she said. "I consent."

She'd hoped the joke might diffuse the situation and, if not prolong the moment, at least prevent it from an abrupt and painfully awkward end. Jack didn't laugh, but he didn't leap out of bed, either. Did that count as a win?

When it came to her dealings with Mr. Prickly, yeah, it did.

He slid his arm away but didn't move otherwise. "What time is it?"

Snow still swirled outside, making the light an indistinguishable soft gray. "Eight, maybe?"

"Eight?" Jack sat up. "I never sleep that late."

She reached for her phone and tapped the screen. "It's actually quarter to nine."

"Seriously?" Jack scrubbed a hand over his face. "Damn."

"I think yesterday counts as both physically and emotionally exhausting." Which was easier to admit than how warm and cozy the bed had been with Jack in it, or how perfectly their bodies fit together. "Yeah."

She liked that he'd own that sort of thing. So many guys—cis or trans—balked at the idea of emotional labor or emotional fatigue. "I'd offer to make you coffee, but until we get power back, I can't pull it off."

"I'll go back out to the garage. Maybe there's a spare gas can I missed last night. We're going to need heat sooner rather than later."

The small red light on the electric radiator caught her attention. "Wait."

"What?" he asked.

She pointed. "I think main power is back on."

Jack threw the covers back and stood. "It does seem warmer in here than it should be."

"And yet not as warm as it could be." Ellie pulled the covers back over her legs, not quite ready to face reality.

He crossed the room and held his hand over the radiator. "Yep. It's warm."

The compressor of her mini fridge kicked on, as though it wanted to add to the conversation. Ellie smiled. "I guess that means I can offer you coffee after all."

"I'm going to take you up on that. Hopefully, the well pump is back on, too, and the pipes didn't freeze. I need to pee even more than I need coffee." Jack disappeared into the bathroom and closed the door.

Ellie got up, adding slippers to the ensemble she slept in. She made it over to the coffee pot before Jack emerged, but no further.

"No water," he said.

"No." She didn't pretend to be calm about it.

"Hopefully, it's just the pressure tank needing to be reset. Give me one minute." He pulled on his pants and boots and disappeared once more, this time into the main part of the house.

She stood there, coffee carafe in one hand and eyes locked on the faucet, as though she might will it to turn on. "Please," she whispered, though she wasn't sure whether the plea was directed at the faucet itself or the man trying to get it to work.

"Try now." Jack's voice, though muffled, carried from the basement.

She flipped the handle. Water and air splurged from the tap, but within a few seconds, flowed freely. "Victory," she called.

She filled the pot and loaded the percolator before heading to the bathroom herself. By the time she emerged, Jack had tidied the bed and washed the couple of dishes they'd dirtied the night before.

"You didn't have to do that," she said.

"Felt like the least I could do." He shrugged, almost sheepish. "After you let me stay with you."

She laughed. "Well, I do my best not to be stubborn on principle. Besides, you brought some nice heat to the party."

His eyes went wide, and she realized how suggestive the comment sounded.

"I mean, I was definitely cozier than I would have been by myself." She dropped her head to one side. "And I wouldn't have known how to fix the water tank."

Jack nodded, all business now. "You should let me show you. It's a simple thing but only if you know what to do. And it can happen anytime a house on a well loses power."

She nodded, not feeling strongly about the well but appreciating the concern it seemed to represent. "So, coffee?"

"Yes, please." Jack pulled out his phone and started tapping at the screen.

"Cream? Sugar?"

"Both, if you have them."

It was an oddly pleasing thing to learn—to know for future reference—the way Jack took his coffee. Not that she would tell him as much. "You got it."

She poured cups and they both stood, sipping and caffeinating and not speaking. Which, honestly, was probably exactly the way Jack liked it. The urge to tease him about it didn't come, though. It turned out this was oddly pleasing, too. Easing into the day in companionable silence.

"I'm still going to head back to the garage. If I can get the generator running, we'll have heat in the rest of the house and work lights wherever we want them."

As tempting as it might be to spend the day cozied up with a movie—or with Jack—that was probably for the best. "I can go with you. I don't want to be completely useless."

Jack smirked, and Ellie tried to ignore how attractive it was. "You're not useless. You're going to keep feeding me."

She laughed at the practicality. Leave it to a guy to consider warmed up soup a fair trade for manual labor. "I am happy with that exchange if you are."

"More than." Jack gave a decisive nod, as if to drive home the point.

Ellie lifted her chin. "Does that mean you want breakfast?"

"Are you offering?"

"Absolutely. I'm not a big breakfast person, though, so your options are pretty much cereal or toast."

He seemed to consider. "Jam?"

"Cherry preserves."

"Sold."

Ellie grabbed the bread bag and fished out two slices. That was easy.

CHAPTER ELEVEN

Jack reshoveled his path to the garage. They'd gotten well over two feet so far and it showed no signs of letting up. He made a mental note to spend an hour or two clearing around their vehicles, just so they'd be able to get out when the plows finally came.

Inside, he flicked on the lights, and damn if it didn't make all the difference. The carpenters' tools took up most of the space—a table saw, a compound miter saw, and a belt sander. Piles of PVC and copper pipe lined the far wall. But tucked behind a stack of cabinetry boxes, the red plastic of a gas can flashed like a beacon. He picked his way over, hoping it wasn't some abandoned empty relic or, worse, one full of stale gas that would do them no good.

It was dusty, but given the sawdust covering every surface around him, that didn't say much. He hefted it, happy to find it full. He added the gas to the generator and primed it. Not that he was superstitious, but he closed his eyes as he pulled the cord, willing it to start. When it roared to life on the first try, he offered a moment of gratitude to the universe. Then he hustled his freezing ass back in the house.

"It worked," Ellie said the second he came through the door.

"Did you think it wouldn't?"

She shrugged. "Big machines scare me. I don't ever assume they're going to do what I want them to do. Except my car. I don't understand her, but I trust her, and she trusts me to pay experts to take care of her."

He couldn't help but laugh at the assessment. "A generator isn't so very different. If you give it fuel, it will generally go."

"I'm glad."

He was, too. Having the generator up and running meant all their work lights and power cords worked, which meant they had the option of working and moving around the house instead of being confined to Ellie's room. It also meant the furnace blower would stay on even if they lost power again, and they could keep the house at a safe, if not entirely comfortable, temperature.

"I looked up the forecast. We're supposed to get another eight to twelve today, but it's going to let up overnight and be clear tomorrow."

All things considered, not the worst news. Once it stopped, plowing and clearing usually happened quickly. "I guess that means you're stuck with me for a bit longer."

She smirked. "I'd be here either way, so I'm happy for the company. You're the one who's actually stuck."

As upset as he'd been at first, spending time with Ellie was shaping up to be not so bad. "I hope it doesn't feel like overstepping to say I'm glad you didn't wind up stuck by yourself."

Ellie's features softened. "Not overstepping at all."

"I think I'll try to get some work done since I'm here. If you're cool with that." He wasn't sure why he added that last bit. Maybe because it felt like her place for the time being, and he was encroaching. Or, at the very least, a guest.

"Yeah, I think that's a good idea. How about we break for lunch around one and I make you that grilled cheese I promised?"

It was a generous offer, all things considered. "I hope you'll let me buy you some groceries when we get out of here."

"Yeah, but you shoveled and got the generator going, remember?"

"Still."

She waved him off. "I stocked up specifically for the storm."

"If you don't say yes, I'll have to figure out something else nice to do for you. Make it easy on a guy."

Ellie laughed, a full and delightful sound. "Fair enough. You can buy me however much fancy cheese it takes to make you feel better about things."

He frowned, not genuinely annoyed, but accustomed to playing the straight man with his siblings.

"I could make you a list, if that would help, of kinds I like."

Jack shook his head. "No, it's not that. I was just thinking about what a silly thing that was. Restitution cheese."

"Technically, it's not restitution because I shared. If anything, it would be reciprocity cheese."

Even he had to laugh at that. And then it hit him. "I know just the ticket."

She made a show of looking intrigued. "Go on."

"I can get you a private tour and tasting at Grumpy Old Goat."

Her eyes narrowed slightly. "Jack Barrow, are you asking me out on a date?"

"Oh." He winced before he could stop himself. "No. I—"

"Can't bear the thought of going out with me?" Ellie shifted to an affronted posture, but her eyes danced with humor.

Jack scrubbed a hand over his face. God, if his sisters could hear this train wreck of a conversation. "I meant that I know the owner. She's engaged to my sister, actually. I thought it would be nice."

Ellie's shoulders dropped and her expression softened. "It would be nice. I'm sorry I can't seem to help teasing you."

He closed his eyes for a second to regroup. When he opened them, Ellie seemed to be regarding him with genuine remorse. He chuckled to show he wasn't a complete stick in the mud. "You might be surprised to hear this, but you are not the first person to say that to me."

She seemed to get serious then. "Does that bother you?"

"I'm used to it." He shrugged, almost as an afterthought.

Ellie shook her head. "That's not what I asked."

He bristled on instinct. He didn't love personal questions from the people he was closest to. Having them come from a woman he couldn't help being attracted to felt downright vulnerable. And yet those eyes—so often teasing and playful—looked at him with this mixture of empathy and genuine curiosity, and he was done for. "I'm not the most social person. I find the teasing preferable to faking it."

"Huh."

"Usually, the teasing comes from my siblings or close friends, so I know there's no malice behind it." If anything, it had become part of the family ethos, and he never failed to experience the underlying affection that came with it.

Ellie smiled. "I always wanted siblings."

"You don't have any? Wait, you already told me you didn't. Sorry." He grumbled on occasion about wishing he was an only child, but not once did he mean it.

"It's okay. I always wanted them, but no."

There was a sadness in Ellie's eyes. Just like that first time. He'd dismissed it then, not wanting to stray into personal territory. This time, it made him want to understand why, made him want to make it better. Even if prying into people's personal lives uninvited was literally the bane of his existence. "Mine are a handful, but I wouldn't trade them for the world."

"How many?" She cleared her throat. "Siblings, I mean."

"Two. You met Logan. She's the youngest. Maddie is my older sister. She's engaged to Sy, who co-owns Grumpy Old Goat. We all work for the family business."

"Wow."

"It wasn't like there was pressure to or anything. We all wanted to. And we all do very different things. I'm an electrician, obviously. Logan does design. Maddie does project management, which means she keeps the trains running. Only we don't tell her that because it would go to her head. Both my parents and my uncle do, too. Technically, they're the owners." Jack stopped, acutely aware that he'd started to ramble.

"It sounds wonderful." Ellie's expression turned wistful. "My parents divorced when I was little. My dad stayed in the picture, but since he died, it's just been me and my mom."

"Are you close?" The second the question left his lips, he remembered that he'd asked her that, too. What had she said then? Complicated.

Ellie nodded. "We are. She's partially disabled, so I've mostly lived at home to help out."

"How so?" He shook his head. What the hell had gotten into him? "I'm sorry. Never mind. That's a really personal question."

"It's okay." Ellie nodded again, this time like she was trying to reassure him. "She has schizophrenia. It's managed with medication mostly. She's just not able to handle a lot of responsibility or stress."

The answer felt genuine but also somehow rehearsed. Like she made a point of being open but didn't want to get too deep in the weeds. It left Jack at a loss. But since he hadn't evolved in the twenty-four hours since they'd had the first version of this conversation, he fell back on his own genuine-yet-rehearsed, "That sounds hard."

Something shifted. Ellie closed her eyes and took what Jack could only describe as a fortifying breath. When she let it out, he'd swear there was the tiniest hint of a shudder. It tugged at every protective instinct he had, even though he had no business feeling that way about her. But before he could tame those feelings into something appropriate to say, she blinked a couple of times and was back—eyes and smile bright. "It's fine, really. She's moved into assisted living and is thriving. And I now get to take jobs like this."

The niggling curiosity left him at a loss. But he didn't trust himself to do or say the right thing, and he'd already pried more than he normally would, so he promptly shoved it aside. "I'm glad it's working out so well."

Ellie lifted her shoulders and let them fall. Jack got the feeling it was her way of closing the conversation. "Shall we get to work?" she asked, driving home the point.

It was weird how relief could feel like disappointment sometimes. "Sounds good."

After a day of plastering and a gloriously hot shower, Ellie headed back to her room to make dinner. It was an odd feeling, cooking for Jack. But not really cooking. Frozen meatballs and jarred sauce got the job done, but hardly flexed her culinary muscles. Or impressed the guy she was hoping to get naked. She said as much to Emily Dickinson.

Emily Dickinson meowed.

Ellie shook her head. "I know, but a girl can hope."

Jack joined her and graciously accepted the offer of a shower, along with a pair of sweatpants she forgot she had, a clean Red Sox tee, and some wool socks.

"You look pretty adorable," she said when he emerged from the bathroom.

He looked down, but it did little for the four inches of ankle exposed below the hem. "I'm channeling all the go with the flow I can muster. The fact that they're clean is helping."

Ellie grinned. "Even if they smell like girl?"

Jack simply angled his head.

"Hungry?" she asked.

"Understatement." He took the seat she'd already started to think of as his.

She handed him a plate and sat across from him at the small table. "I feel compelled to state for the record that I do know how to make a proper meatball."

"Noted." He eyed the pile of pasta. "But now I feel compelled to state for the record that I have no complaints."

"Yeah, but would you say that if you weren't relying entirely on me for your sustenance?"

"Yes." Jack looked genuinely offended by the question. "One, because when someone cooks you a meal, whatever the circumstances, complaining is a dick move. Two, because frozen meatballs are the foundation of party meatballs, which are the best part of any party or potluck. They should never be disparaged."

He'd spent the better part of the day surprising her, and it seemed like he wasn't going to stop now. "When you put it that way."

Jack speared one of the meatballs and popped it into his mouth whole. Yes, it was small, but the gesture made Ellie laugh. It was nice to finally feel at ease around him. Or maybe it was more accurate to say it was nice to feel like Jack was finally at ease around her. She'd hoped a chill and charming guy lived under the crusty exterior he presented to the world, and it was satisfying to be proven right. "Are you happy with what you got done today?"

"Yeah." He nodded affably. "I should be done with the upstairs this week. You?"

She mirrored the nod. "I'm about halfway through the plaster repair. It's exciting to be able to work on some of the painting now."

He chuckled. "It makes sense, even though I'm the opposite. I'm in it for the guts behind the walls. Fixtures and stuff are just gravy."

"I can see that."

"Fortunately, Logan deals with all the deciding and making sure it'll look good. If I had to do the shopping or the back and forth with clients, I might have looked for a new line of work." Jack shuddered, punctuating his feelings on the subject.

"It's reassuring to know you have a brand." As opposed to his prickliness being unique to interactions with her.

He hung his head briefly, but when his gaze returned to hers, it was relaxed. It wasn't just relaxed, though. It was…appreciative. Appreciative in that way she'd been looking at Jack since day one. Appreciative enough that Ellie would bet her favorite set of brushes Jack wanted her. Was that possible? Or perhaps the more apt question was whether there was a chance in hell he would act on it.

She resisted the urge to make a joke, to flirt overtly. That hadn't gotten her anywhere. If anything, it made Jack close up like a clam. Instead, she went for a smile. Not coy, exactly. Soft. Inviting.

They ate in companionable silence, leaving Ellie to wonder if Jack's thoughts were anywhere near hers. Specifically, about spending another night in the same bed and whether she'd be able to keep her hands to herself.

"One more?" she asked after noticing Jack had drained his wineglass.

Jack winced. "I probably shouldn't."

"Shouldn't why?"

He didn't answer.

"I mean, you're not driving anywhere. You don't have anywhere to be in the morning."

Jack dipped his chin slightly, and the resulting pseudo stern look had her stomach doing flips. "Because if I have another, my judgment will get fuzzy, and I'll be tempted to act impulsively."

She swallowed, the flipping sensation settling decidedly lower than her belly. "Would that be so bad?"

His eyes narrowed. "You tell me."

"I don't think it would be bad at all." She took a chance and topped off both their glasses.

Jack carried their plates to the sink. "Say more."

Ellie swallowed a laugh. "Why do I get the feeling that's typically the last thing you usually want to say?"

He leaned against the counter, sexy as fuck even in her borrowed clothes. "I don't like idle chitchat. When there's something to be discussed, something to be settled, it's different."

She stood, picking up both glasses. "And this is one of those times?"

Jack simply nodded.

She felt warmed from the inside out, and the edges of her mind went soft. A far cry from being drunk, but it made her feel light. Like the ropes and strings she used to inhibit herself had been loosened, and she could float free. Like the overwhelming responsibility to act like a logical, rational adult suddenly didn't exist.

"I'd love to know what you're thinking right now," Jack said.

If he was opening that door, no way in hell would she miss the opportunity to walk through. She handed him his glass. "I'm thinking that I'd love it if you kissed me."

One brow raised slightly, more a show than real surprise. "Were you planning to tell me that?"

She smirked. "I was waiting to see if you felt the same."

"And how were you planning to determine that?" He seemed equal parts amused and curious now. So different from the gruff and grumpy guy she'd met a few weeks prior. And yet, so quintessentially Jack.

"I'm pretty good at reading people." Which wasn't always a good thing, she'd learned, but no need to get into that now.

"Yeah?"

"Totally. I'd pay attention to the way you looked at me. I'd touch you." She trailed a finger down his arm. "See how you responded."

"I see." Jack's pupils dilated slightly, and his irises darkened. Did he know that?

"I'd drop enough hints that I might get you to kiss me first, but I wouldn't be afraid to initiate if I knew you wanted it as much as I did." She was pretty sure he did at this point, but it was a game now. Foreplay as much as figuring each other out.

"What if I told you flat out that I wanted to kiss you?"

Not that it was supposed to be hard, but this was almost too easy. "I'd ask what you were waiting for."

He shook his head slowly, without breaking eye contact. "Not a damn thing."

She'd meant what she said. She wasn't afraid to do the initiating. But there was something extra delicious about feeling desired, pursued. For all their arguing and getting on each other's nerves, that was exactly the way Jack made her feel in that moment. Desired. Pursued.

He took his time, setting down his wine and doing the same with hers. He tucked a stray wisp of hair behind her ear and ran his thumb along her jaw. He had a callous, just above the joint, and she wondered what the roughness would feel like on more delicate skin.

"I've been thinking about this a lot," he said.

"Tonight?" she asked, not needing to know but wanting to.

"Way before tonight."

Nice to know the feeling was mutual. Even as her hold on the thread of their banter grew tenuous. "And why didn't you?"

"Because we're working together. Because you drive me bananas. Because we never seem to be alone together for more than two minutes at a time."

Would he talk himself right out if it? "That's a lot of reasons not to."

He brushed his thumb over her lips. "They all seem pretty insignificant now."

"Oh, good." Her voice had gone breathy and completely gave her away. Not that she was still trying to play it cool. Not really.

"Very good," he said.

Jack moved in. Closer and closer, until Ellie's eyes instinctively closed. Jack's mouth moved slowly over hers, as though giving Ellie a chance to acclimate. Or maybe he was simply taking his time. Either way, the kiss was confident, sure. Jack Barrow might be loath to admit it, but damn. The man knew how to kiss. That realization, the sudden confidence that he knew how to do a lot more than kiss, shot a lightning bolt right to her core.

As though he could read every pheromone pulsing through her, Jack took the kiss deeper. When she gasped, he slipped inside, his tongue teasing hers. Just like with the callous on his thumb, the sensation sent her mind racing to other places his tongue might go. Her clit throbbed in response, making her gasp.

Jack broke the kiss, pulled just far enough back to scrutinize her face. "Yes?"

Ellie nodded. "Oh, most definitely. Yes."

CHAPTER TWELVE

Is this a mistake?" Jack asked, not entirely sure he wanted the answer. They'd stopped kissing long enough to stand and start tearing at each other's clothes.

"Maybe." Ellie didn't stop hitching up the hem of his shirt. "Are you saying you want to stop?"

He could think of little he wanted less than to stop what was about to happen between them. "No."

"Good." She yanked his shirt the rest of the way off.

"Do you?" He could have inferred her answer—from that or from the way her hands stroked his bare chest. But he needed her to say it, to agree that even if they both thought better of it in the morning, tonight they were on the same page.

"No." She looked from his torso into his eyes. "No, I don't want to stop."

"Good."

Because she still wore a shirt, he went for her neck, kissing and licking and biting with just enough force to make a point. She dropped her head to the side and arched forward—an erotic display of consent that left him wanting to explore every inch of her with his lips, tongue, and teeth.

"More." She wiggled her arms between them and pulled up her shirt.

He grabbed the hem and tugged it over her head. "More."

Her breasts, still covered in a froth of hot pink satin, heaved against his palms. Even through the fabric, her nipples hardened.

Desperation threatened to overtake him, and he dipped his head to take one into his mouth. Ellie gasped and buried her fingers in his hair.

The gasp did him in. He reached behind her to flick the clasp of her bra, releasing her just long enough to toss it to the side. Her breasts were creamy and pale, a stark contrast to the tanned and freckled expanse of skin above. "Someone seems to make a habit of forgetting sunscreen."

"I don't," Ellie said with a pout. "I'm just so pale I get freckles anyway."

"I'm not complaining." He lightly bit the curve of her shoulder, then traced her collarbone with his tongue.

"Damn right you aren't." She laughed.

The comment made Jack chuckle and kept him from getting overly serious, which he'd been known to do with sex. Maybe this was a bad idea, but maybe it didn't matter. They were stuck, they'd been dancing around each other for weeks, and he didn't know if he could make it through another night of sleeping next to Ellie and not touching her.

In a flurry of hands and limbs, they stripped each other of their remaining clothes. Ellie threw the bedcovers back and pulled Jack with her onto the mattress. He used one knee and one arm to brace himself and settled his other leg between Ellie's. With his free hand, he roamed every inch of her he could reach—her belly and sides, the swell of her hip, and that perfect little crease where the top of her thigh met her abdomen. She was soft and lush, and the more he touched her, the more he wanted.

"I might combust if you don't touch me soon," Ellie said with a laugh.

"I am touching you." Jack gave her ass a squeeze to drive home the point.

"You know what I mean." She pinched his side hard enough to make him yawp.

He considered giving her a taste of her own medicine, of teasing her and playing dumb until she begged for him. But as much as he might enjoy that, his own need demanded more immediate satisfaction.

Jack slipped his hand between Ellie's legs and slid the pad of his middle finger over her clit. She was hot and wet and the way her body arched into his was absolute perfection. Her hands, that had been roaming over his back, gripped his shoulders.

"Yes?" he asked, loving that he already knew the answer.

"So much yes."

He continued to stroke, and Ellie continued to move against him. Deliciously hypnotic, and yet not enough. When she asked him to be inside her, his cock twitched with equal parts excitement and longing. He settled for his finger and wasn't disappointed with the way she tightened around him and pulled him deeper.

"More." Her voice was breathy now, but no less insistent.

He added a second finger but kept his thrusts slow. Exploring the curve and shape of her from the inside, learning the way her muscles clamped around him. God, he could spend hours doing this.

"Please." Insistence gave way to desperation as she began to thrust against him.

He increased the pace, curling his fingers slightly to test the sensitivity of her G-spot. Ellie groaned, pumping her hips faster. She came hard, a flood of wetness spilling into his hand.

"Fuck." She took a few shaky breaths. "You're really good at that."

"Thanks." He settled on his side next to her to give her some air. "Your body is amazing. You're amazing."

Her body trembled with an aftershock. She closed her eyes and let out a soft moan. "I haven't come like that in a while."

"So sexy."

"You are." Ellie chuckled. She rolled to her side and pressed a hand to his chest, nudging him onto his back. "Okay. So. What do you like? What can I do?"

The fact that she asked instead of jumping right in ramped up his desire even as it helped him relax. "I like hand jobs."

She smirked. "Are those the only jobs you like?"

The insinuation had him imagining Ellie on her knees, looking up at him through those impossibly thick lashes. Maybe they'd get there. But not yet. "I consider them a good place to start."

"Acceptable." She did come onto her knees but remained next to him rather than crawling on top. She cupped her hand around his cock and stroked fingers along each side. "Any particular kind of hand job?"

"That's good," he said, voice strained. "Really good."

She continued stroking, adding just the right amount of pressure. "I love how hard you are."

It took every ounce of restraint he had not to come right then and there. He groaned, since there was no chance of words much less a complete sentence. Ellie hummed her pleasure—or was it satisfaction?—and rocked her body in time with her hand. Even without her on top of him, the sensation intensified her touch, and he exploded. "Fucking fuck," he managed after the orgasm swept over him.

"A good fuck I hope." Ellie swung her leg over his hips and straddled him.

"Good. Fuck."

"Is this okay?" She undulated slowly, sending aftershocks rippling through him.

"So good." He settled his hands on her hips, not to control but simply to appreciate them more deeply.

"I'm not going to lie, feeling your cock on my clit like this is enough to make me come again."

And just like that, he was back to hard and horny. He dug his fingers in with a little more force. "Yeah?"

"Especially when you grab me like that." She canted her head. "Makes me feel used, but in a good way."

Seriously, did this woman have a playbook for turning him on and getting him off? He guided her with more intention, letting the pressure build low in his belly. "Keep that up, and you're going to make me come again, too."

She folded forward, bracing a hand on either side of his shoulders. She slid her hot, slick, perfect pussy up and down his cock, over and over. "Yes." Her movements bordered on frantic. "Yes. Please."

The please sent him over the edge. He bucked, held her to him, and swore. She came against him, flooding the space between them with another wave of liquid heat. His own orgasm tumbled into another, or maybe it never stopped. But it exploded through him, blurring his vision and leaving him disoriented and weak.

Ellie sagged over him, still on her knees but with her breasts against his chest and her face nuzzled into his neck. "Holy crap," she muttered.

"Uh-huh," was pretty much all he could manage.

Ellie lingered for a long while before shifting to Jack's side. She kept one leg draped over his thigh and her breasts pressed to his ribs. It was blissful. Until it wasn't.

The wet spot on the sheets was large and grew cold beneath her. She didn't even want to think about how gross it must feel to Jack. It was nice that he didn't immediately bound out of bed and demand a shower, but she honestly wouldn't have blamed him. "Sorry about the mess," she said.

"I'm not." Jack didn't move or even open his eyes.

She smiled. "Well, I'm not sorry I made it, but I am sorry we're now lying in it."

He remained still. "I'm not."

"I have clean sheets."

Jack rolled his head to face her and opened his eyes. "Is that your way of asking me to help you change them?"

"Offering." She poked him lightly in the ribs. "I'm being nice and offering to change them so you don't have to sleep in a cold, wet spot."

He gave her a smug smile. "I'm perfectly happy to throw a towel over the situation and call it good, but I will happily help you remake the bed if you prefer."

She hadn't expected him to be a jerk about it, but this super laid-back vibe caught her off guard. "Are you trying to be considerate or do orgasms make you placid?"

"Yes."

Even as her skin started to itch, she laughed. "I like that."

"As much as you like clean sheets?"

"Maybe." She lifted her head. "Does it amuse you that there's something I'm fussy about that you aren't?"

He mirrored the gesture. "Maybe."

"What if you help me change them and then we take a nice hot shower together before crawling back in?" She could imagine little appealing more after amazing sex.

"One condition."

She tipped her chin. "What's that?"

"Neither of those things preclude middle of the night shenanigans should the mood strike."

Who was this guy and what had he done with grumpy Jack? Ellie stuck out her hand. "I accept these terms."

Rather than shake on it, Jack shifted, rolling Ellie onto her back and bracing over her. He studied her for what felt like eternity before breaking into a grin. "Good."

In a disarmingly graceful move, Jack pushed off the mattress and stood. He extended a hand to her, but instead of finishing the handshake she'd attempted to start, he hauled her to her feet. "Smooth," she said.

"I have my moments. Now, where are these sheets? Even with the heat back on, it is not warm enough to stand around naked."

He was right, of course. Though she would have tolerated a couple more minutes to appreciate him standing naked in front of her. It was her first real look at the gorgeous oak tree tattoo that spanned his chest, complete with intricate roots that covered his surgery scars. "Sorry, I was busy objectifying you."

"Can't you do that in the shower?"

The question, with all its serious delivery, made her laugh. "I guess I'll have to make do."

She hurried over to the closet and pulled out the spare set of sheets. With one of them on either side of the bed, it took all of two minutes to strip off the dirty and tug the clean ones into place, even with Emily Dickinson jumping on the mattress and deciding each move of fabric was something to be batted at, rolled over, or pounced on.

Ellie led them to the bathroom and got the water going. The shower fit both of them, but barely. That meant little opportunity for looking, but plenty for sudsy skin-on-skin action. Jack made a show of being efficient, but when she grazed her hand over his cock, he didn't hesitate to pin her against the shower wall and kiss her until her knees threatened to buckle.

By the time they stood on the little rug toweling off, Ellie was hot, bothered, and totally horny again. She debated saying so, wanting

Jack to know how much he turned her on but not wanting to come across as demanding. Not yet at least.

Jack hung his towel on the hook and pointed to it. "Do you have spare ones of those, too?"

"Yes?" She cleared her throat. "Yes. Do you need another?"

"I figured we should bring one to bed with us."

The meaning behind his words spun into place and it was all she could do not to laugh. She should have known better than to worry about her own horniness around a guy on T. "I like the way you think."

Jack looked her up and down slowly, and there was no mistaking the hunger in his eyes. "In that case, grab two."

CHAPTER THIRTEEN

Ellie woke to the rumble that only came from one thing: a plow pushing snow. She opened one eye, then the other. Sunlight streamed into the room, bright and full of promise. Too bad what she wanted was the promise of another day snowed in with Jack. She reached over to the spot where Jack had been the last time she had consciousness and found it empty. Apparently, she was alone in that feeling.

"Good morning," Jack said, sitting on the edge of the bed and holding out a steaming cup of coffee.

She sat up and accepted the mug, inhaling deeply before taking a sip, decidedly less disappointed than she'd been ten seconds ago. "How late did I sleep?"

"Not very. I think the plow crews started early now that the snow has finally stopped." He drank from his own cup, looking oddly relaxed in her sweatpants and shirt.

"If I tell you again how adorable you look in my clothes, will you be annoyed with me?" she asked.

He stuck out his chest, spread his arms wide. "I am secure enough in my masculinity to take that as a compliment."

"You should be more than secure after last night." She had an ache between her thighs that would undoubtedly linger all day.

Jack cocked his head, and his smile held more than a trace of arrogance. "I try not to hang my worth on what I do in bed."

"No? Why is that?"

"Because sex is subjective and bragging about having lots of practice is gross."

Ellie tsked. "I disagree. While there might be some inherent or learned skill, really good sex comes with paying attention and being more invested in your partner's pleasure than your own ego."

He set his coffee down and folded his arms. "And you're saying that's what I did last night? Paid attention?"

The attention he was paying her right this second had her libido revving despite the soreness. "I'm pretty sure you know the answer to that."

"I do my best never to assume." He looked her up and down slowly. "But I'm glad to hear you're feeling good about it."

Good wasn't the half of it. "Did you worry I wouldn't?"

"I mean, I'm pretty sure you had a good time. But we had more wine than I would consider ideal for a first time. I was worried you might feel differently about your choices in the light of day."

Seriously, who was this guy? "My consent was enthusiastic. I wouldn't try to take it back after the fact."

"No, but you might acknowledge that it was your choice and still regret it."

She reached for his hand. "I don't regret it."

He gave a tiny but brisk nod, and his features relaxed. "Good."

"You?" she asked, not entirely certain she wanted the answer.

"What about me?"

"Are you regretting what we did?"

Jack gave her another slow, appreciative once-over. "No. I don't regret it."

Ellie nodded, not quite wanting to admit how badly she needed him to say that. "We should probably—"

A loud knock interrupted her half-baked thought and just about sent her out of her skin.

"Hello? Anyone alive in there?"

Ellie didn't recognize the voice, but it definitely belonged to a woman.

"That would be my sister." Jack stood. "I'll go thank her for plowing us out." He stepped into his boots.

"Did you want to"—she flicked her finger up and down to indicate his legs—"put on real pants?"

"Nah. She's seen me in worse."

He left the room, and Ellie debated staying where she was or attempting to make herself presentable. As much as she'd like to thank whichever of the Barrow siblings had come to their rescue, she wasn't sure she could play it cool, and she had a feeling Jack didn't want to advertise what they'd gotten up to. And there was no hiding her sex-tossed hair.

In the end, she dragged herself from bed and threw on leggings and a hoodie. But she lingered in the room, giving herself a minute to be sad the last couple of days were over. Silly, really. Being stuck was never a good thing, even if the company turned out better than expected.

Jack returned, cheeks flushed from even that short time in the cold. Ellie studied him, fondness and arousal swelling in equal measure. "Well, what's the verdict?"

"Roads are clear, and thanks to Maddie, the driveway is, too."

She nodded, reminding herself to be grateful. "That was very kind of her."

"Well, I'm guessing we aren't a priority for whoever Pablo contracted to plow here, so it means we don't have to wait around for them to show up."

"They'll come, but it might be middle of the afternoon if they think no one's working." And calling Pablo to try to get ahold of them would have been more trouble than she wanted to make.

"I don't like that. Pablo should have checked on you, out here by yourself."

She was used to not being checked on, but she couldn't think of a way to say so that didn't make her sound either pathetic or stubborn.

"We'll have to dig out our vehicles, but she brought an extra shovel so we could both make progress on that front."

Ellie laughed, happy to change the subject and for the spare shovel. "Yay."

"We all take turns with the family plow." Jack chuckled. "I owe her breakfast for making her come all the way here, though. She was adamant this place falls beyond her coverage area."

Ellie's instinct was to feel bad, but based on what Jack had shared about his siblings, about their relationships, she realized bartering favors was simply one of the ways they showed affection. "I hope you expressed my gratitude."

"She knows," he said with a grin, like it was the most obvious thing in the world. "Speaking of breakfast, can I take you out for some?"

Was he asking her out? Or was it simply his own way of showing appreciation? How much should she overthink it? "How about I make us some toast and we do lunch? I have a feeling the shoveling is going to take a while."

"I like the way you think."

Would he if he knew her thoughts were actually tangled up with digging out and then tumbling back into bed together like they were still stranded? "I'm pretty smart."

He lifted a chin. "It's hot."

After second cups of coffee and toast with extra butter and jam, they bundled up and headed out. In addition to the sun shining, the wind had died down, making for a day that felt almost balmy. Great skiing weather. Not that she skied, but still.

They worked side by side, unburying Jack's truck and then her SUV. Jack cleaned up the path to the garage, and she worked on the front walk and widening the path to the back door. Chipping away at thirty inches of accumulation was no joke and, by the time they were done, she had half a mind to tumble back into bed for a nap instead of more sex.

She tidied her space while Jack showered. He went out to warm up his truck while she got ready. It was surprisingly companionable, given how much they'd bickered up until a couple of days ago. She had no idea what would happen next, or even what she wanted to happen, but she could worry about that later. For now, her thoughts turned to whatever soup and grilled sandwich combination awaited her at the diner in town.

Apparently, Jack and Ellie weren't the only ones with a case of cabin fever. He'd suggested the Little Gem Diner since it was the closest restaurant to Hampstead House, but when they arrived, the parking lot was packed. He literally got a space only because someone was leaving.

"I bet it's clearing out from a late breakfast rush," Ellie said.

"You're probably right." He hoped so.

"One day, I'm going to get you to say I'm right without any qualifiers." She grinned and didn't wait for him to reply before sliding out.

Jack followed. "I'm not opposed to admitting when other people are right as long as they are."

He held the door and Ellie ducked past him. "Is that a literal quote from the stubborn guy rulebook? Because if it's not, it should be."

"More of a personal mantra," he quipped, rather than defending the logic of his position.

"Of course it is," Ellie said.

The diner was crowded, but several groups hovered near the register to cash out, and no one else appeared to be waiting for a table. In short order, a middle-aged woman with two pencils in her hair pointed them to a booth in the front corner by the window. They settled in, facing each other.

Ellie picked up the massive menu and opened it like a book. "I'm starving."

He laughed "Same. Are you a breakfast anytime you're at a diner person, or do you flip a switch at a certain time?"

"Lunch. All the way. As soon as it's an option. I've never met a sandwich I don't like." She lowered the menu just enough to peer over the top. "That's a lie. I've had some crappy sandwiches, but I'd take a turkey club over a pile of eggs every time."

"That hurts," he said. "Truly."

She shook her head, clearly unfazed. "Haters gonna hate."

He'd barely perused the options when the woman who'd seated them came over. "Start you with something to drink?"

Ellie set the menu down and offered her a bright smile. "I'll have a Diet Coke, please. And a patty melt with fries if my friend here is ready to order."

"I thought you wanted soup," Jack said as he scrambled to decide.

"Changed my mind. Because patty melt."

Liz, the server, pointed at Ellie with her pencil. "She makes a valid point."

Jack folded his own menu. "Well, at the risk of your derision, I'll have the tall stack of blueberry pancakes with a side of bacon."

"Also legit," Liz said.

Ellie nodded like it was a reluctant concession. "I find no fault."

"And a cup of coffee, please." He handed his menu over.

"You got it, doll face."

Liz headed to the kitchen, leaving Ellie regarding him with curiosity. "Do you ever max out on coffee?" she asked.

Jack laughed. "I'm not sure I understand the question."

"Okay, then."

He tapped a finger to the table. "Don't judge me, Diet Coke."

Ellie lifted both hands. "I know. It's awful. But also, so good."

"I won't judge you if you don't judge me," he said.

She pursed her lips one way, then the other. "Deal. About this, at least. I reserve the right to judge you about things I learn about you in the future."

"How do you say things like that and make them sound cute and charming? I try anything close and one of my sisters smacks me for being a jerk."

Liz came back with their drinks, including two little pitchers of cream. Ellie took a long swig and let out an audible "ah" before saying, "I'm obviously a cuter and more charming person than you are."

"That must be it." He was sort of joking but sort of not.

"I think you're pretty charming." Ellie smirked. "In a consummate fuss bucket way."

"Fuss bucket?"

"Technical term." She downed another massive swig of soda with another audible "ah."

Jack stirred way too much cream and sugar into his coffee and indulged in an "ah" of his own. "I see."

"It's okay. You do you. Plenty of people find me too perky to be charming." She shrugged. "I'm not going to turn into a sourpuss to make them happy."

She made it sound so damn simple. In his experience, things might be, but people never were. At least not when it came to relationships. And especially not when it came to relationships involving sex. Could a grumpy and a sunshine—as Logan so effectively put it—make a go of it after the sex endorphins wore off? Or was last night a one-time thing?

"What? Is this where you tell me I'm too perky and you don't want to hook up with me again?"

He flinched, wanting to be annoyed that Ellie was putting words in his mouth, but mostly annoyed that he was already thinking about hooking up with her again. "You're not too perky."

"Does that mean you do want to hook up with me again?" Ellie leaned forward, elbows on the table and chin propped on her fists.

"I—"

She fell back as though wounded. "Undecided? Secretly married?"

Jack was used to teasing but not like this. Ellie had this way of poking fun, then making his brain go fuzzy with sex images before he could form any semblance of a comeback. All of which was exacerbated by the fact that they hadn't actually discussed what last night was—what it meant, how they felt, whether they were going to do it again. Not that he was old-fashioned or anything, but he didn't make a habit of one-night stands. Especially with women he had to see again.

"What? Too much? I didn't mean to get carried away." Ellie tucked a lock of hair behind her ear and looked away, making Jack wonder if it might be a tell.

"No. You didn't. It wasn't." Jack ran a hand through his hair and forced himself to look at Ellie rather than the table. "I guess, I don't know. I figured we should check in."

"Check in?" she asked.

"About last night. I mean, I know we established that we didn't regret it, but I feel like there's more to it than that. And you made that comment about hooking up again and it made me think it was the right time. To check in. That's a thing, right?" He stopped talking and hoped she'd give him points for substance if not style.

"It can be. It's not required or anything, though."

"Yeah, but dudes who don't are jerks." And he might be a grump, but he wasn't a jerk.

Ellie smiled. "Not all of them. But I know what you mean. And I appreciate it."

That twinge of unease blossomed. "Are you making fun of me again?"

"No." Ellie grabbed his forearm. "Not at all. I think it's really sweet actually. I just didn't…"

When she didn't finish, Jack took a stab. "Expect it?"

She laughed. "Something like that."

Their food arrived and provided just enough distraction that Jack thought maybe there wasn't anything to talk about after all. Though, if he was being honest, watching Ellie unabashedly go to town on her burger and fries made him want to talk and do a whole lot more. He didn't want to be weird about it, but Ellie felt like the most genuinely authentic woman he'd ever met. He liked it—liked her—a hell of a lot more than he'd bargained for. And if seeing her outside of being snowed in together was on the table, he was interested.

After Ellie polished off half her food, she wiped her fingers on a napkin and took a long swig of her soda. "Sorry. I really was starving."

Jack laughed. "We shoveled a lot of snow."

She cocked her head. "And did a lot of other things to work up an appetite."

"That, too." He told himself not to be disappointed that she didn't want to talk. It didn't necessarily mean things were off the table.

"I'm glad you asked to check in. You're right, it usually falls to the woman, or the more feminine identified person, to bring up. I wasn't sure how, and that fact was not helped by low blood sugar." She picked up a fry and bit it in half. "I didn't mean to turn into a goofball."

"It was charming." He polished off his bacon.

"Debatable. Either way, I'm well fed now and ready to talk for real."

"I didn't mean to make it sound urgent." He winced. "Or ominous."

Ellie laughed. "You didn't. So, what are you thinking? How are you feeling?"

"Uh-uh." He wagged a forkful of pancake at her. "I broached it, which means I'm off the hook for going first."

"Ooh. Touché." Ellie tapped a finger to her lips. "Okay. I like you. I think you're hot. And underneath that grumpy exterior, I think you're a standup guy."

He wasn't sure she meant that last part entirely as a compliment, but he took it as such. "That's the nicest thing a woman has said to me after spending the night together."

"I'm pretty sure that's not true."

"I said nicest, not most ego stroking."

Ellie stuck out a hand, feigning offense. "Hey, I said you were hot."

"You're pretty hot yourself." He pounced on the chance to shift the focus to her. "Oh, and I like you, too. Beyond that incessantly chipper exterior is a woman of substance."

Ellie blushed.

"Oh, so you can dish it out, but you can't take it."

She chuckled. "I can take it just fine, thank you very much."

They might have been having a genuine heart-to-heart, but his testosterone-enhanced brain raced to all the ways she had taken it. All the ways she hadn't but might be open to.

"I've lost you, haven't I? A double entendre too far."

He laughed at the accuracy. "Sorry."

"Don't be. My thoughts aren't so very different from yours, I'd wager," she said.

"No?"

"No. So, I think that means we should spend some more time together, see what unfolds." Her eyes held so many promises.

"Maybe not at Hampstead House?" he asked.

"As you may have gleaned, I'm otherwise homeless at the moment. I need to start looking for a place, but I haven't yet."

So many questions popped into his mind. But for now, only one mattered. "Well, you know where I live. Can I interest you in dinner at my place?"

"Depends. Do you cook?" She lifted her chin in playful challenge.

"Does your answer really depend on mine?"

Ellie nodded slowly, like she appreciated having it tossed back to her. "No."

"Good." He drained the last of his coffee. "But for the record, I do."

Chapter Fourteen

Jack pulled into his driveway and smiled. He had no idea if Rhett had shoveled the front porch and walk, or if Logan or Maddie had when they'd come over to plow. Either way, he owed someone a beer.

He let himself in, Dorothy and Sophia in tow. He'd barely unhooked their leashes when they made a beeline for their beds. "Did you girls miss being home? I sure did."

Dot stopped digging at her blanket long enough to give him a curious look.

"I know. You had fun with aunties Logan and Kathleen. I had some fun of my own. But there's still no place like home."

Sophia snuffled and Dot picked up her favorite toy, a sloth wearing overalls.

"Yeah, but first I want a shower." Which he'd technically done at Ellie's—twice—but he'd been stuck using her body wash and now smelled like strawberries and hibiscus. Well, strawberries, hibiscus, and sex. There were worse things, but still. A guy got used to his twenty-in-one gel that was supposed to evoke an alpine forest.

Upstairs, he stripped off the clothes he'd worn far too many days in a row and tossed them in the hamper. In the bathroom, he cranked the water nice and hot and turned the shower head to massage. Under the spray, he let out a groan—pleasure and relaxation and a couple of choice images reminding him why his muscles ached in the first place. Images that had nothing to do with pulling wire or fighting with the breaker box. Or shoveling snow.

As he worked the soap into his hair and over his body, his hand strayed south. One brush was all it took to get his cock standing at full attention. It was as though, in fewer than forty-eight hours, Ellie had made him insatiable. Which wasn't entirely fair. Thanks to weekly injections of T, it never took much to turn him on. But usually a couple good orgasms took the edge off for a few days at least. This? This was bananas.

Rather than indulging in the quick release his hand could bring, Jack turned his attention to scrubbing, rinsing, and toweling himself off. If there was a chance of being with Ellie again any time soon, it would be worth the wait. He said as much to Dot and Soph, who'd taken up residence on the bathroom rug while he showered.

They seemed far less interested in his sex life than the prospect of dinner, which he served them while contemplating his own choices. Something from the freezer, probably. A hunk of lasagna, maybe. Too bad he hadn't bothered to stop for fresh bread on his way home.

He almost missed the knock on the front door courtesy of the dogs crunching in stereo. But he heard it again, unmistakable now that he was paying attention. He peered through the window, surprised to see Rhett peering back. He opened the door. "Please don't tell me something isn't working."

Rhett laughed. "I promise I'd start with a text if that was the case."

A relief, though it didn't shed light on why Rhett was at his door. "Thanks."

"I wasn't sure if you'd managed to get supplies or had the energy to do anything with them. I've got a pot of gumbo on the stove, and I'm happy to share if you're interested."

He'd never had gumbo, but he knew enough to know it was hearty, hot, and probably on the spicy side. "Yeah?"

"You're welcome to come over, but I'm also perfectly happy to bring you a bowl if you're feeling antisocial."

He and Rhett had already bonded about being introverts with borderline hermit tendencies, so he took both offers as genuine. But if Rhett really didn't want company, she could have showed up with a Pyrex and insisted there was no pressure to take it. As much as he hated admitting it, he had a What Would Clover—or Logan or

Maddie—Do moment and said, "I'd love to come over. Can I bring beer?"

Rhett grinned. "I'll never turn down that offer."

"Should I come now?" he asked.

"If you're ready. Rice is just about done. But it'll hold for a good half hour, too." Rhett shrugged. "Whatever."

Jack couldn't tell if it was a Southern thing or a Rhett thing, but the easy-going vibe seemed natural. He couldn't even pretend to pull it off. "Now is great. I'll be right there."

A few minutes later, he found himself at a gorgeous antique table that barely fit in what passed for a dining room. "Damn, this is good."

"Okra is what scares people off. I use filé because that's what my mawmaw did. And because it's easier to get my hands on up here."

Jack nodded, vaguely aware of what okra was, if nothing else. "Your mawmaw taught you well. This is fantastic."

"I'm glad you like it. Maybe I can convince you to take some home. Even sharing with Ellie and putting some in the freezer, I've got more than I can eat without getting sick of it."

He chuckled. "The plight of the big pot. I've got the same issue with chili."

Rhett tapped her fingertip on the table. "Now, see, I'd happily agree to a trade."

"Deal."

"Speaking of Ellie, she was good when you left earlier?" Rhett's tone was almost too casual, even for Rhett.

They hadn't been, but Jack could appreciate the attempt to be smooth. "Yeah. We grabbed lunch together after digging out our cars, then stopped at the store so she could get some groceries since I ate most of hers."

"I'm glad she wasn't snowed in alone. I know I'm squeamish when it comes to blizzards, but still." Rhett shuddered.

"Yeah, but no matter how bad they are, they're never as destructive as hurricanes."

"Oh, I know. It's just the idea of being buried alive." She shuddered again.

"Well, we weren't anything close to that." He considered how much to say. "And I never mind getting stuck in for a few days here at home, in town. But even I can admit I wouldn't love being stuck alone out in the middle of nowhere."

"Exactly." The concession seemed to make Rhett feel better.

"You fared okay here? I know one of my sisters plowed, but thank you for shoveling the walk and the porch."

Rhett shook her head. "Logan did that. I told her she didn't have to, but she said you'd do it if you were here."

"Then I'll save all my gratitude for this." He pointed at his bowl.

"So, not to make things weird, but Ellie did mention you two had, you know."

Jack kept his cringe internal. At least he hoped he did. "Oh."

"We don't have to talk about it or anything, but I didn't want you to feel weird wondering whether or not I knew."

In the grand scheme of things, the wondering would be weirder than knowing. That didn't lessen the weird in the moment, though. He stared at his bowl and tried to decide what to say.

"Too much?" Rhett asked.

"No. I mean, yes, but no." Jack laughed. "I'll have to tell my sisters at some point, so it's only fair."

Rhett's eyes narrowed. "Have to?"

He laughed again. "Not like that. More like, we all share stuff and I'm usually off the hook by virtue of leading a very boring existence."

"There's something to be said for boring."

"Right?" His siblings—including Clover—didn't seem to get that.

"As someone who spent the better part of a year slogging through a crumbling relationship and another six months trying to tease apart the wreckage? Yeah, boring is good."

"I'm sorry you went through that. Relationships are the worst." The second the words were out of his mouth, he realized they were the exact wrong ones to say to the best friend of the woman he'd just spent the night with. "Not all relationships, obviously. The doomed ones. The doomed ones are the worst."

"I'll drink to that." Rhett lifted her beer. "And to being better at figuring out the doomed part before the doom begins."

He didn't try to hide his cringe then. Instead, he clinked his bottle to Rhett's and took a long swig of the hoppy ale. And maybe, just a little, he thought about Ellie and hoped they'd be able to enjoy each other for however long and come to a mutual decision about parting ways when the time came.

❖

FYI. Jack knows I know.

Ellie frowned at her phone. *How did you manage that? It literally just happened.*

Well, not literally. Because I literally had dinner with him, got a good night's sleep, and am on my second cup of coffee. Rhett added a winking emoji, the one with its tongue out.

Ellie rolled her eyes, then replied with the emoji expressing that sentiment.

I'm sure he was wondering or would have wondered. Preemptive disclosure. It's the way to go.

She shook her head this time. *That's such a poly thing to say.*

That got her a string of emojis, all expressing some variation of anger, annoyance, and despair. Rhett punctuated the collection with the green one on the verge of puking. Poor Rhett. She'd been through the wringer—from her wife declaring she wanted an open marriage, to embracing poly as a lifestyle, to having her wife change her mind and marry the woman she'd had an affair with in the first place.

I'm sorry. Ellie wished there was more she could say.

Oh, I'm fine. Just indulging a momentary flair for the dramatic.

Rhett would be fine. Ellie knew it with more conviction than she had for her own fineness some days. But it was possible to be fine and bruised at the same time. *I love you.*

Love you, too. Now, get to work so you have time to flirt with Jack later.

Ellie checked the time before tucking her phone in her pocket. Jack usually rolled in by eight thirty—an impressive feat given that he lived an hour away. She'd no sooner wondered if he might be late today, given the last few days, when she spied his knit cap out in the parking lot.

Just the knowledge of his proximity had warmth radiating through her. She clenched her thighs, blew out a breath, and reminded herself not to jump him in the middle of the study. She did, however, prop the drill she'd been using to mix plaster on the edge of the bucket so she could say a proper hello.

She waited a beat, then another. When he didn't appear, the hot and tingly sensation gave way to something sinking and left her feeling foolish. Jack didn't owe her a good morning kiss. And even if he might be inclined to greet her with one, the house was already swarmed with carpenters, tile guys, and any number of other subcontractors. She didn't have to know him any better than she already did to guess he wasn't a PDA sort of guy.

Resigned was better than foolish at least. Ellie picked up the drill, placing a foot on either side of the bucket to hold it steady. She pulled the trigger and worked the mixing paddle up and down. She'd see him when she saw him.

"Hey."

Ellie jumped, sending her bucket of plaster flying in one direction and herself in the other. The bucket landed on its side, its contents oozing onto the floor. She landed on her ass, about as graceful as a newborn giraffe. The drill clattered to the floor, sending splats of plaster everywhere, including her arm, her overalls, and her cheek. "Fuck."

Jack let out a snort of laughter. Ellie glared on principle. Jack had the sense to cringe.

"Sorry," he said.

"Damn right you are." She laughed, though, and took the hand he extended. Back on her feet, she surveyed the damage. Most of the spill landed on a drop cloth. She could let that dry and then scrape it off. Her overalls had seen worse. Her hair was a different matter. At least one blob had landed in her bangs and another right above her ear.

"Are you okay?"

Did she admit why she'd been so stubbornly focused on the task at hand? Probably not. "I'm fine. Just in my own little world."

His expression softened and he smiled. "I'm familiar with the condition."

For all her feeling foolish about being eager to see Jack, now she felt foolish for succumbing to the flash of insecurity. "I, um, didn't hear you come in."

The whine of a table saw punctuated the sentiment, and Jack rolled his eyes. "Everyone's back to work."

He seemed slightly saddened by the fact, which gave her a case of the warm and fuzzies. Not quite as fun as the warm and tinglies, but she'd take it. "Yeah."

"I just wanted to say good morning. I'm sorry I made you make such a mess."

She shrugged. "There are worse things."

He gestured to the toppled bucket. "What if I clean up here so you can take care of yourself?"

Ellie dropped her chin and turned her head, one way then the other. "Not a good look?"

"Not your best."

She touched her fingertips to her hair again. "This is already starting to dry. I need to get in the shower."

Jack folded his arms. "It was an accident, you know. There's no need to torture me in retaliation."

Confusion lasted only a second, giving way to warm and tingly after all. She smirked. "I don't think it'll hurt you to suffer a tiny bit."

He looked her up and down. Slow. Knowing. "Well, I'll have some nice images to keep me company at least."

Ellie could have happily stood there flirting. Or tried to coax Jack into playing hooky and joining her. But a crash sounded overhead, followed by yelling and swearing, and served as a jarring reminder they weren't alone. "I'll see you later I guess," she said with more than a little reluctance.

"I really am sorry about the mess."

"I'll let you make it up to me." She sauntered to the door, willing herself to play the vixen even if she looked ridiculous. A glance over her shoulder told her he was eating it up, plaster splats and all. "When you make me that dinner you promised."

"Name the day," he called, his voice following her from the room.

She smiled, wondering if the upcoming weekend would be too soon.

CHAPTER FIFTEEN

With Ellie not due until seven, Jack spent a leisurely Saturday morning at home, then headed over to Logan and Kathleen's. Kathleen had offered Logan the basement to use as a shop in exchange for first dibs on the trash Logan had a habit of bringing home and turning into treasure. And Jack had offered to help with the wiring, since many of said projects turned out to be joint efforts.

When he arrived, the whole house smelled like a bakery—yeasty and warm. "What magic is this?" he asked Kathleen after kissing her cheek. "And more importantly, do I get some?"

Kathleen smiled. "I got bored when we were snowed in and made bread."

"And now she's obsessed," Logan said, emerging from the basement.

"I'm not obsessed," Kathleen said.

Logan raised a brow. "Three loaves in three days?"

Kathleen smiled with the affection of a woman so in love she didn't mind being teased. "Maybe a little obsessed."

"I'd point out that not all obsessions are bad," Jack said.

Logan raised a hand. "Yeah, I'm definitely not complaining over here."

Kathleen jutted her hip, bumping it to Logan's. "You can complain when I jump on the sourdough train and start fussing over my starter like a baby."

Logan laughed. "If it means I get fresh bread on the regular, I'll feed it and change its diaper."

"And I'll babysit." It made Jack happy to know Logan and Kathleen had arrived at a place of joking about such things. Babies, not bread. It had been a source of tension and almost unraveled their relationship. Well, not actual babies. Just talking about them. How was it that talking about hard things turned reasonable and sane adults into zombies? He might not win any relationship trophies, but that seemed foundational for anything of substance.

"I'll keep both those things in mind. Today, however, we have a nice ciabatta and some minestrone." Kathleen tipped her head toward the table she'd already set. "Grab your bowl. We're serving from the stove."

Jack had two bowls of soup and three big chunks of bread, each smeared with more butter than would qualify as reasonable. He told himself it was because he was still running at a deficit from his time with Ellie—all that physical activity plus not wanting to wipe out her entire food supply. Really, though, Kathleen was a phenomenal cook, and he simply didn't want to stop. Plus, he needed energy for later. Working in the basement, sure, but also another night with Ellie. If their first time was anything to go on, he'd need all the strength and stamina he could muster.

He debated telling Logan as much when they headed down to the basement, but he couldn't think of a way to broach the subject that didn't make him feel like a lothario. Fortunately, Logan launched into a series of stories about their friend Leah's baby, which turned into a discussion of Maddie and Sy and gratitude that their plan to get married and have babies took the pressure off them for the time being. Which led to updates about Uncle Rich and his impending nuptials.

"I'm just glad Cherry talked him out of selling his half of the business to the first willing buyer," Logan said.

"Yeah, we could have found ourselves up shit creek." Jack shook his head. "I don't like the idea of my future being susceptible to a guy thinking with his Viagra prescription."

Logan let out a snort. "Seriously."

He grimaced. "Not a mental picture I need, thank you."

"Hey, older people deserve a rich and satisfying sex life as much as the rest of us."

"They absolutely do. That doesn't mean I want to think about the specifics. Especially when one of the parties is Uncle Rich." Rich had one of those overly friendly salesmen vibes that counted as a plus in his line of work, but it made Jack feel gross after spending more than a couple of hours with him.

"I'll give you that," Logan said.

Rich and Cherry had come up to Vermont to meet the family and drive Rich's car back down to Florida. But what everyone thought would be a quick and dirty sell-off of Rich's life had turned into Cherry falling in love with New England and discussions of whether they could swing a semi-retired snowbird lifestyle. A win for everyone, at least in the short term. Jack and his siblings, along with their parents, still spent most staff meetings discussing if, how, and when they'd be able to buy out Rich's half.

Logan and Jack rehashed a version of that conversation, then slipped seamlessly into companionable silence. It was their unspoken pattern when working together—catching up and chewing the fat, then taking a breather. It satisfied Logan's need for interaction without sending Jack's introverted self into overload.

Jack installed new breakers on the panel while Logan tacked wire to the exposed beams and joists. Jack connected the new outlets; Logan followed behind, securing them in the boxes and screwing on plate covers. In a matter of hours, they'd added eight new outlets, installed half a dozen can lights, and expanded the electrical load of the house by twenty percent.

Jack tucked his tools away while Logan surveyed the results. "I had a bet with Kathleen that we'd finish in one day," Logan said.

"Did she think we wouldn't?"

Logan tipped her head back and forth. "She figured we'd get distracted by my recent estate sale finds that I want your help with."

"There are finds? I wasn't told there were finds." He stuck out both hands. "Show me these finds."

She laughed. "See?"

"Yeah, but we got our work done. We earned some play." Jack lifted his chin toward the pile Logan had assembled in the corner. "Let's play."

Logan made a sweeping gesture. "After you."

The finds consisted of a few lamps, a vintage tabletop greenhouse, and a side table whose top could be flipped to reveal a chess board. Not all required his expertise but all things he'd be happy to get his hands on. They sorted and prioritized, and Jack pulled out a couple of the lamps to take home for rewiring.

"I'll bring them back and you can make them not hideous," he said.

"Deal." Logan grinned. "Hey, do you want to stick around for dinner, too? I'm sure Kathleen's not sick of you yet."

"I can't," Jack said.

Logan scowled. "Why not?"

"Hot date."

"You can't call it a hot date if it's with your dogs," Logan said without missing a beat. She knew him too well.

"I'll have you know I have plans with an actual human female."

Logan's eyes narrowed. "Is it Mom?"

"No," he said, slightly offended, though he'd tried that move at least once in the past.

"Oh. Clover, then. Tell her I said hi."

Irritated on principle if nothing else, he squared his shoulders and lifted his chin. "It's someone I've recently had sex with."

Logan's mouth fell open. "You slept with Clover? Dude."

Though he and Clover had a certain chemistry—that plenty of people had picked up on throughout the years—they'd never acted on it. Mostly because their relationship philosophies couldn't be more different. Clover embraced a solo poly identity with strains of relationship anarchy thrown in. Jack appreciated that in theory but considered it far too much work to maintain. So much seeking out of people and making new connections. Blech. "I did not sleep with Clover."

"That's a relief." Logan laughed. "Not that I don't love you both. So, who was—wait."

Since Logan seemed perfectly happy to have a one-directional conversation, Jack wasn't about to stop her. He folded his arms and waited for her to continue.

"Ellie. The artist. The one you were stuck with." Logan nodded slowly. "Who's best friends with your new tenant."

He neither confirmed nor denied, content to let his sister marinate in her theories for a moment.

"Yes?" Logan asked. "Am I right?"

Jack blinked, his version of a reluctant confirmation. Though, really, he wasn't all that reluctant. For all his grumbling, he wasn't opposed to a night of mutual enjoyment with a woman he found attractive. And however annoying he found his siblings from time to time, he shared the details of his life with them and loved that they did the same.

"She's beautiful." Logan frowned. "But I thought she got on your nerves."

"She's cool. Just, you know, perky."

"Right, right. Grumpy and sunshine." Logan nodded knowingly. "Did she wear you down with her good mood or did you find a way to bring out her inner bah, humbug?"

His mind conjured the highlight reel of the hours leading up to tearing each other's clothes off. "I'd say we met in the middle. With wine."

Logan laughed. "Who doesn't love a little social lubrication?"

He didn't make a point of relying on it, but he didn't turn his nose up at it, either.

"You cooking?" Logan asked.

Jack feigned offense. "Do you have to ask?"

"Let me rephrase. What are you cooking?"

He'd considered just about everything in his repertoire—not professional caliber but varied enough to keep himself well fed and impress when the moment presented itself. Cooking for a date was tricky. He wanted the meal to be nice but not heavy. Not helping his plight was the meager selection of good produce at this time of year. "Risotto with asparagus and peas." Neither were in season locally yet, but beggars couldn't be choosers.

"Nice."

It had worked for him in the past. Not that he was keeping score. "I do what I can."

"You know, it's a good thing you don't put in more of an effort on a regular basis. The women would be falling at your feet."

The thought sent a shudder through him, this evening's company notwithstanding. "You say that like it's a good thing."

Logan chuckled. "There's the Jack I know and love."

He let out a simpering laugh.

"I hope it goes well for you. And I hope this Ellie gives you a run for your money."

❖

After spending the morning at Riverdale Estates, Ellie headed back to Hampstead House for a full-body pamper. Even though it added to her driving around time, she liked the reset, allowing her to shift gears from the version of herself she showed her mom to the one she was the rest of the time.

She dillydallied with makeup and dawdled over what to wear before settling on a plum-colored sweater dress, black leggings, and ankle boots. Casual, but nicer—not to mention more feminine—than what Jack typically saw her in. Plus, since she'd be spending the afternoon with Rhett, it wouldn't get her too much ribbing in the meantime.

Rhett greeted her with a big hug hello and compliments about the clingy fabric accentuating her boobs. Not ribbing, exactly, but so totally Rhett. They caught up on the odds and ends of life. Rhett had contracted with a couple of new shops to carry her pottery and successfully fended off an invitation to the gender reveal party for her sister's new baby.

"I've never been so grateful for twelve hundred miles," Rhett said with a shudder.

"I'm rarely grateful to be an only child, but that might count as a tick in the column."

"So," Rhett said, promising an unsubtle conversation shift. "Is it weird to come hang out with me, then go next door to get laid?"

"Well, when you put it that way." Ellie grinned and sipped her tea, then shook her head. "No. Not weird."

"It's a rather poly arrangement, if you think about it. Though I'm not sure which of us is the metamour."

She rolled her eyes. "Neither of us is. Not unless I start sleeping with you or you start sleeping with Jack."

Rhett made a face. "Yeah. Bad analogy. I take it back."

"But I appreciate you playing emotional support human to both of us." She'd decided to frame it that way in her mind rather than get bogged down in the weeds of potential weirdness.

"It's a great distraction from the train wreck of my love life." Rhett cringed. "Or thinking about what Gillian is doing right now."

Ellie curled her lip. She'd stopped cussing at every mention of Rhett's ex—at Rhett's insistence—but she couldn't let it go completely. "Being a narcissistic jerk face, probably."

Rhett gave her a stern look.

"What? She is. Best friend prerogative allows me to say that even if you've decided to be graceful about everything."

"She's just living her truth."

Ellie had a plethora of opinions about that categorization, but rehashing them didn't seem to make Rhett feel better. She opted to change the subject instead. "Speaking of living one's truth, do you think it might be time to wade back in?"

Rhett shook her head with force. "Nope."

Ellie covered Rhett's hand with her own. "There are a lot of amazing women out there who aren't Gillian."

"I know. And I will meet some of them and date some of them and maybe even settle down with one or two of them. I'm just not there yet. I promise I won't check out completely."

She let out a sigh and, since some things bore repeating, said, "Fucking Gillian."

Rhett smiled, and there almost wasn't any sadness riding with it. "Fucking Gillian."

They sat in silence for a minute. The ability to do that was one of her favorite things about being friends with Rhett, since it didn't come naturally to her.

"All right," Rhett said eventually. "No fucking for me since I'm still getting over fucking Gillian, but Jack is waiting and I imagine the fucking will be fucking fantastic, so you should go."

Ellie laughed even as her heart ached for what Rhett had been through and would continue to go through for the foreseeable future.

"I am, but I'm channeling so much good energy into the universe to heal your heart and make you better than ever."

Rhett sighed. "Thanks."

She stood. "I love you. You know that, right?"

"More than I know a lot of things." Rhett made a shooing motion. "Now get. Let me get laid vicariously through you, in the most platonic and non-creepy way possible."

"I hope you have a good night," she said as she slipped into her shoes and grabbed the jacket she didn't bother putting on.

"I will. Just don't be too loud, okay?"

Ellie cringed. "I'll do my best."

"That good, huh?"

"Oh yeah."

"Well, good. You deserve it."

She wanted to say something about Rhett deserving it, too, but held back. For now, at least. "Thanks."

"And don't worry about keeping it down. I'll put in my earbuds and spend my evening in blissful oblivion."

She thought about what she and Jack got up to in the less than ideal setup she had at Hampstead House—cramped bed, minimal heat, plus having to overcome the exhaustion of the day and the bottle of wine they'd downed. At the risk of jinxing herself, she expected tonight to be even better. And she wasn't afraid to own it. She went to the door but turned to blow Rhett a kiss. "You're the best."

"You are, too."

She waved goodbye and let herself out, making the twenty-foot trek from Rhett's front door to Jack's.

CHAPTER SIXTEEN

Jack knew it would be Ellie on the other side when he opened the door, but the sight of her made his breath catch. Well, not catch. That was the sort of phrase Kathleen would write into one of her books. But damn. She had her coat folded over her arm, giving him a full view of the dress she wore. It showed off all the curves usually hidden by overalls, and her dark hair fell softly over her shoulders. He had to resist the urge to run his fingers through it, to yank Ellie inside and into his arms and take her straight to bed. Kathleen would probably write that sort of thing into one of her books, too, and he didn't even care.

"Why do you look surprised to see me?" Ellie regarded him with amusement.

"I'm not." He shook his head. "I'm happy to see you."

She quirked a brow and his emphatic, if uninspired, declaration. "Does that mean you're going to invite me in?"

He stepped back and held the door wide. "Of course."

Ellie crossed the threshold and, before setting down her bag or her coat, leaned in for a kiss. A slow, lingering kiss that assured him he'd been as much on her thoughts as she'd been on his. She pulled back with a smile. "Hi."

"Hi," he said, wishing he was better at banter. "Um, I'll take your coat, and you can leave your stuff on that bench for now."

She handed over her coat, and he busied himself with hanging it while she took off her boots and rooted around in the duffel. "I took the liberty of bringing slippers. I hope you don't mind."

When she pulled out a pair of fuzzy, leopard-print slides, he didn't try to hold back a smile. "I'm glad you did."

In the time it took Ellie to slip them on her feet, Dot and Sophia extricated themselves from their blanket pile and ambled over to say hello. Ellie immediately dropped to her knees and lavished them with greetings and pets. "They're so sweet," she said briefly to him before shifting her focus back to them. "You're so sweet. And cute. And I bet smart, too."

They all stayed like that for a minute, then Jack suggested they move to the living room so everyone could be more comfortable while he finished making dinner.

"Will they follow us to the kitchen? It feels rude to abandon you completely."

Before he could say he didn't mind, Ellie stood and started in that direction. "Yeah, that's pretty much their third favorite place, after the sofa and bed," he said.

They moved as a ragtag pack, Ellie settling back on the floor as soon as she spotted the oversize dog bed in the corner. Dot and Sophia followed, fully blissed out by the combo of attention and a soft place to sit.

"I'd offer to help, but I'm too busy falling in love with your dogs." Ellie looked up at him from the floor, her eyes as bright as her smile. "You're okay with that, right?"

"I couldn't be more delighted. You're having fun, Dot and Sophia are in heaven, and I get to cook without anyone in my way."

Ellie's lips pressed together, like she was debating whether to laugh or tell him to go fuck himself. Eventually, she let out a chuckle. "I'd take offense, but I know exactly what you mean."

He hadn't truly worried about her reaction, but his shoulders relaxed. "I'm sure you're great in the kitchen, but I have my routine, you know?"

She remained cross-legged on the floor and folded her arms. "What makes you think I'm good in the kitchen? I served you canned soup and pasta sauce from a jar."

"Yeah, but you were self-conscious about it and apologized for your frozen meatballs. Either you're a good cook or all your friends lie to you."

She laughed for real then. "Okay, yes. I am a decent cook. And those are legit measures. I'll cook you something nice if I manage to find a place to live."

Jack paused, ladle full of stock midair. "Are you struggling to?"

"Oh." Ellie laughed again. "No. I haven't really tried yet. The last few months have been all about getting my mom settled, then clearing out the house and getting it on the market. When I negotiated staying onsite at Hampstead House, I gave myself license not to think about it for a while."

He couldn't imagine preferring uncertainty, even if the alternative was a lot of work. "It can be tricky, especially if you're not looking in one of the cities."

"Yeah. I'm hoping to avoid even the suburbs of Springfield," she said. He must have looked confused because she added, "That's where my mom is."

"Close but not too close?" He lived five minutes from his parents, but he got why that was a thing.

She smiled. "Exactly."

"Are you hoping to buy or rent?"

"Rent for now, because I don't feel ready to commit to any place yet. But buy eventually. I have feelings about making a space my own."

It was Jack's turn to laugh. "Yeah. Logan and I bought this place as soon as she finished college. I was barely twenty-five and already over living in a rental."

"That's really cool. Did you two do a lot to it?"

"It was a disaster. Because that was pretty much what we could afford on our budget. We were lucky, though. Our parents cosigned the mortgage, and we were able to get materials at cost and do a lot of the work ourselves." It struck him just how privileged that sounded. Which it was, in a way. Hopefully, the context helped.

Ellie sighed. "I love what I do, but I sometimes wish I was more handy."

"You could be." Jack resumed stirring. "I'm trained as an electrician but know the basics of everything else. I'd be happy to teach you anything you wanted to learn."

"Really?"

He didn't want to come across heavy-handed, but it frustrated him how many people—women especially—felt helpless when it came to their homes. But Ellie's reaction held nothing but enthusiasm, and it was easy to imagine installing light fixtures together or showing her the basics of repairing a faucet or drain. "The offer stands, whether or not we keep sleeping together."

Ellie got up from the floor then and sauntered over. "I hope that's your way of being a standup guy and not a hint that you don't want to have sex with me again."

"The former." Jack gave a bobblehead nod. "Definitely the former."

"Oh, good." Ellie kissed his neck, right below his ear. "Because I'd love to pick up some do-it-myself skills, but I'm far more interested in you doing me."

The snort escaped before he could stop it. "That's a terrible come-on."

"Is it?" she asked. He'd turned to face her, and she took advantage, pressing her breasts to his chest.

Jack groaned. "Yes."

"Seems like you like the way I'm coming on to you just fine."

"Not fair." He shook his head. "You can't chase a bad line with your breasts and expect me to hold firm."

Ellie tipped her head. "I don't think you have any issues with how firm you can be."

The line might be even worse than the first one, but the innuendo worked. He was hot and horny, and they hadn't even sat down to dinner. "I guess you'll have to wait and see."

She licked her lips and sent his imagination to some particularly X-rated places. "I'm looking forward to everything you want to show me."

Ellie eyed the serving bowl—still more than half full of risotto—that sat between them. "I'm resisting seconds solely because of what I hope to be doing in an hour."

"I'll happily send you home with leftovers if you'd like."

It was sweet, the sort of thing a boyfriend would do. Though, in her experience, it might be more accurate to say girlfriend. She'd had mixed results with guys through the years—cis and trans alike. Jack seemed different, especially now that she'd gotten to know him. Definitely a guy, but more thoughtful than the ones she'd encountered. "I'm not going to say no."

"I'm not much of a baker, but I picked up some brownies from the Sugar Shack if you're wanting something sweet."

Rhett had been going on and on about that place, but she hadn't had the chance to check it out. "I'd love a brownie, but maybe not just yet?"

"Yeah, of course." Jack nodded. "Just say when."

She chewed her lip, debated how forward to be. "About everything? Or just the brownie?"

His expression turned quizzical.

"Sorry. I was trying to be clever."

"Ah," he said. Then his eyes lit up. "Oh."

"I mean, we could watch a movie or something. I'm not only here for the sex." She gestured to the food that remained. "And the dinner."

Jack smirked. "We've established I'm not one for sparkling conversation."

"You're not so bad." She looked him up and down. "Though I have to say I might enjoy some of your other skills a bit more."

"Yeah?" he asked, clearly pleased with the statement.

"Oh yeah."

"So." Jack swallowed but didn't continue.

"So, I'd love to see your bedroom." No point pretending otherwise.

"Yeah. Okay. It's upstairs."

Ellie lifted her chin. "I'll follow you."

They barely made it through the door before Jack had his hands in her hair and his lips on hers. Knowing what was about to happen—knowing it was going to be good—spurred Ellie on. She started pulling at Jack's clothes, wanting the sensation of his skin on hers.

Jack took the cue, shedding his shirt and pulling Ellie's dress up and over her head. She smiled at the sight of his naked torso and traced her fingers along his scars. "Tell me about the ways you like to fuck," she said.

Jack paused and pulled back enough to make eye contact. "I like lots of ways."

She held his gaze. "Me, too."

"Are you asking me if I like to strap?"

"Do you?"

His smile spread slowly. "Wait right here."

He grabbed a bag and went to the bathroom. Ellie used the moment of privacy to wiggle out of her leggings. While she was at it, she shed her socks and underwear. "I need you inside me, the sooner the better," she called.

"I'm moving as fast as I can," Jack hollered.

Ellie perched on the edge of the bed. "For the record, I'm usually a very patient person."

"Is that so?" Jack sauntered into the room, cock at full attention.

"Usually." She stood and licked her lips, not even pretending to be subtle.

"But not now?"

She merely shook her head.

"What do you want now?" Jack asked. "Right this very second."

Ellie lifted her chin. "You. Doing whatever you want."

"Whatever I want?"

She nodded, thrilling at the prospect, and of trusting him enough to let go. "Yes."

"So many options." He ran a hand down her side and around to cup her ass.

It was enough of an invitation for her. Ellie turned around, leaned over, and planted her hands on the bed. She looked over her shoulder at Jack, whose mouth hung ever so slightly open. "How about this one?"

He spanned his hands over both sides of her ass. "I like that one a lot."

She thought he would and was delighted to be proven right. She shifted her weight side to side, making her hips sway.

"Lube?" he asked.

She looked over her shoulder and shook her head. "Just a little warmup."

Jack raised a brow. "Just a little?"

She wiggled her butt back and forth, more playful than sensual this time. "You'll see."

His hand moved between her legs. Ellie widened her stance to give him better access, and he took full advantage, sliding a finger on either side of her clit. She shifted back, more instinct than intent. Wanting more. Needing more.

When he dipped those two fingers inside, she clenched around him. It had only been a couple of days, but her desire bordered on desperate. She tried to convey that with her body instead of words, rocking against him with purpose. He turned his hand left, then right. Massaging her from the inside.

"You are wet," he said without stopping his slow exploration.

"Yep," she managed.

His fingers slid away, and Ellie braced herself for what was to come. When the tip of his cock pressed against her opening, it took every drop of restraint she had to wait. Jack made it worth her while.

He pushed the head in. Ellie groaned. He slid in further, stroking her G-spot along the way. She gasped. He pulled out and thrust in deeper. Again. Deeper. Again. Inch by glorious inch.

Before long, he'd filled her completely. The base of the cock and the warm leather of the harness pressed against her each time. And when Jack pulled back, he pulled out almost entirely. The length of him was perfection. The rhythm hypnotic.

When Jack's hands grasped her hips, she let out a hum of pleasure. He used his hold to guide their bodies—together, apart, together, apart. Over and over.

God, she loved being taken like this. She dug her fingers into the mattress and pumped her hips back to meet him. Each thrust stroked all the right spots, and it was a struggle to keep her knees from buckling.

When the orgasm began to build, she let it. "I'm close," she said, thinking it only right to give him fair warning. "So fucking close."

He groaned. "I've got you, baby. Come for me."

Whether it was the endearment or the demand, she couldn't be sure. But his words sent her tumbling over the edge. The orgasm crashed over her in waves. His own body bucked, and she knew he was tumbling with her. She rode it, rode him, until her legs gave out and she collapsed onto the bed. Even then he stayed with her, half lying and half braced over her. His cock stayed buried deep.

"Fucking fuck," she said, though her words got somewhat lost in the mattress.

"Uh-huh," Jack mumbled into her hair. "You okay?"

"So good."

"Does that mean you're done?" he asked, easing out of her and taking a step back.

Ellie pushed herself upright and turned. She pointed to the cock. "With that? For now. But otherwise no."

He gave her a quizzical expression but worked at the buckles and shed the harness. He stood there, wide stance and hands on his hips. Sexy as fuck but like he didn't quite know what to do with himself.

"You should sit." Ellie angled her head toward the bed. "Make yourself comfortable."

He did, but his eyes remained wary. Ellie sashayed over and kneeled in front of him, resting her hands on the tops of his thighs. Understanding dawned, and Jack's lips parted.

"Is this okay?"

He merely nodded.

Ellie leaned forward, looking up at Jack through her lashes. She wrapped her lips around his cock and sucked gently. Jack groaned, and his eyes drifted closed. Ellie allowed hers to do the same. She worked him slowly, swirling her tongue around the tip and bobbing her head as she sucked.

Jack's hands returned to her hair. He fisted them but didn't pull. He guided her, but gently. She could tell he was holding back, holding firm to his awareness of her and not wanting to be too rough.

Ellie wanted him rough, wanted him to let go. To trust that she could handle herself and wouldn't be sorry to feel a little used. She increased her speed and dug her fingers into his quad muscles, trying to communicate that but unwilling to break contact long enough for words. It seemed to work because his grip on her hair tightened, and he pushed into her with more force.

Ellie ate it up, feeling completely powerful and utterly at Jack's mercy at the same time. He came in a torrent of swear words, his whole body going rigid with it. She ate that up, too.

Jack flopped back onto the bed. Ellie sat on her heels and smiled. "Thank you."

"Not fair," he said, breathing heavy.

"No?" Ellie stood and batted her lashes.

Jack propped on his elbows. "Not unless you let me reciprocate."

Oh, that's how it was going to be. "I wouldn't want to deny you. I know fairness is important to you."

He pushed himself the rest of the way up and stood so that they were face-to-face. "So important."

"What exactly did you have in mind?"

Instead of saying anything, Jack grabbed her and all but tossed her onto the bed. He slid a hand under each knee and spread her legs, settling his torso between them. "Something like this."

Before Ellie could speak, Jack's tongue slipped into her. She arched, overwhelmed by the intensity of the sensation and yet wanting more. Needing more.

She couldn't quite manage words, but Jack didn't seem to need them. In fact, he seemed to know exactly what would drive her to the edge and send her careening over. And that's exactly what he did.

When the world finally stopped spinning, Ellie sucked in all the oxygen her lungs would hold and flung an arm over her head. She blew it out slowly and dropped her head to the side to look Jack in the eye. "That was amazing."

"I'm glad you approve," he said with the most perfect lopsided grin.

"Understatement."

"I feel like I should say thank you, since that's what you said to me."

"You're welcome." She laughed. "Reciprocation is the best."

Chapter Seventeen

When Jack arrived at the soon to be opened Grumpy Old Goat tasting room, he found Sy frowning over an iPad. "Do I want to know?"

Sy shook her head. "I realized I should figure out how to use this before I attempt to train the staff."

"Always preferable to know what you're talking about."

Sy laughed. "Exactly."

"So, we're going over there?" Jack pointed to the butcher block peninsula Maddie had built to serve as the register for both the tasting room and shop.

"Yep. Maddie said the pull would be minimal and you should be able to run off the line for the wine fridge."

"Did she now?" She was right, of course, but he didn't need her telling him.

Sy lifted both hands. "I think she only told me that so I wouldn't freak about tearing holes in the wall after the fact."

Jack laughed then. "I guess that justifies her being a know-it-all. But just this once."

Sy snickered. "I won't tell if you won't."

"Deal." He headed over and started calculating. "Do you want me to put in two outlets just in case?"

Sy abandoned the tablet and came over. "The more, the merrier?"

He shrugged. "That sounds nicer than adding one for a rainy day."

"I'm hoping rainy days bring in people looking to get out of the house, so that works for me, too."

Jack grinned. "That's the spirit."

Sy lifted her chin. "You're awfully chipper this morning. You get laid or something?"

"Depends. Is my answer going to stay just between us?"

"Ooh. You drive a hard bargain." Sy drummed her fingers on the counter. "How long am I keeping this secret?"

He laughed. Sy wasn't legally part of the family yet, but she might as well be for how well she fit in. "You aren't actually. I was yanking your chain."

"Wait." Sy shot her a side-eye. "Is that a confirm or deny?"

Sy wasn't in the business of harassing him to the degree his sisters did, but even she poked fun at his stalwart ways. He lifted his chin back. "You tell me."

"Nice. Ellie, right? The artist from your current project?"

While he appreciated some degree of privacy, Jack knew better than to think he'd get away spending two nights trapped with a woman he'd admitted to having chemistry with and keeping the details to himself. Big picture details, at least. And since he'd invited Ellie to the opening of the tasting room, it would be pretty obvious pretty quickly that they were dating. "Yep."

"I'm glad, dude. Everybody deserves some action."

He frowned at the phrase. Not because Sy meant anything derogatory or dismissive by it, but because it implied a lack of something more. And as much as he wasn't looking for a relationship, the thought that Ellie might consider him not much more than a hookup left a bad taste in his mouth. Since he had no desire to dig deeper into that—in the moment or with his soon-to-be sister-in-law—he offered a vague nod.

"You'll holler if you need me, right?" Sy asked.

"Go learn your POS. I got this."

It was Sy's turn to offer a vague nod. She returned to tapping at the screen, and Jack got to work. After flipping the breaker to that part of the room, he made a couple of choice cuts into the drywall and spliced the wire into a new junction box. Adding the outlets themselves took all of twenty minutes and, fortunately for him, Maddie would swoop in to do the patching and painting.

He tucked his tools back into his bag, thinking he might have set a record for time to finish a job. It was a minuscule job, but still. He stood and dusted off his hands. "I think you should be good to go."

Sy blew out a breath. "I can't thank you enough. I can't believe we didn't factor in the POS system when we did the wiring."

"To be fair, I didn't think about it, either." He shrugged. "The price you pay for hiring an outfit that does mostly residential work."

"I like the price I paid very much, thank you." Sy smiled. "And I'm pretty fond of the outfit."

He couldn't help but walk through the door Sy left open. "The outfit, or one particular woman in it, whose outfit usually contains a pair of tight jeans?"

Sy straightened her shoulders. "Both. Though, damn, she looks amazing in those jeans."

Jack laughed. He obviously gave little thought to the fit of Maddie's jeans, but he wasn't so much of a prude as to balk at Sy's appreciation.

Maddie strode in, cordless drill in hand. "Who looks amazing in those jeans?"

Sy grabbed her around the waist and pulled her close. "You do."

"Oh." Maddie smirked. "I thought there might be a hot delivery person or something. I didn't want to miss it."

Sy rolled her eyes but planted a noisy kiss on Maddie's neck. "You're supposed to like my ass in jeans."

"I do." Maddie nodded eagerly. "That doesn't prevent be from appreciating another fine specimen in passing. They're not mutually exclusive."

"True story," Sy said. "Just promise me we'll talk if you ever want to do more than appreciate in passing."

Jack didn't think Sy and Maddie were seriously considering poly, but they all spent enough time with Clover to know better than to dismiss it out of hand. "As much as I enjoy all this conversation about nice asses in jeans, I need to get to my other job."

Sy stuck out a hand for Jack to shake, which he did. "Go, go. I owe you one."

He grinned. "I will happily take payment in cheese."

Sy swept both arms wide. "By this time Saturday, every case in here will be filled. You can help yourself."

"I'm looking forward to it," Jack said.

Maddie pointed her drill his way. "Speaking of Saturday and nice asses, are we finally going to get to meet this mystery woman of yours?"

"That was the worst segue ever." He shook his head. "I'm refusing to answer on principle."

Maddie stuck out her tongue. "Whatever. I know you RSVP'd two, so unless you're counting the mouse in your pocket, I'm assuming she'll be here."

Jack rolled his eyes. "Fine. She will be. Try not to give her the third degree, will you?"

"Moi?" Maddie pressed a hand to her chest.

Sy let out a snort, and Jack merely shook his head. "I like her, okay? But it's been barely a couple of weeks. I know how you can be."

Maddie's hand swept from her chest to a Scout's honor salute. "I'll be completely chill." She smirked. "To her at least. No promises when it comes to grilling you after the fact."

Sy jerked her head to the side. "Ooh."

"I expected nothing less." He finished packing his tools away. "Hey, Sy, can I grab a plain chèvre now? Ellie's coming for dinner later this week, and I want to make that chicken thing with the sun-dried tomatoes."

"I got you." Sy disappeared to the main storage area and returned with two logs. "I hope she likes it, and you get lucky."

At the rate things with Ellie were going, he had every expectation of getting lucky regardless of what he served for dinner. Not that he intended to say that to his sister and soon to be sister-in-law. But it filled him with a certain satisfaction as he finished cleaning up and went on his way.

"I think this might be the one." Ellie turned a slow circle and looked to Rhett. "What do you think?"

"I think it has character without feeling like it's going to fall apart in a stiff breeze." Rhett tipped her head one way, then the other. "So, if that's our criteria, yeah, maybe."

She scowled on principle, but Rhett was telling the truth. They'd seen two white-walled, beige-carpeted boxes, three apartments that had been hacked out of once gorgeous Victorians, and a carriage house conversion that she didn't entirely believe had a valid certificate of occupancy. She'd known her options would be sparse in the mostly rural stretch between Bedlington and Springfield, but the actual listings were even worse than her lowered expectations, especially after crossing off those that didn't allow cats. It had gotten so bad the day before that she genuinely considered buying something even if she had to turn around and sell it in a couple of years.

Today, though. Today brought this charming two-bedroom unit in Grovener, a tiny town half an hour from Bedlington and just over the border from Massachusetts. It was the first floor of a house that had been divided, but thoughtfully. The original kitchen and sitting room remained charmingly intact, along with an enclosed sun porch off the back. The two bedrooms shared a bathroom, but considering how often she anticipated guests, it was an arrangement she could live with. And it was in the budget she'd set for herself—one that would allow her to keep her savings intact for when she did want to buy.

"Be honest." She planted her fists on her hips. "Do you like it?"

"It's charming. Cozy but not cramped. So you. And best of all, reasonably close to me."

"It is charming. That's the perfect word." She clasped her hands and pressed them to her chest. "I wanted charming."

"You deserve charming." Rhett grinned.

Deserve was such a funny word. She didn't use it much, and when she did, it was usually in reference to things in the little treats category. An iced mocha in the middle of the afternoon. A manicure after a project that left her nails and cuticles wrecked. The twenty-dollar bottle of wine instead of the twelve. The idea of deserving bigger things, things that mattered, left her uneasy.

Not because she didn't, but because it opened a can of worms from her religious childhood that she'd just as soon not wrestle with. Like whether it was wrong to want big things in the first place. Or whether she'd made the right decision about not continuing to live with her mother.

"Not the right thing to say?" Rhett asked, as though she understood her comment carried more weight than it might seem on the surface.

She smiled. No point ruining a perfectly good moment. "A lovely thing to say."

Rhett's eyes narrowed, and Ellie could tell she was deciding whether or not to push.

Rather than wait her out, Ellie gave Rhett's forearm a squeeze. "I'm going to go talk to the owner."

Since the owner—a weathered-looking white guy who appeared to be in his seventies—was waiting for them outside, and since the weather had started to hint at spring but not much more, it was a move she could get away with. She went to the postage stamp of a front porch and found him staring into the distance. It struck her, which in turn made her wonder about her generation and how much of a lost art that had become.

"What did you think?" he asked.

"I'll take it."

He seemed surprised by her answer. "Yeah?"

She certainly didn't owe him an explanation, but her default was to put people at ease. "I've looked at a half dozen places already. This is definitely the one."

"Alrighty then. I'll go get the lease forms from my car." He started to go but paused. "It's first and last month's rent, along with one month rent for the security deposit."

She patted her purse. "I've got my checkbook."

He didn't question her further, though it looked like he wanted to. Rhett joined her on the porch and Mr. Franklin returned with the paperwork. She read through the legalese, signed on the dotted line, and gave him a check for more than what she'd earn on the entire Hampstead House project. Questions about deserving things popped back into her mind, but she pushed them aside. She didn't have anything to do with the financial cushion her father had provided her with, so the best she could do was be grateful and use it responsibly.

"I hope you're going to let Jack help you move," Rhett said when they were back in her car.

"I hadn't really thought about it." Not entirely true, since she'd given more than a passing thought to hiring the same movers who'd handled getting her mother's things to her new place and loading up a storage unit with hers.

"I think he's probably the sort of guy who'd be offended if you didn't."

That hadn't occurred to her. She'd dated her share of butches and mascs and trans guys, and they all definitely seemed to have a code of some sort. But most of them had been artists or academics. Okay, and one ill-advised investment banker. None of them had a lot to offer in the manual labor department. She didn't want to assume Jack would want to help on that front, but she also realized she shouldn't assume he wouldn't. "I'll ask him."

"When are you gonna move?"

She had a few weeks left on her arrangement to live at Hampstead House. But it was getting weirder and weirder to live in the servant's quarters as the house neared completion. Plus, there was some work to be done in that space, and it was on hold until she cleared out. "Next weekend if I can swing it. The Grumpy Old Goat party is Saturday night, but maybe Sunday?"

"Might as well, right?"

Her new digs were technically closer to both Jack and her mother. So, while she'd be picking up a work commute, there were some benefits. More importantly, they were hers. Well, as much hers as she was going to get for the time being. She'd actually never had more than a room to herself, and now she was about to have four. Five if she counted the sun porch. She absolutely wanted to move in sooner rather than later and had no doubt Emily Dickinson would share that feeling. "Might as well."

CHAPTER EIGHTEEN

Ellie stepped out of Jack's bathroom wrapped in a towel and found Jack lounging on the bed scrolling his phone. The casual, almost domestic vibe of it struck her. And not in a bad way. "I hope I haven't been keeping you."

He looked up and smiled. "I need exactly five minutes to shower and trim my beard, and another three to get dressed."

"Show off."

"Being a dude has some perks."

She waved a hand. "You can keep them."

"Don't mind if I do." He stood and crossed the room to her. "Do you need anything?"

She'd packed not only her outfit for the party but all the bits and bobs of female adornment she'd had little occasion to use lately, save the handful of times she'd primped for Jack. "Maybe more than eight minutes?"

Jack laughed. "We've got forty-five before we need to leave, and you can have all of them."

"I promise I'm not the girl to need that many." At least not with her clothes picked out and her shower already done.

"I like that about you."

"You would."

He kissed her briefly and headed to the bathroom. Ellie did her makeup and hair, taking pleasure in the process as well as in the sight of her lipstick and mascara next to Jack's watch and the other personal items arranged on his dresser.

She slipped the dress over her head and tugged it into place. The wrap style accentuated her cleavage, and the dark teal of the fabric made her eyes look several shades darker. A pair of dangly gold earrings and her favorite, if rarely worn, black heels finished the look.

Jack didn't have a full-length mirror, but Ellie turned one way, then the other, in front of the dresser, checking her reflection from as many angles as she could finagle. She smiled, pleased with the result.

The problem with working on a site like she was, and living out of a suitcase on top of it, was just how much she'd resorted to variations on jeans and T-shirts. It was nice to let her girly side out to play, especially now that she was getting laid on the regular.

She didn't have to see Jack come in to know the whistle belonged to him. "Damn," he said when she turned around and struck a pose.

"Not too much?" she asked.

"Even if it was, I'd be tempted to lie. Because, again, damn. But, no, you look perfect."

"Good enough that you'll take me home and have your way with me at the end of the night?"

He crossed the room and slid an arm around her waist, pulling her to him. "Good enough that I have half a mind not to leave the house in the first place."

"Stop." She swatted his arm, admiring the fit of his wool blazer and loving the way it turned his own look of jeans and a button-down into a delicious concoction of casual and classy. "Clover is one of your best friends. And Sy, too."

"And they're both, along with Maddie and Logan, dying to meet you. If we didn't show, they might literally turn up on the front porch." Jack shook his head. "I'm not even kidding."

Ellie smiled. "If Rhett didn't already know you, she'd be the same."

Jack made a show of rolling his eyes. "Friends. They're as bad as family."

"Especially the ones who fall into the chosen family category."

Jack's expression softened, then got serious. "Yeah."

"Why do you look so stern?"

He shook his head, as though chasing away cobwebs. Or perhaps thoughts he'd rather not have. "I gripe, but I wouldn't trade them for the world."

"Chosen family or the one you're born with?"

"Both." Jack chuckled. "But don't tell any of them I said that, or they'll give me such crap."

From the affection in his tone, it was clear he didn't really mean it. "Your secret is safe with me."

"Does that mean we have to go?" He didn't pout, but it was close.

Ellie lifted a shoulder. "Yes. But it doesn't mean we can't have a little fun before we do."

She might as well have suggested they rob a bank given the scandalized look on his face. "What kind of fun?"

She could have given him options, or perhaps tugged off the dress she'd just pulled on. But both those things would have wasted precious seconds. And when she only had a few to play with, she had no intention of wasting them. Instead, she went for a kiss. One of those long, hot, messy kisses that would have her scrambling to fix her lipstick before it was all said and done. To his credit, Jack kissed her back without missing a beat.

She kept her mouth on his, wiggling a hand between them so she could go to work on his belt. Jack either didn't notice or didn't have the wherewithal to stop her, and when she slipped her fingers into his boxer briefs, his only reaction was a groan. She worked him slowly, enjoying the way he hardened against her hand.

Only when she broke the kiss did Jack seem to show any hint of rational thought. He blinked a few times, confusion clouding over lust. Ellie simply smiled and dropped to her knees.

Jack looked at her dumbly, then. Like he wanted what was about to happen more than anything, but any hope of forming words to that effect was futile. He swallowed visibly, eyes fixed on hers. Ellie held her smile as she tugged his pants and boxers down to his knees. And then, without hesitation or buildup, she took him into her mouth.

Jack let out a moan that made her clit throb, and the muscles in his thighs tightened. Ellie sucked, bobbing her head slowly for extra effect. She wrapped her arms around Jack's legs, sliding her hands up to grab hold of his ass.

"Fuck," he whispered as his hips began to work forward and back.

Ellie hummed her pleasure, reveling in how powerful she felt. She switched her rhythm—slow to fast and back to slow. She licked and sucked, swirling her tongue up and over the length of him. She closed her eyes and let instinct guide her. Well, instinct and her own lust. Her own desperation to get Jack off. To make him hers.

When he threaded his fingers into her hair, she looked up. Jack's eyes had gone dark and there was something almost dangerous in them. And yet she couldn't remember a time she'd felt safer. Certain that he was giving himself to her as much as taking what he wanted.

It spurred her on, made her want to be everything he desired. And more. She held his gaze, even as Jack's eyes drifted closed, then snapped open as though he was afraid of missing something. He held her head more firmly then, thrust harder.

Ellie did what she could to spur him on. Moans and little whimpers of surrender. She quickened her pace and held it, working him with everything she had and hoping the frenzied quiver in her own body translated.

Jack pushed against her, hard. Once, twice, and then a third time. His whole body tensed, and the sound he made was primal. Ellie stayed with him until his body sagged, as though remaining upright took all the strength he had. She let go of his legs, eased her mouth away gently, and sat back on her heels.

He took a step back and practically staggered. "Damn, woman."

Ellie smirked, trying to remember a time she'd felt more smug and coming up short.

Jack slumped against the edge of the bed, worried he might actually fall over without some support. His body continued to quake, even as his need to be inside Ellie surged.

Ellie stood, swiping her thumb across her bottom lip. Her satisfied smile practically begged him to fuck her back. She locked eyes with him, satisfaction dancing in her eyes. "Thank you. I needed that."

"I think I'm the one who's supposed to be thanking you."

"In that case, thank you and you're welcome."

He hauled himself upright. "You look awfully pleased with yourself."

"I am." She sauntered toward the door, tossing a playful look over her shoulder. "We should probably get going. Don't want to be late."

The part of his rational brain that had returned knew she was right. For better or worse, it was no match for the part still fueled by adrenaline and sex endorphins.

Jack reached Ellie in the short hall at the top of the stairs, grabbed her wrist, and spun her around. He pressed her into the wall with his body, finding his own satisfaction in the small gasp that escaped her lips. "You don't think you're getting off that easy, do you?"

"At this rate, I'm going to get off the second you touch me, so consider yourself warned."

Challenge? Threat? A fine line in this situation and not one he was overly concerned about. "Then I guess I'll have to see if I can get you off twice."

Ellie started to laugh but stopped short when Jack yanked the hem of her dress up around her hips. He thrust his hand into her panties and found her clit. "Fuck," she said.

"I intend to." He circled her a few times before sliding a finger into her wetness.

She clamped around him with such force he almost couldn't move. But even as he prepared himself to go easy, her muscles relaxed. He added a second finger, and she tightened around him again, the sort of contract and release that seemed to draw him in deeper. His own cock pulsed with it, despite the release only minutes before.

Ellie lifted one leg, hooking her ankle behind his thigh. The shift gave Jack even better access, and he took advantage, angling his wrist so his thumb could graze her clit each time he plunged into her. Ellie grabbed his shoulders tighter and thrust back, meeting him and demanding more, even without words.

When he added a third finger, Ellie cried out and he stilled. But before he could ease up or offer an apology, she leaned in close. Through her ragged breaths, she whispered in his ear. "Don't stop."

Relieved, aroused all over again, and with half a mind to drag her back to bed, he forged on. Curving his fingers inside her each time he pushed in, coaxing her higher. She started swearing then, encouragement laced with command. Just enough meaning for him to give her exactly what she wanted.

When the walls of her pussy started to spasm around him, she went silent. The rest of her froze, then quaked against him. She let out a shuddering moan that lit him from the inside and made him feel like he could conquer the world.

Her body went lax, so much so that he had to wrap his free arm around her for support. "Just lean into me. I've got you."

Between his own efforts and the wall, she remained standing. Perched on that one gorgeous high-heeled shoe. "Mm-hmm," she murmured eventually.

"Do you need to sit? Do you want me to pull out?"

The lolling shake of her head became a slow, exaggerated nod. He'd regained his own wits enough to make sense of it and gently eased his fingers away. Ellie brought her other foot to the ground and shifted her weight.

"You okay?"

Another slow nod. "You're an animal."

He tensed instinctively.

Ellie lifted a hand to his cheek. "In a good way."

"Yeah?" He didn't typically need reassurances about his skills, but the thought of going too far sure as hell gave him pause.

"So, so good."

He wouldn't have thought it possible, but she looked even more satisfied than after giving him the best surprise blow job of his life. Different sort of satisfied, though. Then, she'd been pleased with herself. Now, she was simply pleased. "You bring that out in me."

"I like that." Ellie smiled, a trace of that earlier smugness returning.

"We really should get going. Are you sure you don't need to sit down for a minute?" Or maybe bail on the party after all.

"I can sit in the car." She tipped her head back toward the bedroom. "I should probably change my underwear."

Jack nodded. "Okay. Yeah. That's probably a good idea."

"You're also going to have to do something about your face."

He rubbed at his lips with the tips of his fingers. "Do I have lipstick on me?"

"No." Ellie smirked. "But if you walk into the party with that look on your face, everyone in the room is going to know exactly what you were doing before you got there."

Jack laughed. Laughed because Ellie was funny, laughed because she was right. And maybe, just a little, he laughed because he couldn't remember the last time he'd had a quickie on his way out the door to what was, for all intents and purposes, a family function.

CHAPTER NINETEEN

Ellie filed away names and details, hoping she'd have occasion to bump into most, if not all, of the people Jack introduced her to. For being such a small town, Bedlington had an impressive collection of creatives and queers. And more than a few queer creatives. It gave her a lovely boost of confidence that Rhett had picked the right place to settle, at least for the time being. And made her glad she'd found a place close without being creepy close, since it would be a bit extra to move to Bedlington after she and Jack had been dating all of three weeks.

It also made it easy to relax. She'd worried Jack would be the type to nurse a drink in the corner. And while he certainly wasn't one to work the room, most of the room seemed to know him already and didn't hesitate to approach them.

"Why do I get the feeling you don't often bring dates to social functions?" she asked after a lovely chat with the woman who owned the Sugar Shack.

He gave her a bland look. "Because you're reasonably observant and it's blatantly obvious."

"It's like every woman here over the age of fifty has auntie vibes and just wants to see you happy and settled down."

Jack's gaze had landed on his sister Logan, who was talking with her girlfriend Kathleen and Rhett. "And some not even over the age of fifty."

Ellie laughed. "Thank you again for inviting Rhett. I confess I've got some of those auntie, or maybe just protective sister, vibes for her."

"Of course. The more the merrier," Jack said.

"Yeah, but it's more than that. This one party will probably introduce her to like half the queers in a twenty-mile radius."

Jack laughed. "Probably more than half."

Ellie nodded. "She needs that. Needs community."

"What do you need?" Jack asked.

"Besides you taking me back to your place and fucking my brains out?" Because despite what they'd gotten up to before leaving, she absolutely wanted him again.

His eyes went ravenous for a moment before turning serious. "Yes. Besides that."

She shrugged, oddly content in that moment. "You're already on the hook to help me move, so not a whole lot."

"I'm glad you asked me."

She was, too, and grateful to Rhett for nudging her to. "I'm really excited to settle in. It's close-ish to Springfield so I can keep tabs on my mom. But not so close that she expects me to come over every day. And I wanted to be close to Rhett. She's chosen family as much as friend."

"Fair. Is your mom cool with it?"

"She's glad I found a place close. I don't get too much into the details with her." Though Ellie wasn't always sure whether that was for her mother's benefit or her own.

"Huh." Jack looked like he might be unsure, too.

"Trust me. It's easier." And not something she cared to analyze. "Anyway. I also want to find my own community beyond hanging around Northampton forever."

Jack chuckled. "Also fair."

Ellie chewed her lip, decided to take a chance. "I like that I'll be relatively close to you for the time being. I'm having too much fun to make getting together a colossal hassle."

"For what it's worth, seeing you would be worth a pretty sizable hassle." He squeezed her hand. "But I'm glad making it not was on your priority list."

She wondered if that had been his aim all along—finding out if they were serious enough to rate in her decision-making. Either way, she liked where they ended up. She'd had so little luck landing on the same page as someone else, much less headed in the right direction. It was nice to have that, and to have it without some unspoken pressure to get anywhere quickly.

People continued to approach them, and Jack continued to navigate each conversation with ease. It made her wonder about his grumpy demeanor when they first met. Was it unique to her? Or perhaps new people. Or work environments? Maybe she could needle it out of him next time she had him in a sex coma.

They hadn't said more than a passing hello to Clover and Sy, who were clearly the celebrities of the hour. As the crowd started to thin, Clover made her way over. "I'm so sorry I haven't had a chance to chat with you more." She took Ellie's hand.

Ellie waved her off. "You needed to work the room. You're fantastic at it by the way. I'm sure we're pretty close in age, but I definitely want to be you when I grow up."

Clover laughed. "Officially the first time anyone has said that to me."

"Totally not true," Jack said. "I've seen you hosting the school field trip."

"Okay, fine. But that has more to do with the goats than with me."

Ellie raised her hand. "I'm also in it for the goats."

Clover's eyes lit up. "You should come to goat yoga next weekend. It's our first one of the spring."

"You do goat yoga?" She'd heard of it but never imagined she'd have the chance to do it herself.

"You don't even have to be good at yoga. It's mostly about the goats."

Jack cleared his throat. "And that's my cue to go refresh our drinks."

He took their glasses and disappeared in the direction of the bar. When he'd gone, Clover leaned in and whispered, "I'm really glad you came."

"It's such a cool place. I'm so going to be a regular."

"I hope you are," Clover said. "But it's more than that."

"I don't follow."

"Jack would kill me if he knew I was saying this, but he doesn't date a lot. For him to be into someone enough to bring them to what is practically a family function? It's a big deal."

She let the significance of that sink in even as its underlying meaning eluded her. "Are you going to give me the 'if you even think about hurting him' speech? Because I'd be okay with that, but I'd prefer another drink first."

Clover laughed long and hard. "I wasn't, but the way you said that makes me feel like you two are perfectly suited for each other."

She knew what to make of that even less than the big deal comment. It seemed like a vote of confidence, though, and she didn't turn her nose up at those. "Thanks." She made a face. "I think."

"High praise, I promise."

Since Jack appeared to be waylaid, Ellie decided to change the subject. "Have you met my friend Rhett?"

"Butch hottie with the Mississippi drawl?" Clover asked without missing a beat.

"That's the one." And she couldn't wait to tell Rhett that's how Clover described her. "Did she mention being from Mississippi or are you that good with accents?"

Clover laughed. "Oh, I asked. I'm not an expert and she mentioned living in New England for more than a decade. I didn't stand a chance."

She was quite fond of Rhett's cadence. She wondered if Clover simply agreed, or if there was possibly more to it. Not that she was trying to rush Rhett into another relationship, but it would be good for her to know someone was into her. Besides, she had no idea of Clover's attractions or relationship philosophies. "She is easy to listen to."

"I wish someone would say that about me." Clover rolled her eyes.

"Say what about you?" Jack asked as he rejoined them.

"That I'm easy to listen to." Clover laughed again. "Though I think I'm easy to talk to, so that counts for something."

Jack leaned in and kissed her on the cheek, more brotherly than possible romantic history vibes. "You're my favorite voice of reason. And so much nicer to me than my siblings."

Clover offered him an affectionate smile. "Sweet talker."

Jack shook his head. "You've saved me from making an ass of myself on more than one occasion. That warrants some sweet talking."

Ellie cleared her throat. "I feel like that's a story I need to hear."

Clover nudged her gently with her elbow. "Come to goat yoga. I'll buy you breakfast after and tell you all the stories."

Jack made a show of groaning.

Ellie didn't hesitate. "It's a date."

Ellie let Emily Dickinson out of the second bedroom where she'd been sequestered. Jack watched the cat sniff and rub herself against pretty much every stack of boxes and laughed. He'd never had a cat, but he'd warmed to the idea since meeting her.

Ellie planted her hands on her hips and turned a slow circle. "I can't believe we did that in one afternoon."

Jack let out a relaxed sigh. "It helps to have able-bodied siblings."

"Thank you for letting me borrow them for the day. And your truck. Do you have any idea how much money you saved me?"

He didn't. He'd literally moved twice in his life—from his childhood home to a house he shared with a couple of guys from the Barrow Brothers crew to the duplex he'd shared with Logan. Each time, there were enough pickups and strong backs to get the job done. Each time, payment came in the form of pizza, wings, and a couple cases of beer. "Are movers ridiculous?"

Ellie nodded. "Not that I begrudge them. I wouldn't want to move other people's heavy crap around all day."

She had a point. "Well, I'm glad I—we—could help."

"I'm planning to have everyone over for dinner once I've unpacked my pots and pans, but I feel like you deserve an extra display of gratitude."

"Display, huh?" He imagined her body on glorious naked display and wondered if that made him creepy.

"Yeah. You know. Like balloons." Ellie stared up at the ceiling. "Or a fruit basket."

He knew she was teasing, but he couldn't help but frown. "Please don't buy me a fruit basket."

"Ooh. What about one of those fruit things that's made to look like a flower arrangement? Those are money."

"One, there's nowhere in a fifty-mile radius that sells those. Two, no."

Ellie scowled. "Are you saying you'd turn your nose up at something I picked out and got especially for you?"

His confidence wavered for a split second. Just enough to make him say, "Of course not."

She smirked. "Right answer."

"I'm no idiot." Jack shrugged. "I mean, I'd rather something that wouldn't cost you a dime, but a gift is a gift."

"Did you have something in mind, then?" The playful look in her eyes made it clear she knew exactly what he had in mind.

"Maybe."

"A striptease, perhaps? Or a scene of some kind?"

Even as his libido revved, he cringed at his complete and utter lack of creativity. "Is that an option?"

She angled her head to one side and jutted her hip to the other. "You sound surprised."

Did he admit how pedestrian his fantasies were? "I'd just never presume to ask for that sort of thing."

Her eyes narrowed. "But you're into it."

It wasn't a question. He nodded anyway.

"I'm not a queen of kink or anything, but I like to be adventurous." She came over and ran a finger down his chest. "And I'm always open to suggestion."

Who was this woman, and what in the world had he done to capture her attention? More, her desire. He normally didn't get caught up in questions like that, but damn. Ellie was unlike any woman he'd ever known, much less been with.

"Your imagination is running wild, isn't it?" Ellie asked.

He nodded. His brain might be floundering for immediate specifics, but he had no doubt it would conjure all sorts of possibilities as soon as it picked its proverbial tongue up off the floor.

She lifted her chin. "Like what?"

Dammit. "I'm experiencing a momentary short-circuit. Perhaps you could share some of the things you like while I reboot."

Her smile came slow and smug, though it was hard to know if she was gloating or liked that he cared about her desires. "Role-playing can be fun. Bondage. Edging. And like I said, I enjoy a little strip show now and then."

"Yes, please," he said.

"To which?"

"All. Any. Yes. Thank you." He was laying it on thick now, but Ellie seemed to dig it.

She tipped her head side to side. "I think we should start with the striptease, then. It involves me actually doing something for you, which was the point of this conversation in the first place."

He'd clearly lost track. "Do you have a lot of experience with that?"

Ellie shrugged, all casual now. "I took a few burlesque classes, performed once."

Christ on a cracker. Was she trying to kill him? "For real?"

"Pasties and everything. But audiences of one are the best. Eye contact, blurring the lines of what's burlesque and what's a lap dance." Her tone remained light, but her expression told Jack she knew exactly the effect she was having on him.

He cleared his throat. "I'd do a lot more than help you move for that."

"It doesn't have to be a trade." She grinned. "Though you did promise to teach me how to rewire a lamp."

Maybe he should be asking her to teach him about plaster or color theory, but the only thought swimming around his brain had to do with her, undulating in front of him to some sexy ass music. For him. Only for him. "I can do that."

"Cool. I'll put a little something together."

Jack blinked a few times, trying to prevent his brain from fixating on the idea. "Cool."

"So, like, did you want to hang out tonight? I'm open, but I'm sure you're beat, and I totally get if you want to go to your place and crash solo."

The abrupt shift helped, and Jack pounced on it. He liked that she offered. Directly, too. Not in some weird roundabout way where she tried to feel him out without revealing her own leanings. He understood why some people did that, but it drove him up a tree. "I'd love a low-key night with you. Do you want help making your bed, or do you want to go back to my place?"

"I so want to go to your place. I'm super excited for mine, but I'd love to not have to deal with any of this until tomorrow." She made big sweeping circles with her arms. "If you're saying I can have that and you won't even judge me for it, total bonus."

He shook his head. "No judgment. You may be surprised to learn this about me, but I sometimes struggle to relax around chaos."

Ellie laughed. "Shocker."

"I don't expect people to accommodate me, mind you. But it's my truth."

"You know what I love about trans guys?" Ellie asked.

"What?"

"A lot of things, but in this moment, I love the fact that most of them understand enough about identity and privilege that they use phrases like 'my truth' in all sincerity."

Jack laughed then, long and hard. "To be fair, I picked it up from Clover. She's all about living her truth."

"I knew I liked her."

"She's a lot for some people, but she's also one of the very best humans I have the privilege of knowing."

"A lot how?"

He considered what to say. Or, perhaps, how much. Clover was super open about herself, plus a firm believer in taking the taboo out of talking openly about sex and relationships. "She's poly, and while I'd never call her pushy about it as the right choice for everyone, she is pushy about how people need to be more honest and communicative about who they are and what they want."

Ellie laughed. "That doesn't seem so bad."

Jack tutted. "It's all fun and games until she starts asking about why you're so scared of being vulnerable."

Ellie folded her arms. "Did you learn that from personal experience?"

"Maybe once or twice. But damn it all if she isn't always right."

"Those poly people, man. They'll get ya."

He squinted, not surprised by the sentiment so much as Ellie having it. "Do you know a lot of poly people? Crap, are you poly? I should have asked."

Ellie smiled. "I don't identify that way, but I'm not unilaterally opposed. Rhett is, but only somewhat recently. We've talked about it. A lot."

"So much talking, right?" He chuckled. "I like the way you put it, though. I haven't tried it, but I'm not one of those people who wouldn't even consider it."

"Nice. And sorry. I didn't mean to send us on such a tangent."

"Pretty sure it was mutual." Jack checked his watch. "What do you say we head over to my place before it gets dark? We can take two cars if you want, but I don't mind bringing you home tomorrow if you're not feeling up for driving now."

"Have I told you that you have the best ideas?"

"You know, I don't think you have." And it carried all the more weight considering how little they'd agreed on at first.

"Well, you do. Let me feed Emily Dickinson and we can go."

Jack considered his own propensity for being single-minded and stubborn—traits he wasn't necessarily proud of but didn't try to deny. Yet, there was something to be said for new ways of looking at the world, different ways of moving through it. Since Ellie had gone to the kitchen, he called out, "Turns out, the feeling is mutual."

CHAPTER TWENTY

Ellie spent most of the following week working and settling into her new apartment. Other than not seeing Jack, who'd mostly finished his work at Hampstead House, it made for a busy but exciting few days. Seeing the murals take their final shape, seeing her possessions turn her empty apartment into a home—the concreteness of it was beyond satisfying.

Getting to spend the weekend with Jack, complete with a jaunt to Grumpy Old Goat on Saturday morning, made her feel like a legitimate adult. And a cool one at that.

Clover gave her a big hug. "I'm so glad you came."

"Wouldn't miss it." She'd actually been relieved when Clover said that both Maddie and Kathleen had prior commitments. She liked them both, but being the newbie in a gaggle of friends could be tricky sometimes. Besides, after Jack's disclosure about Clover's relationship leanings, Ellie wanted to feel her out. Not as a potential partner for Rhett, necessarily. Just as a fellow queer poly person in a place where there probably weren't too many.

"Now, you're not super serious about your yoga, are you? I don't want you to be disappointed in the caliber of the class." Clover shrugged. "It's mostly about the goats."

"Rest assured, I'm not super serious about much." She'd given that up a long time ago, after deciding it was a sure-fire way to wind up disgruntled or disappointed.

"Oh, good." Clover hooked her arm through Ellie's. "Let's go set up our mats."

They did, and Clover left Ellie to make friends with Delilah—one of the half dozen goats wandering around—while she went and saw to getting the other students and instructor situated. Ellie scratched the Nigerian dwarf under her chin and surveyed the space. It was a large room, with a high ceiling and exposed beams. Not a full-on dairy barn vibe, but close.

She contemplated talking up other people in the class but thought better of it. This was a moment to center, and to relax. Oh, and to love up on some goats.

Class started and, despite Clover's warning about it not being overly serious, it covered the essential bases of moving, breathing, and holding poses that tested her muscles in both strength and flexibility. But with comic relief. Like when she came into a cobra pose, only to have her chin licked by one of the kids. She smiled. He bleated and bounced away.

By the end of class, she'd managed to break a sweat and have a good time, even if the meditative state she usually tried for remained elusive. But movement was movement, and she'd downright giggled at one point.

"So, what did you think?" Clover asked, wiping her face with a towel and scratching Delilah behind the ears.

"Definitely the most chaotic yoga class I've ever been to." Ellie lifted a hand. "But I mean that in a good way."

Clover laughed. "Could you please put that in a Google review?"

"Um, yeah. I could. I could probably say it nicer though."

Clover shook her head. "No, no. We believe in truth in advertising here."

"Fair enough."

"Do you have to run? We're doing a pseudo brunchy thing in the tasting room if you wanted to stick around."

Other than doing some laundry—and maybe doing Jack—she had nothing on her agenda. "I'd love that."

"Yay. Go find a table. I'm going to touch base with the instructor, and I'll be there in a minute."

She'd barely settled when Sy came over and offered her a big smile. "Hey, Ellie. Can I get you something?"

"Hey. I'm just waiting for Clover." The second she spoke the words, Clover appeared. Ellie waved, though the room was small enough that she probably didn't need to.

Clover headed over but was stopped twice on her way—once by a group of women who'd been in the class and once by an older gay couple who fawned over her and the tasting room and the food.

"I'm going to go rescue her," Sy said. "Or it could be a while."

Ellie smiled. "You two make a good team."

"I like to think so." Sy's voice held affection. "If I don't catch you before you leave, I hope we can all get together soon."

"We should." Even as Ellie agreed, she wondered if all was code for the three of them. Or perhaps Sy meant a double date with Jack and Maddie. Either way, she was game. She liked Jack's family, his friends. She didn't quite think of them as her friends yet, but it didn't feel like a reach. That was nice.

"Sorry I kept you waiting." Clover slid into the seat across from her. "I forget how many people know who I am now."

"It's such a tradeoff, isn't it?"

Clover looked around and let out a happy sigh. "Technically, yes. But it's a freaking fantastic one."

She let Clover pick some items from the menu. Nothing fancy—bagels and pastries from the Sugar Shack, some locally smoked salmon with Sy's version of cream cheese, and a quiche of the day with micro greens. It covered the bases, though, and having both a mimosa and a fantastic cup of coffee made the experience downright indulgent.

As they ate, Clover studied Ellie. Ellie, knowing full well what came with that sort of scrutiny, braced herself for the well-intentioned interrogation. Clover abandoned her bagel and circled the rim of her mimosa glass with the tip of her finger. Ellie smiled.

Eventually, Clover said, "So, your friend, Rhett. Is she open to dating?"

Ellie barely held in a laugh. Not the interrogation she was expecting. Still, she noticed Clover's choice of phrase. Not "single" or "seeing someone." Not what their relationship status was, but what they might want it to be. "She's getting there."

Clover raised a brow. "That feels like a loaded answer."

"She went through a pretty traumatic divorce, and I don't think I'm betraying any confidences when I say she's still licking her wounds. But I think she's thinking about it."

Rather than looking put off, Clover shook her head, all sympathy. "Divorce can be such a nightmare. It's one of the reasons I have no intention of getting married to begin with."

"Never?" Ellie asked, more curious than surprised.

"I'm what you call solo poly. I like forming deep and intimate connections, but I'm not looking to get married or nest with anyone."

She chuckled before she could help herself. "Rhett's the opposite. She craves the companionship of a primary partner but doesn't feel like committing to someone has to be at the expense of all other connections."

Clover tutted. "Perhaps not my type after all."

"I hope you two can be friends, at least. She picked Bedlington on a whim, and I think she's missing having a friend group and sense of community."

"I'm always happy to offer both to a fellow queer. You should give her my number." Clover winked. "And encourage her to use it."

"I will." Rhett likely wouldn't, not because she hesitated to make the first move but because she was afraid of making any moves at all these days, even of the platonic persuasion. But it didn't mean Ellie couldn't orchestrate some casual run-ins. Again, not playing matchmaker, just helping Rhett get back on her feet as a cool, outgoing artist in a community of people who were primed to embrace her exactly as she was.

"Good."

"I confess I expected you to needle me about my intentions toward Jack."

Clover laughed. "Oh, no. Maddie might if she was here. Big sister prerogative and all. Me, I generally expect people to behave like mature adults with integrity unless they're displaying signs to the contrary."

"Ah."

Clover lifted her chin. "I've got my eye on you, though."

It was Ellie's turn to laugh. "I'd expect nothing less. And for what it's worth, I'd do the same."

Clover seemed to consider that. Whether she was doing so in the context of their earlier conversation about Rhett, Ellie didn't know. Either way, Clover gave a satisfied nod. "I'll keep that in mind."

"Thank you for the invite this morning. It was fun." And nice to break out of her routine of spending all her non-work time with her mother, Rhett, or Jack.

"I'm so glad you came." Clover glanced at the clock over the bar. "I hate to eat and run, but my weekend help called in sick and I've got some stalls to muck before evening milking."

"Not all fun and games, is it?"

Clover canted her head. "The good stuff never is, right?"

She'd never have said it like that, but Clover's words resonated. About work, about relationships, about so many things. She gave one of those slow, deep truth nods. "Never."

"You want to get married here?" Maddie asked the question Jack was pretty sure everyone was thinking. Even though Rich had literally just said as much.

Rich's face dominated the screen, like he was sitting too close to his own laptop. "Cherry loves all of you. And she's decided a New England summer wedding would be much nicer than waiting until winter down here."

Jack looked at his parents' and siblings' faces rather than his uncle. Dad looked incredulous while Mom seemed amused. Maddie seemed suspicious, but she often did when anyone behaved in a way she didn't expect.

"What exactly did you have in mind?" Mom asked.

"Backyard, close friends and family. End of July, after the worst of the biting flies have come and gone."

"Is this really Cherry's idea?" Dad lifted his chin. "Or is it your way of saving a few bucks?"

Rich rolled his eyes, more exasperated than offended. "It's all her. She insisted I talk with you without her on the line so you could veto it without having to hurt her feelings to her face."

Jack didn't care one way or the other—aside from what Rich's decisions said about his grand plan of cashing out his share of the business. That said, he couldn't help but have a soft spot for the woman his uncle had fallen head over heels in love with in a matter of weeks. The whole family had been dead set on disliking her, and she'd turned out to be one of the sweetest humans any of them had ever met.

"Of course you'll do it here, if that's what the two of you want." Mom shot Dad a stern look. "And we'll do it at our house since the yard is bigger."

Rich blustered. "Cherry had hoped for that, but she didn't want to impose."

"Nonsense. She's going to be family. There's no such thing as imposing." Mom gave the sort of nod that settled things—decisions, arguments, and all manner of things in between.

"I tried to tell her, but she was all in a tizzy about it." Rich shook his head. "I'm going to have her call you to talk details. You know all this wedding planning business is over my head."

Everyone laughed because it was true. And because it was just the sort of thing a boomer getting married at sixty could get away with.

They moved to the actual business of the meeting. Mostly updates on jobs and leads on new ones. Rich had been zooming in since he and Cherry had gone back to Florida, but it remained to be seen if that was his way of reengaging or keeping tabs. As far as Jack was concerned, every week Rich didn't bring up selling his half was another week they had to figure out how to buy him out with the reserves they had on hand.

He and Logan had looked into refinancing the duplex. Maddie had sold her house to move in with Sy. They were in better shape than they'd been six months prior, but it would still be a stretch to buy Rich's share outright. Maybe with his bride-to-be so enamored with Vermont and the Barrow clan, it wouldn't come to that. He didn't like to count on things working themselves out in the end, but it didn't hurt to put good vibes out into the universe.

When Rich logged off, Jack debated heading to Hampstead House to check on the punch list or trailing after Maddie to a basement refinish in town. He and Ellie felt a little bit like ships in the night lately, with Ellie racing to finish the murals and him pretty much done with the electric and focused on other jobs.

They'd managed to spend a couple of nights together, but even those consisted of late dinners and tumbling into bed exhausted. The exhaustion didn't prevent them from getting up to all manner of hot sex, but it made mornings inevitably brutal. The cumulative effect had him longing for a weekend with nothing but low-grade project puttering and time with Ellie.

Jack decided to text Ellie as much, then head out with Maddie. She responded immediately. *If you trust Rhett to watch Dot and Sophia, I want to make you dinner at my place.* Followed by: *Yes, I already asked her. She's happy to, in general but especially for hot dates.*

He wasn't in the habit of using the phrase "hot date," mostly because it implied a cool factor he didn't even pretend to aspire to. But Ellie's playful tone—the same one he would have found grating only weeks before—made him smile. It must be all the sex. That would make anyone a little softer around the edges. Not that he made a point of being unnecessarily hard, but he had enough self-awareness to know this was a departure from the norm.

As was relying on people who weren't family. But Rhett was a great tenant, and they'd become friendly if not full-on friends, a distinction he made mostly because Rhett was Ellie's best friend, and he knew a thing or two about boundaries. In any case, everything about Ellie's offer felt good and, curmudgeon or no, he wasn't in the business of shutting down anything that sat safely in the realm of good. *Sign me up.*

Chapter Twenty-one

At the sound of her mother's designated ringtone, Ellie rested the paintbrush on the edge of her palette and fished her phone from her back pocket. She swiped her thumb across the screen and lifted the phone to her ear. "Hi, Mom."

"Ellie, honey, I have some bad news," her mother said instead of a hello.

Since bad news typically dealt with things like a pair of pants coming back from the laundry with bleach stains or an elderly resident of her facility passing away, she didn't instantly switch into worry. "Oh, no. What is it?"

"It's your dad. He was on his way here to pick me up and he hit a patch of ice and his car was involved in a head-on collision." Her voice pitched with each additional detail.

"Mom, Mom. Calm down. Take a deep breath. It's okay."

"He died, Ellie. Your father is dead." Donna practically yelled the last bit, and her sobs came through with wrenching clarity.

Ellie squeezed her eyes shut, remembering all too clearly the day her father actually died. He'd already left, and she resented him enough at the time that their required visitation was a chore she did under vocal duress. She'd done enough therapy that the guilt and regret she'd experienced in the aftermath didn't haunt her on a daily basis. But this? This brought it all crashing back, but with the added panic that her mother's delusions had given way to a full-blown psychotic break. "Mom, we're going to figure it out. It's going to be okay."

Her mom continued to cry, giving Ellie's mind a moment to race in a variety of directions. Her first instinct, obviously, was to remind Donna that Bill had died years ago. That they'd mourned him and, in whatever ways possible, moved on. But when Donna was in the clutches of a full episode, trying to reason with her, much less correct her, often only served to fuel the paranoia that accompanied her loss of touch with reality. "Okay, what do you need right now? Do you need me to come over? I can be there in a couple of hours."

"Betty Parker said she'd call the prayer line. Do you think you'll be able to make it to the funeral? Calling hours are going to be from five until eight on Monday and the Mass will be Tuesday morning at nine. I think I'm going to wear my navy-blue dress since I don't have a black one, and blue was Bill's favorite color."

Ellie sucked in a breath and blew it out slowly. She'd been through this at least a dozen times in her life, with six of those times being in what she considered her adulthood. But it struck her every single time the way her mother's mind could weave together fact and fiction, hold almost microscopic details of her lived experience while its tether to reality strained. "That sounds nice. I'm sure he would have loved that."

"I'll have to tell the kitchen that I won't be here for dinner so they don't make a plate for me and it ends up going to waste."

She almost laughed at the level of consideration, even as her mind ran through the interventions that would need to happen as soon as she ended the call. "Don't you worry about that. I'm sure they know. You just focus on taking care of you. We need to make sure you stay well with all this going on. Maybe say a rosary and try to lie down for a little while?"

"Okay, honey. I am a little tired. I only had one cup of coffee this morning because my roommate Mary needed me to help her put her laundry away and I got to the dining room late."

"Now, you know the staff is there to help her with that. You shouldn't feel like it's your responsibility to take care of her." Especially since some of Mary's paranoia manifested as the belief that people were stealing her things, and she didn't hesitate to yell first and ask questions later.

"I know. I'm sorry."

"You don't need to apologize. I'm just reminding you not to worry about things you don't need to worry about." And inadvertently create a brouhaha that required staff intervention.

"Do you think you'd like to go out to lunch this weekend? I've been craving shepherd's pie."

She had no idea whether her mother would be in any state to go out come the weekend. But the question implied that the hallucination that began their conversation might have waned, at least for the moment. "That sounds like fun, especially now that the snow finally seems to be done. I'd love that."

"You should invite Jack, that nice man you said you've been seeing. We could all go, and it could be my treat." Her mom's voice was almost back to normal, the excitement of an outing and meeting a new person overcoming the anguish of only a few moments before.

"I'll see if he's free." She had no intention of letting those worlds collide just yet, but that was a fact she'd keep to herself. And she would want her mom to meet Jack eventually, of course. She just needed it to be when she could manage both sides of the situation and make sure everything went smoothly.

"Okay. Well, it's almost time for bingo, so let me let you go."

"I hope you win."

"Me, too. Bye, honey."

"Bye, Mom."

The line went silent. Once again, Ellie sucked in a breath and blew it out slowly. She tried to focus on the relief of averting a complete spiral, but the gnawing knowledge that things likely wouldn't resolve themselves remained front and center. Her own feelings—the lingering sadness about her father's death, the anxiety spike from her mom's brush with hysteria, and the nagging guilt that these episodes might be avoided if she was somehow more present in her mom's life—got boxed up and set to the side. She'd have to deal with them, of course, but that's what her therapist was for.

She pulled up the number for the social worker at her mom's facility. In a matter of minutes, they'd activated a care plan that included close monitoring, a visit with the consulting psychiatrist, and authorization to transport Donna to the hospital if the situation worsened. It was a comfort to have a team of qualified and caring people at the ready, even if it made her feel less like she was in the driver's seat.

"Let's try to minimize excitement," Lily said. "Why don't you plan to visit her later tomorrow or Sunday?"

Ellie paced the length of the study, still clutching her palette and brush. Her instinct was to go over as soon as she could get herself cleaned up, but Lily was right. Besides, that plan would mean she didn't have to cancel on Jack. Lord knew she could use the distraction of good company and even better sex.

With her brain already in high gear, it didn't take long to formulate a plan. She'd make dinner for Jack, as promised. But she'd give him that little show she'd promised for all his help getting her moved in. It would be perfect. Then she could send him home happy and deal with everything else.

Jack should have known better than to think having one aspect of his life going great meant the good vibes would simply rub off on everything else. What a day. Everything that could have gone wrong had. Flat tire on his way to a job, wrong materials ordered when he finally got there. And after going to the trouble of making a nice salad for lunch with the chicken he'd grilled up for the week, he forgot it on the kitchen counter. Which meant the salad was trash and lunch consisted of gas station pizza. Not that gas station pizza didn't have its place, but it was the principle.

On the drive over to Ellie's, he put the windows down and blared the radio, hoping to clear his head and reset his mood. What he got was a bug in his mouth and the knowledge that a country music star he already disliked was rocking the airwaves with a blatantly racist anthem masquerading as a tribute to Americana. He arrived at Ellie's even crankier than when he'd started out.

Hopefully, she'd take pity, feed him, and put him to bed early.

Jack knocked lightly but didn't wait for Ellie to come to the door. Inside, he hung his keys and pulled off his boots. But he only made it a step further before stopping. He hesitated, then scanned the room.

The coffee table was gone, and the ottoman had been pushed to a far corner. Weird. "Are you rearranging already?" he asked in lieu of a hello.

Ellie emerged from the kitchen, dressed to the nines. "Only temporarily."

"Shit. Do we have plans I forgot about?" Jack drank her in, even as his mind scrambled. The black wrap dress was cut low, and her hair was all pulled up in some sort of twist, leaving her neck exposed. Even across the room, he could tell the heels made her as tall as him. And even though he knew they were uncomfortable and impractical, the things they did to her calves made his mouth water.

"None that require leaving the house," she said with a smile.

Confusion replaced panic, but both gave way to a heady mix of understanding and lust. "You're going to strip for me."

Ellie sashayed across the room. "I was planning to. Assuming you're still interested, of course."

Interested. Such a woefully inadequate word. Even in his current funk, he'd have to be dead not to be interested in what Ellie was offering. "Oh, I'm interested."

"Something's wrong, though." Her eyes narrowed and she took his hand. "I can tell."

"Just a bad day," he said perhaps a little too quickly.

"Bad how?"

"A million minor annoyances. Nothing big, I promise. And this?" He swept his finger up and down to indicate her. "This is making that a distant memory."

Ellie studied him for a good five or six seconds. Like she was scanning to see if his words matched his aura. Eventually, she nodded. "I can take a raincheck if you'd prefer. I know it can be hard to shake off that sort of thing."

It was a sweet offer, especially given the trouble she'd obviously gone through to get ready. "I can't think of anything that would improve my mood more."

"How about a steak salad with strawberries and bleu cheese?"

"Shut up." His stomach rumbled and his mouth watered at the prospect.

"I try not to buy strawberries out of season, but they looked so good and I'm definitely developing spring fever." She grinned. "I figured if I put a big piece of meat with it, you'd be game."

"Big salad with steak is definitely one of my love languages." He didn't always need meat, had actually made a point of doing a couple of meatless days each week. Still. The combination was one of his favorites. Like the lunch he hadn't gotten the chance to enjoy, only more extravagant.

"We should eat first, then, because I have plans for after."

Knowing what those plans entailed gave him half a mind to forget about dinner. But she'd gone to the trouble. And he wasn't such a hormone-addled teenager that he couldn't contain himself for the next hour or so. "What can I do to help? Do you want me to man the grill?"

"How about you turn it on while I pour you a glass of wine, then you can put your feet up and relax?"

Jack had never put much stock in the fifties housewife vibe, but her phrasing hinted at it and damn it all if it didn't sound enticing. He picked at the underlying meaning of that while he went out to the back patio and lit the grill. Then he shook it off. It was a game, not some statement on what he thought he deserved. And Ellie was the one who'd started it.

He'd just settled into the idea when Ellie joined him outside with a gorgeous ribeye and an oversized pair of tongs. As promised, she shooed him in, pointing at a glass of red on the side table and snapping the tongs at him for emphasis. He couldn't help but laugh. The woman might be looking to wait on him tonight, but there was nothing docile or demure about her.

Ellie swayed to the music in her mind while she stood over the grill. She sashayed around the kitchen, slicing strawberries and toasting up fresh croutons. It wasn't the show she promised, but he enjoyed it all the same.

He moved to the table she'd already set, and she set down an artfully composed platter that would have rivaled most of the restaurants he'd been to. "I'd say this is the most beautiful thing I've seen in a while, but you're here, so there's really no comparison."

She paused, fork suspended between her plate and her mouth, and smirked. "I haven't even taken my clothes off yet."

"If I say you're beautiful fully dressed, do I still get to see you naked?"

"Always."

Although tempted to rush through dinner, he resisted, both to savor the food and the time Ellie took to make it. Even without the promise of what was about to happen, it would have turned his mood entirely. But Ellie—happy, playful, impossibly sexy Ellie—wasn't asking him to choose.

They finished eating, and Ellie directed him back to the living room. He sat on the sofa, suddenly unsure of what to do with his hands. He rubbed them along his thighs, which only served to rev his imagination and his libido. Would Ellie slink into his lap at some point? Would she tell him he could look but not touch?

"Comfy?" Ellie asked, pulling him back into the moment.

"Uh-huh." He swallowed, present but no less filled with anticipation.

"Good." Her index finger hovered over the screen of her phone. She gave it a single tap and turned to face him.

The horns started first. Trumpet, maybe? Sensual and insistent. Bass followed, pulsing and sure. Ellie struck a pose, held it. Held his gaze. When she started to move, he had a momentary crisis over where to look. But she was there, only for him. So he drank in the lines of her body, the way her hips and breasts undulated in time with the music.

The song wasn't slow, and Ellie didn't make her dance overly serious. She bit her lip and jutted her chest forward, sort of like an old school pinup. She shimmied and wiggled, leaning close enough for him to touch but then wagging her finger to deny him.

After a minute or so, she kicked off the shoes and inched up the hem of her dress, giving Jack the most delicious view of black garters and the tops of her sheer stockings. She flicked the front clasp, then the back, then jiggled her ass while she worked it down her leg. But instead of simply removing it, she bent her leg behind her and pulled the stocking off over her shoulder.

She repeated the move with the second stocking before going to work on her dress, untying the bow that held the fabric in place and giving him a few playful peeks before sliding it off and letting it pool at her feet. She continued to dance around in a sheer black bra that showed off her nipples and a pair of cheeky lace panties that covered only about a quarter of her ass.

His hand itched to touch, to pull her onto him so he could kiss and lick and bite every inch of her. But just when he thought she might let him, she slipped away and turned her back to him. With surprising skill, she unhooked her bra one-handed, and in a single fluid motion, she turned around, whipped it off, and let it drop to the floor.

The music ended at that exact moment, driving home just how much she'd rehearsed her routine. Jack nodded and clapped, unsure the appropriate way to show appreciation for a private strip tease. "Wow."

Ellie stood before him, in nothing but those lace panties, looking pleased with herself. She stroked circles around her nipples, making Jack's already hard cock strain. "I considered pasties but decided you'd probably rather a full view."

He nodded. "I like this view very much. Also, wow. Seriously. And thank you. No one has ever done that for me before."

Ellie extended a hand and he took it, letting her help pull him to his feet. "I like being your first for something."

He wanted to be her first for something, too, though he couldn't fathom what. A problem for another day. "Do I get to take you to bed now?"

She dipped her chin, playing shy all of a sudden, before looking up at him through thick lashes. "I sure hope so."

Chapter Twenty-two

Ellie expected urgent, maybe even rough. Jack didn't seem to be in a hurry, though. If anything, it was as though he had all the time in the world. Time and care.

It was the care that threw her. Soft, open-mouthed kisses along her shoulder. Caresses across her ribs that she'd swear took days.

Ellie tugged at Jack's hair, willing him to hurry up and fuck her already. But he didn't seem to get the message. Or he did and took his sweet time anyway. Like she was something precious to cherish. To revere.

"Please," she said, knowing the effect that usually had on him.

"Please what?" He'd ventured somewhat south, posing the question between lazy tongue swirls around each nipple.

"Please take me. Be inside me. Fuck me." Not exactly distinct options, but hopefully he'd get the picture.

"I will."

"Soon?" It was almost comical at this point, how desperately she needed him and what she was prepared to do to have him.

"Eventually."

She worked her fingers into his hair again, scratching lightly at his scalp and the back of his neck. Perhaps a taste of his own medicine might do the trick. Jack merely hummed his pleasure, sending the vibration from her nipple right to her clit.

Ellie squirmed. She writhed. She thrust her hips up to meet him, rubbing herself against his thigh.

Jack made his way down her body with a slowness that proved both excruciating and erotic. While she so often relied on urgency to drive herself to the edge, Jack's attentiveness had her coming apart at the seams. She was everywhere and nowhere, mind racing and yet disarmingly still.

When Jack's tongue pressed into her center, she fully expected to launch from the mattress into orbit. But he seemed to ground her instead, tethering her to the moment and awakening every cell, every nerve ending. She'd never been so aware of herself, and yet she was so overwhelmed with pleasure, she didn't have the wherewithal to feel exposed.

Time spun out. Minutes could have passed. Hours. She succumbed to Jack's will, followed wherever he beckoned.

After a while, his fingers joined his mouth. Slow, come hither strokes with each pass of his tongue. Ellie moved against him, with him. Climbing ever higher but no longer seeking the peak. It would come, eventually. It wasn't about that anymore, though.

The pleasure was the moment. The fact that no one had ever been attuned to her body the way Jack was now. As though he knew her inner workings, her wiring. As though he knew how to bring her to life.

When the orgasm started to build, Ellie didn't chase it or try to keep it at bay. She simply let it come to her, like a gift. Like so many gifts Jack had given her in the short time they'd been together.

It might have started out effortless, but her climax exploded, like being shot from a cannon, zipping through her like lightning and setting every nerve ablaze. Ellie rode it, powerless to do anything else. The exhilaration left her breathless.

It took ages to even begin to come down from the high. But instead of the satisfyingly wrung-out feeling that usually came with orgasm, Ellie felt energized and full. Like she'd had the full tune-up after having her systems flushed, and every muscle and joint hummed like a beautifully designed and well-oiled engine.

She rolled to her side and slung a leg over Jack's thighs, using him to leverage herself on top. The room spun and dark splotches peppered her vision. "Whoa."

Jack's hands came to her shoulders. "You okay?"

His grip steadied her. She blinked a few times. "Yes. It appears normal blood flow to my brain hasn't happened yet."

"Lie down. Relax. Dizziness is the worst."

There were lots of things worse than getting dizzy. Nausea, for example. Or a killer headache. In this moment, though, the only point of comparison in her mind was not being able to touch Jack. And it was no contest. She needed to feel him, taste him. She needed to give him at least a fraction of what he'd given her. "I'm okay."

"Ellie."

The sternness in his voice had the opposite effect Jack intended. Or at least what Ellie assumed was his intent. Rather than sending her scrambling to obey, it turned her on even more. If she didn't do something with that, she honestly didn't know what would happen. "I'm good. Trust me."

His hold on her remained, but he didn't force her away. She slowly started to rock. Back and forth, back and forth. It was almost soothing at first, but with each shift of her body, she grazed his cock.

"Ellie."

The sternness was gone. In its place, that same sort of reverence she'd sensed before. Like he was in awe of her. Headier than any drug.

She braced a hand on each of his shoulders and used the leverage to increase the pressure and pace. Despite teetering on the brink of overstimulation, her clit began to pulse, and she'd swear she could feel Jack's cock doing the same.

Just like when he was going down on her, her grip on time wavered. Sensation was all that remained, along with this expansion in her chest that made it difficult to breathe. But unlike the scramble for oxygen that sometimes came with chasing an orgasm, this fullness was pure joy. And even as Jack's fingers dug into her thighs with his own tumble into release, the thing coursing through Ellie felt like an entirely different kind of falling.

Ellie set down two plates of French toast and joined Jack at the table. "Bon appetit."

"Woman, you're spoiling me."

"You deserve to be spoiled," she said.

"No more than you do." He did his best to reciprocate, but he'd need to up his game at the rate they were going.

"Okay, well, I wanted French toast. I probably wouldn't have made it for just myself, so I'm technically spoiling both of us."

"You wouldn't?" he asked around a bite bigger than he should have taken.

She lifted a hand. "Not on a workday, I mean. Weekends deserve French toast at the very least. Weekends deserve waffles."

He chuckled at the vociferous tone. "Agreed."

"What's on your agenda for the day?"

A simple question, but it had this cute, domestic vibe to it. It felt weird to admit, but he was digging that vibe more and more. Like, have this exact conversation over coffee every morning kind of vibe. Was it too soon to say that? Or was she right there with him?

"Are you having a brain fart right now?" Ellie reached across the table and grabbed his hand. "Because I was starting to think you never did and it was making me kind of nervous."

It wasn't not a brain fart, right? Just in a very specific direction. "Oh, no. I have them all the time. You should see me trying to put together something I took apart literally ten minutes ago."

She laughed. "I feel better about life now."

"Happy to oblige. So, to answer your question, I'm starting the electric on a house Maddie's taking lead on."

"Let me guess. Taking out walls to make an open concept."

"Ha! The opposite. This couple is overwhelmed by the fact that their entire downstairs, save the half bath, is one big room. We're putting up some walls so they have an office and guests can't see whether there are dishes in the sink the minute they walk in the front door."

Ellie sipped her coffee. "I wondered when that would start to happen."

He thought about the chopped-up spaces that had come before. "I'm hoping we land somewhere in the middle."

"Why does it not surprise me that you'd say that?"

Jack shrugged, not bothered by the prospect of being predictable. "What about you?"

Ellie blew out a breath. "I've got probably three days of work left at Hampstead House, but today I need to head down to Springfield.

My mother has been struggling. Having delusions, yelling at the staff. I'm going to visit her today so I can help her care team assess whether she needs to be hospitalized."

"Wait. What?" He understood the words, but they didn't mesh with her almost casual delivery.

Ellie took what appeared to be a fortifying breath. "It happens sometimes. I think now is one of them. I don't need you to do anything. I just wanted you to know that I might need to spend some extra time down there."

"I mean, yes. I absolutely want to know. But I want to help, too."

She shrugged and smiled. "You're sweet. There really isn't anything to help with, though. Her facility will handle the transport if that needs to happen. I'll need to talk with her doctors and go and visit her and stuff, but it'll all be handled."

They hadn't really talked about the specifics of Ellie's mom's condition, only that it was mostly managed. But he didn't think it was overreacting to consider being in the hospital a big deal. Sure, a psychiatric condition might not be life threatening the way cancer or a heart attack would, but it felt no less intense. For Ellie's mom or for Ellie herself. "What can I do for you, though?"

"Don't make me talk about it too much?" She laughed. "I'm kidding but not."

Jack shoved away the little red flags that waved in the periphery of his mind. This wasn't about him, or even about them. This was about Ellie. And figuring out how to support her through an obviously stressful time. "No pressure. Truly. But I'm here if you need to unload or process or anything. I can even drive you if that would help."

She sighed again and stared at her food. "I don't mean to sound like a jerk, but it's actually less stressful to do it myself."

Since she'd let go of his hand, he grabbed hers. "I want to lower your stress, not add to it."

She looked into his eyes. Hers seemed a little glassy, but she kept her smile firmly in place. "I know. I also know that if you're there, I won't be able to stop myself from worrying about what you're thinking or how you're feeling."

It made sense, for now at least. He hadn't even met Ellie's mom. He'd have a problem being shut out by a wife or even a long-term girlfriend, but Ellie wasn't that. Not yet. Hopefully, they'd get there, and they'd figure out how to be there for each other. For now, he'd respect her wishes and leave it be. "I'm tougher than I look, but okay."

She dropped her head to the side, an affectionate look on her face. "You're an outstanding tough guy. I'm glad you're in my corner."

It was a small concession. "Don't forget you can tag me in sometimes. It's not just for show."

"I know," Ellie said.

Did she? Now probably wasn't the time to press. "What's her name?"

Ellie gave him a quizzical look. "Donna."

"Donna." Jack nodded, committing it to memory. "I hope she feels better soon." He tried for a reassuring smile, though it struck him he didn't even know if that was the right thing to say.

"Thanks." Ellie cut a large bite of French toast and stuffed it in her mouth. She tipped her head back and forth as she chewed, like doing so took all her concentration.

Jack took the hint and did the same. He might not be able to help, but he could at least follow her lead.

Chapter Twenty-three

As Ellie expected, things didn't improve. Her mom's outbursts worsened, and she'd even slapped one of the nurses who'd gotten too close while attempting to calm her down. She'd never been violent before, so it triggered immediate hospitalization. Ellie spent two full days going back and forth with the case manager before finally getting the okay to visit.

She signed in at the front desk and was shown into one of the visitation rooms. It was one of the nicer hospitals of the ones her mother had stayed in through the years. Fresh paint and lighting that managed to be bright without feeling sterile. It still smelled like a hospital, though. There was no getting around the harsh cleaners and overcooked food that seemed endemic to medical facilities.

She took a deep breath and swallowed the wave of anxiety that came a little too close to nausea for her comfort. It was fine. The visit would be hard, but it was important for her to be there—whether or not her mother was lucid enough to know it. The doctors would recalibrate her medication and she'd be back to her usual self within a couple of weeks.

She'd just finished the pep talk to herself when an aide wheeled her mom in. A precaution more than anything else, but knowing that didn't stop her mind from racing to the very real possibility her mother would lose mobility at some point. All the medications, all the things that passed for treatment before many of the modern medications were options. They took a toll.

It was a conversation she'd had with her dad during one of their stilted attempts at having a relationship before he passed away. "You need to be prepared," he'd said. "You can't put your whole life on pause to make hers more comfortable."

The advice had come from a good place, even if she'd resented it at the time. And in the end, her mom had embraced the lower maintenance lifestyle assisted living had to offer. Donna no longer had to think about cooking or cleaning or laundry. And she was a joiner, which meant she got more social interaction at her residence than she would if she and Ellie still lived in the house together.

Ellie had hoped having less to worry about might increase the time between these psychotic episodes. But despite what Donna's sister had insisted through the years about shielding Donna from things that might upset her, Ellie didn't actually buy it. Sure, major stress could trigger things, but so could hormonal shifts or even an ill-advised prednisone shot meant to quash a nasty case of bronchitis. Chemical imbalances happened and there was little modern medicine could do to predict it.

Fortunately, the opposite was true in terms of managing symptoms. The cocktail of antidepressants and antipsychotics her mother took kept her on an even keel most of the time. And when they didn't, minor adjustments usually did the trick.

"Hi, Maureen."

The greeting snapped Ellie from their reverie even as her mom's use of the wrong name made her sigh. "No, Mom. It's me. Ellie."

Donna laughed. "Oh, silly me. I thought you were Maureen for a second. You look so much like her."

Ellie smiled. She did bear a striking resemblance to her aunt, or at least to the pictures of her aunt from a couple of decades prior. "Nope, you're stuck with me today."

"I'm never stuck with you, sweetheart."

The sentiment and the pet name gave Ellie a familiar pang that she struggled to identify precisely. "How are you feeling today? Did you sleep well?"

"Well, my roommate was yelling and that woke me up, but the nurses came and took care of her and the next thing I knew, they were bringing me my breakfast tray."

Ellie nodded. She'd never been able to pinpoint whether it was causation or correlation, but good sleep seemed to go hand in hand with her mother's mental health. "I'm glad it didn't keep you up too long."

"The food here is terrible, though. My toast was burnt, and the oatmeal was cold. And who serves toast with oatmeal anyway? All those starches."

Since it was a perfectly reasonable thing to complain about, Ellie didn't try to deter her. If anything, it was a point that grounded her in reality. "The kitchen is probably short-staffed. You know how that seems to be the case everywhere."

Donna shook her head. "It's because not enough people are going to church anymore."

If she closed one eye, she might be able to follow the thread of that logic. But since getting Donna going on church often led to questions about when she'd last been to church herself, she opted to skirt the matter as much as possible. "Hopefully, you'll be back at Riverdale soon. You really like the food there."

"And they need my help to take care of all the babies that the mothers didn't want until they can be adopted by the couples who couldn't have babies."

Ellie pressed a finger to her forehead, right above the bridge of her nose. Babies were a common theme in her mother's delusions, fueled by the pro-life stance that aligned with her religious views. She knew better than to argue about it, even when Donna was well. "You know what we always say, though. You have to take care of yourself first. You can't help anyone until you're good and well."

"That's true." Donna nodded.

"That means lots of rest and taking your medicine when it's time. We'll worry about everything else later."

Donna seemed to be on board, but something in her demeanor shifted, and her eyes filled with tears. "But one of the babies was crying and I couldn't pick it up and it died."

"It didn't die, I promise. Someone else took care of it and rocked it to sleep."

"It did die." Donna's voice rose. "It did."

Every instinct told Ellie to drive home the truth, to console her mother with the fact that no babies died on her watch. And yet she knew better. Being doubted or corrected only created a spiral of agitation that could escalate to the point that Donna would have to be sedated. She placed a hand on her mother's arm. "Then it's with God and the angels now. We should say some extra prayers for it."

Just as quickly as the switch flipped on, it flipped back off. Donna wiped her eyes and nodded her agreement. "You're right."

They said a Hail Mary together, and Donna calmed down enough to tell her about a movie she'd seen. Ellie grasped at the diversion, and they spent the remainder of her visit talking about their favorite movies through the years. It was the funny thing about psychosis. Even as her mom lost some of her tethers to reality, others remained. Memory was usually one of them, along with religion. Ellie carried a certain ambivalence about the latter, but she'd come to accept working with her mother's parameters instead of against them.

By the time Ellie left, Donna was in good spirits and looking forward to lunch. She managed to catch one of the social workers in the hallway, who was able to get her a list of the adjustments that had been made to Donna's medications. The changes were minor, but hopefully that would be enough. It was so much better now than when standard practice was to stop all medication and start from scratch. She offered her thanks and signed herself out.

She got into her car and checked her phone. She had one text from Rhett, laced with the perfect blend of encouragement, empathy, and snark. Another from Pablo, asking if she'd be interested in a job at a boutique hotel in Boston the following month. And a trio of messages from Jack.

How's your mom?

How are you?

Do you want company tonight?

She sighed, a weird mix of gratitude and discomfort turning in her stomach. She answered Pablo first, thanking him for thinking of her and asking the scope and pay rate of the job. She texted Rhett next with thanks of a different nature and a summation of her visit. And then she pulled up her thread with Jack.

She's okay. Doctor hopes she'll be stabilized in the next couple of weeks. And I'd love that. Can I come to you?

When Jack didn't immediately respond, Ellie got on the road. She could intrude on Rhett's afternoon until Jack was free and hopefully shake off the heaviness that always threatened to envelop her after an hour in a psychiatric unit.

Jack had just started up the porch steps when Rhett's door opened. But instead of Rhett on the other side, it was Ellie. "Hi," he said, happy to see her but a little relieved, too.

"I'm so glad to see you." Ellie stepped out, slid her arms around Jack's neck, and kissed him.

"Uh, that feeling is definitely mutual."

"One sec." She turned her head and called over her shoulder. "Good night, Rhett."

"Good night," Rhett said.

Ellie pulled the door closed. "Sorry, I should have asked if you needed a minute first."

"Not at all." Jack unlocked his door. "I need to let the dogs out, but come on in and make yourself comfortable."

She followed him in, setting her things on the bench by the door the way she always did. He headed for the back door, so Dot and Sophia could make their evening patrol of the backyard. It took them all of two minutes. He had a feeling that would change when the weather got really nice, but for now, they were all about doing their business and getting back inside as quickly as possible.

When he returned to the living room, Ellie had flopped onto the sofa—full slouch, legs sprawled, and feet on the coffee table. "How are you?" he asked.

"Meh?" Ellie shrugged.

"How's your mom?"

"Meh?" No shrug this time, but she looked away.

"Tell me about it." Rather than joining her on the couch, he sat on the coffee table and pulled one of her feet into his lap.

Ellie groaned when his thumb pressed into her arch, so he worked the spot. Her eyes drifted closed and her breaths seemed to mellow. Her shift into relaxation highlighted that it was the most stressed he'd ever seen her. "That's nice," she said.

He stayed with that foot for a while, then switched to the other, figuring she'd talk when she was ready. When she remained quiet, he haggled with himself over the line between showing concern and being pushy. It was a line he'd struggled with in life, given his propensity to go down the internal reflection rabbit hole when he had things on his mind. "Do you want to talk about it?"

"Meh?" Her choice to use it a third time conveyed a lot more than the word itself.

"You don't want to talk?" he asked.

Ellie blew out a breath. "I really, really don't."

Her default of keeping things bottled up raised all sorts of red flags, but he knew better than to tell her what she needed. And it wasn't like he relished hashing through emotional distress. So, he pressed a kiss to her cheek and smiled. "Okay, then. What do you want?"

"Distraction?"

Under normal circumstances, he'd take her hand and take her right to bed. But something told him that wasn't the right move. "How about dinner and a bad movie and a shoulder rub?"

She let out another sigh, but this one was a little shaky. "That would be great."

He made pasta—because comfort carbs were called that for a reason—and a small salad. They ate on the couch with one of the *Star Trek* movies. He'd never hopped on board that wagon, but Ellie had grown up with the franchise and was slowly winning him over. "No whiny anti-heroes here," she'd declared after convincing him to give it a try the first time. The memory made him smile even as he worried over saying or doing the right thing now.

When the credits rolled, Ellie swung a leg over his thighs and straddled his lap. "I'm ready for the next level of distraction."

"Yeah?" Jack's body responded even as his brain held back.

She gave an eager nod. "I'd prefer to not think anymore tonight."

He could appreciate that. Hell, he'd been there himself a few times. But something in her eyes made him wary. A distance he'd not seen before. A flatness almost. "What exactly did you have in mind?"

Ellie tipped her head, gave him a playful smirk. Then she circled her hips suggestively. "If I have to tell you, I must not be doing it right."

Jack smiled. "Your signals are nice and clear. I just, I don't know. You seem lost in your head a little. I'm totally fine to crawl into bed and cuddle."

She shook her head. "I need to get out of my head."

"I know, but—"

"I'd like you to fuck me until I can't think. If you're not up for that, it's fine, but it's what I want."

Her voice had an edge to it. A challenge. He could read it as more red flags, but he didn't want to. Because her words turned him on. And because he didn't borrow trouble. "I want nothing more than to give you what you want."

"Good." She stood and took his hand. "Take me to bed."

A handful of lights remained on, and the dogs still needed their bedtime walk. But he set that aside and let Ellie pull him up the stairs.

In his room, she started tugging off his clothes like she couldn't wait to get him naked. He soaked it up and gave it right back. She did things to him, his restraint. Revved him up and left him practically blind with desire.

He leaned into that, letting the worries fall away. Who was he to tell her what she needed right now? He'd certainly had his own moments of using sex to forget about a crappy day. If he could give her that, why wouldn't he?

Chapter Twenty-four

Jack slept badly, but Ellie had passed out right after she came and slept soundly most of the night. It was almost enough to convince him that Ellie had been right, that not being nudged to talk about her mom or her feelings had been what she needed. Only she woke up the next morning and went right back to acting distant and distracted.

It wasn't that she wasn't entitled to be those things. Hell, he'd be a wreck in her shoes. But her fake smiles and insistence that everything was fine pushed every button he had. He could practically see Clover and his siblings shaking their heads over it. And without the sex endorphins to take up all the space in his brain, he couldn't pretend any longer.

So he poured them each a second cup of coffee to go with the bagels he'd toasted, and tried again. "What do you need? What can I do?"

Ellie shook her head. "There isn't anything."

He bit back the flare of frustration. "I know there's nothing I can do for your mom. I trust she's in the best possible place for her right now and getting the care she needs. I'm asking about you."

"I'm fine," Ellie snapped. Then she huffed out a breath. "I'm fine."

The second delivery was calmer but no more convincing. "Ellie, this is really hard. You don't have to be fine."

"But I am." Her smile—not too bright and the tiniest bit wry—was so convincing he almost believed her. "I promise."

He might have let it go if it hadn't been for that last bit. *I promise.* A patent lie. Though he couldn't tell whether she was lying to him or to herself. "I don't believe you."

Her shoulders stiffened, but she didn't say anything.

"I think you're worried and hurting and used to putting on a brave face when it comes to your mother. And for some reason, you don't want me to see any of that."

Ellie's eyes went cold. "What makes you think it's a face? Maybe I'm just experienced enough with all of this to know what I need to do to get through it."

"I'm sure you do. What I'm saying is that you don't have to do it alone." Surely she couldn't argue that.

"I don't need you to hold my hand."

The retort packed a dose of snark, but he'd take fiery over frigid any day. "Maybe I want to hold your hand."

Ellie merely rolled her eyes.

"Come on. Would you take that answer if the tables were turned? What's good for the goose—"

"I've got it. It's easier to keep it all separate." She shrugged, as though that was the most obvious thing in the world.

"I'm pretty sure you'd be the first to say easier isn't necessarily better." Jack regretted the words the second they left his mouth. What he'd meant as a gentle prod to Ellie's straightforward and openhearted worldview had come out as a sarcastic dig. And one look at Ellie's face confirmed that's exactly how it landed.

"Would you like me to yell and throw things? Fall apart so you can play hero?" Ellie folded her arms. "It sounds like this conversation is actually about what you need."

He expected her to call him out. He didn't expect her to do it with such vitriol. "I need you to be honest."

"Well, I need to figure out if my mom's facility will take her back after she hit a member of the staff. So, unless you can make that happen for me, I've got it covered."

He winced, the magnitude of her stress hitting him at a new level. "Can they do that? Not take her back?"

"Yeah." Ellie pinched the bridge of her nose.

"I'm sorry." He reached for her, feeling utterly helpless but wanting to offer something.

"It's not your fault. It's just one more thing I have to deal with." The fire was gone. In its place, simple resignation.

"I want to help," he said, hating just how unhelpful he sounded.

"How can you help when you don't even understand?"

"Help me understand. Please."

Ellie shook her head, and suddenly she seemed a million miles away. "I can't, Jack. I've got a million things to deal with and teaching you intro to having a parent with mental illness just doesn't make the cut right now."

He opened his mouth but closed it without saying anything. Because what could he say to that? It might be harsh, but it was true. In this moment, Ellie saw him as one more problem needing her attention instead of a partner. And whatever good intentions he might have, he didn't know how to help.

"I'm sorry," she said.

"You don't need to apologize." He suddenly felt like he did. "I'm sorry if my attempt at making things better just feels like more work for you."

"It's not that." Ellie dropped her head back, stared at the ceiling, and sighed.

"What is it then?" Because even more than he wanted to help, he wanted to understand.

"I love my mom, and I'm protective of her. I don't like it when people feel sorry for her."

Jack wanted it to make sense. With enough mental gymnastics, he might get it to. But that wasn't how Ellie operated, and something told him to go with his gut. "Are you worried about people feeling sorry for her, or sorry for you?"

Ellie gave an almost imperceptible shake of her head. It felt a lot more like denial than disagreement. "I'm not the one with the debilitating illness."

Was she really playing the tough card? "That doesn't mean you're not profoundly affected by it."

"But it does mean I get to go about my life and have my work and my friends and my"—she gestured vaguely at him—"you."

"You should have those things. And I'm guessing your mom wants you to have them, too."

Ellie sighed again. "She does."

"Do you feel guilty for making a life for yourself?"

"No."

The fast and flat answer told him he'd hit a nerve. Only he didn't know where to go next that wouldn't make her lash out. Or, worse, shut down entirely.

"I feel guilty that I don't want the messiness of that part of my life to seep into the rest. I like being the fun and easy person that people want to be around. I like being insightful and optimistic and fun. The person people can count on who doesn't bring a whole lot of baggage to the table." She shrugged. "What you see is what you get, you know?"

It struck him that, for all the ways he came across as quiet and closed off, it was Ellie who kept the most fragile parts of herself locked firmly away. "That might work for casual friends or the occasional fuck buddy, but I'm neither of those things. I don't want to be either of those things."

"Are you giving me an ultimatum?" Ellie asked.

"What? No." Jack scrubbed a hand over his face. "I'm asking you to open up to me. To trust me."

Ellie nodded, but again, it registered as resignation more than anything else. "And I'm asking you to let me decide how to handle a very personal part of my life."

It felt like an impasse, though he didn't want to call it that. Especially when Ellie was so emotionally wrung out. "I can give you space, if that's what you want."

Ellie's eyes narrowed briefly. "Yeah, okay."

Jack reached for her hand, but she stood before he could take it.

"I think I'm going to go," she said.

"Go?"

"Yeah. Home. Or maybe to Rhett's. I need to decompress from all this. You know. Space."

That wasn't at all what he'd meant, but trying to clarify would be asserting his truth over hers—the exact opposite of what he was going for. "Do whatever feels best for you. I'm here, though. I'm not going anywhere."

"Thanks." She gave him a small smile then turned her attention to the dogs. After some pets and promises to see them soon, she headed for the front door.

Jack got up and followed. She put on her shoes and picked up her purse. "I'll text you later."

"Sounds good." He resisted the urge to pull her into his arms, to tell her everything would be okay. Because platitudes were rubbish, and in this case, he didn't actually know if things would be.

Ellie opened the door and stepped out. "Thanks for trying."

She didn't wait for him to respond, to say he'd like to do so much more than try. She didn't linger for a goodbye kiss or say she loved him. He didn't say it either, not because he didn't feel it but because they hadn't said it at all to each other yet and this would be a really shitty time to lay it out there. And because, he realized with a heaviness in his chest, saying it wouldn't fix the gaping divide between what he wanted from a partner and what Ellie seemed interested in giving.

Ellie left Jack's only to walk the length of the porch and knock on Rhett's door. Rhett was smiling when she opened it. "Are you just going to go back and forth between my place and Jack's? We could get you your own mailbox."

She let her shoulders slump. "At the rate I'm going, I won't be spending much more time at Jack's."

Rhett's look became her signature mix of concerned and stern, an expression she referred to as her Southern special. "Girl."

Ellie shrugged. "Can I come in?"

Rhett opened the door wide and made a sweeping gesture. "You know you didn't have to ask. Or knock, for that matter."

Ellie skulked in, dropping her bag and collapsing dramatically onto Rhett's sofa.

"Okay, then." Rhett closed the door and nodded slowly. "Would you like a cup of tea? Something stronger than tea?"

"He's so fucking stubborn," Ellie said. She stomped her foot, a move made extra ridiculous by the fact that she was sitting down.

Rhett winced. "You're probably going to kick my ass for saying this, but it takes one to know one."

She glowered. "I'm not going to kick your ass."

"No, but you'll probably get huffy and try to change the subject since I'm not agreeing with you." Rhett lifted a finger. "For the record, I'm not disagreeing with you. It's a both and situation."

Ellie huffed, then realized she'd played right into Rhett's prediction. "Well, can we talk about Jack's stubbornness first?"

"Of course."

"He's so fucking stubborn," she said again. "I've been through this. More times than I care to count. I know what I'm doing. Why won't he just trust me to handle it?"

"I don't think he thinks you can't handle it," Rhett said.

"Then what?"

Rhett took a deep breath and let it out excruciatingly slowly. "I think he thinks you shouldn't have to handle it alone."

Her shoulders slumped. "He said that. Essentially, at least."

"Yeah?" Rhett's tone was gentle.

She hated when people tried to be gentle. It implied she was fragile. "He said that I act open to the world and all about embracing vulnerability, but when it comes to myself, I don't."

"That's a big assertion."

Ellie laughed. "He actually used the phrase 'what's good for the goose.' Like a freaking ninety-year-old."

Rhett laughed, too.

Ellie stopped laughing.

Rhett did, too.

Ellie scowled.

Rhett smiled.

"Is that your way of telling me he's right?" She really didn't want to entertain that possibility.

"Not necessarily. Why don't you tell me how he's wrong?"

Ellie squinted. "That's sneaky."

"Is it?" Rhett asked, all innocence.

"Yes, because I'm trying to be indignant and you're busy poking holes in my logic." It was like getting emotionally pantsed.

Rhett dropped her head to one side. "Am I poking holes or simply pointing to ones that are already there?"

She sniffed. "Same difference."

Rhett didn't say anything then. She simply blinked.

Ellie weighed her options and landed on the side of playing dirty. "Why do I think you learned that look from your mother?"

"I did," Rhett said without missing a beat. "But she uses her powers for evil, and I only use mine for good."

She laughed because how could she not? It broke a little of the tension, which was nice, but mostly left her back where she'd started. "So, you're saying you think Jack is right. And I'm wrong."

"I'm saying no such thing. I'm saying you need to think about the kind of person you want to be."

"What the hell is that supposed to mean?" Other than to imply the kind of person she was now was the wrong slash not good kind.

"You're one of the most generous, kind, and delightful human beings I know."

"Aw, thank you." Ellie smirked. "Even though I know you're about to slap a big ole but on there."

"And. I'm slapping an 'and' on there." Rhett gave a haughty chin toss and cleared her throat. "And…I think you're so attached to that version of yourself that you hesitate to show anything else."

"You say that like it's a bad thing." She knew she was setting herself up but couldn't seem to help it.

"It's not bad. But it's not authentic." Rhett didn't elaborate, knowing full well she'd achieved mic drop in seven words.

Ellie scowled again. "Just because I compartmentalize doesn't mean I'm not authentic."

Again, Rhett merely blinked. Slow. Intentional. Effective.

Ellie let out a string of swear words.

"Hey, don't shoot the messenger."

She wouldn't. And she trusted Rhett more than anyone else. God, she hated being wrong. She was about to say as much when an even more unpleasant thought landed. "Do you think I do that with you?"

Rhett didn't answer, which proved more damning than anything she could have said. Ellie pressed the tips of her fingers to her forehead.

It didn't do much to chase away the headache she had brewing, but it spared her having to look Rhett in the eye.

"Hey, it's okay." Rhett grabbed her hand and gave it a squeeze. "I don't think you mean to shut me out."

"But you think I do. Shut you out I mean." Ellie shook her head before braving eye contact.

"Well, it's like you said. You compartmentalize. The thing is, I love you. All of you. And I want you to show me all those messy, not always a good time parts. I bet Jack feels the same."

They were talking about her messy parts, but she couldn't help but wonder at the love part. Did Jack love her? Did she love him? She always considered herself quick to fall in love, but it struck her now that her way of being in love was very specific—lots of chemistry and affection, mutual curiosity, and support anytime the other person needed it. But how often did she let herself need it in return?

"I didn't mean to make you cry," Rhett said softly.

Ellie swiped at her eyes and laughed. "I didn't even realize you did."

"There haven't been a lot of people in your life you could count on. Not for the hard stuff at least."

She nodded slowly. As much as she hated the phrasing, it held truth. She didn't count on people because it meant she wouldn't have to be disappointed if they wouldn't—or couldn't—come through. And most of the people in her life, romantic partners included, either hadn't noticed or didn't have a problem with it.

"I think you can count on Jack." Rhett elbowed her gently. "And you sure as hell can count on me."

Ellie grumbled, then she chuckled. "Yeah."

Chapter Twenty-five

With Ellie's car still parked out front, Jack had no choice but to sit and stew that she was next door spilling her guts to Rhett while shutting him out completely. Well, that wasn't entirely true. He had choices. And after an hour of pussyfooting, he hauled himself over to Logan and Kathleen's for an afternoon of basement puttering.

"So, did you break up?" Logan asked not twenty minutes after they'd settled on refurbing a couple of their side-of-the-road finds.

Jack ran the planer over the cabinet surface, then followed with his hand to check for rough spots. He should have known better than to think they could simply work in companionable silence. "I don't think so?"

Logan looked up from where she'd been filling tiny nail holes with her secret blend of wood putty and sawdust. "Are you asking me or telling me?"

"We didn't break up, but we didn't resolve anything, either."

Logan shrugged. "That feels like standard fare for a couple fight."

Jack grumbled on principle. He was perfectly prepared for couple fights with Ellie, along with everything else that being a couple entailed. Only he wasn't at all certain that feeling was mutual.

"I get that it sucks, but not everything can be resolved in a single conversation."

"I don't need it to be." He hadn't meant to snap, but he refused to take on the stubborn and grumpy mantle when he'd been neither.

"No?" Logan didn't pretend to be anything but dubious.

"Yes, I like things to be concrete, but that's not the same. There's no plan for what next. No, hey let's cool off for a couple of days and try to talk. You know?"

"Did you have such a heated argument that you need a couple of days to cool off?"

"No?" There he went with questions disguised as answers again. "No. It was barely a fight at all. Strong words. I think Ellie felt hurt, but also like she didn't want to get into it."

"Oh," Logan drawled in that knowing way she had.

"What do you mean, 'oh'?"

"You like to state grievances, come to consensus, clear the air, and move on."

He tried and failed to find fault in that approach. "And?"

"And not everyone works that way."

"What other way is there?" He lifted a hand before Logan could reply. "That's not passive-aggressive and dysfunctional."

"Feeling heard, having your feelings validated even if they're somewhat irrational. Some people need that before they can get to the logic."

"That's just it. I all but asked her whether she wanted empathy or problem solving."

Logan laughed at the phrase they'd all learned from Clover. "And?"

"And it was like she didn't want either. She wanted to pretend like nothing was wrong and go about her business."

"Huh." To her credit—or maybe to his relief—Logan seemed stumped. "Like, stubborn and independent?"

That he could have worked with. Thanks, Maddie. "More like she didn't trust me with her feelings enough to share them in the first place."

"Ouch."

He hadn't put it in those words before, even in his own mind. But they seemed to hit the nail on the head. "I don't know if it's specific to me, or if she doesn't trust anyone."

"That's tough," Logan said. "Both options kind of suck."

And didn't leave him with a whole lot of room to work. "She did call me out on expecting her to educate me on her mom's condition."

"That doesn't feel like an unreasonable ask."

"Yes and no. I mean, it's definitely insensitive to expect her to hold my hand while she's trying to keep her head above water. But her experience is unique, and that's what I want to understand."

"I guess."

Logan didn't seem convinced, and Jack wondered whether he felt compelled to swoop to his own defense or Ellie's. And then it hit him. "It's like how I resent it when people I barely know ask me about trans stuff they could easily learn by reading an article. Hell, a blog. A TikTok video."

Logan made a sweeping gesture with her sanding block. "Okay, see, that makes sense. Did you just come up with that?"

He nodded.

"I guess that gives you something concrete to do?"

Another nod. "At this point, I'll take what I can get."

It didn't do anything about Ellie's reticence to let him into that part of her world, but when it came down to it, that would be her call to make. Hopefully, he could do his homework and lay a better foundation. With something solid in place, hopefully he could convince her to land on the side of navigating hard stuff together.

Ellie needed to talk to Jack. She knew it as clearly as she knew her own name. She also knew it was going to suck. Nothing about being messy or vulnerable appealed to her. Even as she prided herself on being someone her friends and partners could be messy and vulnerable with.

She didn't relish being a woman of contradiction, but it was what she had. Unlike her actual work. When it came to that, she was a goddamn genius.

She stepped back from the last Hampstead House mural and smiled. She would have regardless. The final touches on a big project always brought a certain satisfaction, and this one was the biggest she'd ever tackled solo. But this work also had the queerness Bea had asked her to infuse, and Ellie couldn't be happier with the result.

As they'd discussed, she'd given a picnicking woman, who happened to be gazing longingly at a man, a five o'clock shadow and one of the gallant gentlemen an unmistakable boob swell. Two women walking together now held hands and gazed at each other with far more than friendly affection. And she'd figured out how to turn an outstretched palm into an implied hand job.

The result was less obvious than the bathroom mural, where she'd worked feather boas and actual glitter into a hunting scene, but that's what made it so special. A passing glance might not even pick up on the gender bending she'd managed to weave into the original. And she'd done such a good job matching the colors and style that it looked as though it had been in the house for a hundred years.

She tapped the wooden tip of the paintbrush to her lips and contemplated any final strokes. But no. It was done. And as far as she was concerned, it was damn near perfect.

"Wow." Pablo appeared beside her, arms cast wide. "It's literally a masterpiece."

He'd been stingy with his praise over the course of the project, though she hadn't been able to tell if it had to do with her skills or Bea's idea. Perhaps it had been the confluence of those two things and whether she genuinely had the skill to make Bea's vision a reality. He seemed plenty pleased now, though, and that's what mattered. Well, technically, it mattered if Bea was pleased, but she'd take Pablo as proxy for now. "Yeah?"

"It's fucking epic." He shook his head. "I'm not going to lie, I thought it was going to look cheap and tacky."

She bristled on principle but knew what he meant. The fact that she'd managed to avoid that felt like a feather in her cap. "I'm pretty happy with how it's come out."

"Bea is going to flip. I can't decide whether I should send her a picture now or make her wait so she can see it in person."

Ellie lifted both hands, a rather comical gesture with a paintbrush in one and a palette in the other. "I'm going to leave that up to you."

Pablo studied the mural. "Wait, I think. It's the detail that really makes it, right?"

"For sure." And Bea hadn't been back since she'd actually gotten to the painting part, so it would be quite the reveal.

He turned to her with exaggerated seriousness. "Do you want to be here when that happens? She's going to be up next week to oversee the decorating."

Ellie shook her head. As much as she enjoyed being showered with compliments, Bea made her uneasy. Uneasy as in borderline creeped out. Not a worthwhile trade in her book. "No, no. I just need to know if she's happy with it or if there are any changes or additions she wants."

"Suit yourself, girlie. Me, I'd want the praise parade."

She chuckled at the phrase and tucked it away for future use.

"You're coming to the party, right?" he asked.

She loved a good party but hadn't been invited to one that she knew of. "Party?"

"Oh, the invites probably just went out. Housewarming. Bea's invited all her friends from the city, but she wanted to include the contractors too. Well, at least the queer ones." He winked.

Other than a couple of carpenters and subcontractors, that pretty much covered the entire crew. It would be nice to see everyone again, to celebrate the completion of the renovation. And she was more than a little intrigued by the prospect of meeting some of Bea's friends. Would they be old money? Powerhouse lesbians? Other eccentric dynasty heiresses? "If I'm invited, I wouldn't miss it."

"Perfect. You'll needle Jack into coming, won't you? Bea is quite enamored with him, but I get the sense he's not one for cocktail parties."

Ellie laughed even as her chest constricted. He'd attempted to be subtle, but she couldn't help but wonder whether Pablo had picked up on the chemistry between them. And if his comment had more to do with getting Jack to the party or finding out if they were together. "I'll see what I can do."

His eyes narrowed slightly, clearly unsatisfied with her vaguebook answer. "And of course a plus-one, if you're seeing anyone."

He was upping the ante, but she refused to take the bait. "Thanks," she said brightly.

Pablo lifted his chin, as though acknowledging she'd taken the point if not the match. "Are you all done? Can I check you off and put your final check in the mail?"

"Yes, and please do." She wasn't feeling strapped, but the influx would give her a sense of security until she figured out her next big job.

"Excellent." Pablo whipped out his ubiquitous tablet and tapped at the screen. "Floor guys are in tomorrow and the appliances are due end of the week. I think that leaves me to schedule movers."

"I wasn't holding you up, was I?" Between moving out earlier than she'd planned and all the time at the hospital, she'd run a couple of days over her estimate.

"Not at all. The main bathroom is still a situation. Bea decided she didn't like the marble she'd picked for the shower after all."

Ellie kept her expression neutral, but it wasn't without effort. She might find people like Bea maddening, but jobs like the one she'd just finished wouldn't exist without them. "Then I will clean up and clear out."

Pablo looked up from the screen. "Can I keep you in mind for other projects? You do paintings from scratch, right?"

She'd never considered herself good enough to be an artist outright. Or, rather, never considered art on its own a viable career path. The prospect of being hired solely for her talent—her vision—as a painter sent a ripple of pleasure through her. She stood a little taller and resisted the urge to be bashful. "I do, and I'd love to work with you again."

Pablo grinned and Ellie wondered if he had any clue the gift he'd just given her. "I've got your number, and I promise I'll be using it."

"I'll look forward to it." If only things with Jack were that simple.

CHAPTER TWENTY-SIX

Jack walked into the house and fought the urge to turn around and go back the way he'd come. It wasn't that he couldn't mingle and make nice. He didn't love it, but he had enough skill to do it passably. And he was genuinely looking forward to seeing a couple of the other queer contractors he'd gotten to know over the course of the project. The thing he dreaded was ignoring the elephant in the room: the state of things with Ellie.

They'd texted, but he hadn't seen her in close to two weeks. She'd claimed busyness, both with a new project Pablo had connected her to and needing to spend time with her mom. Both were legit. And he'd been plenty busy himself with overseeing the electric for a new residential build and reading up on what it was like to have—or love someone who had—schizophrenia. On top of that, she'd asked for space, so he wasn't going to go inserting himself where he wasn't wanted.

Of course, knowing all that did little to alleviate the fact that he missed the hell out of her.

"Hey." Ellie sidled up to him, smile firmly in place and glass of wine in hand.

"Hey," he said back, not wanting to sound sullen but truly unsure of what else to say.

"Looks great, huh?"

"Yep." He nodded but felt like an ass. "Your murals are spectacular. I hadn't gotten the chance to see them finished."

"Thanks." The smile reached her eyes this time. "I've never had the chance to queer a historical work before."

"Yeah. It's like new and fresh but also like it's always been here." He might not be an art aficionado, but he didn't have to be to understand what Ellie had accomplished.

"That's quite the compliment." Ellie shot him a sideways glance.

"You sound surprised that I'd give you one."

Her shrug said more than any words could have.

"Ellie, you're an amazing artist." He could have let it go at that. Maybe should have let it go. But he didn't. "You're an amazing woman, too. The fact that you're emotionally closed off and stubborn as a mule doesn't change that."

Her mouth fell open. Literally. Like a cartoon character, or a smallmouth bass.

Jack figured she was debating whether to walk away or smack him, but Bea didn't give her the chance. She swept in and slung an arm around each of them. "My two favorite magic-fingered queers."

He barely resisted a cringe, and even Ellie's smile faltered. "Everything looks fantastic," he managed.

"You have some beautiful pieces." Ellie gestured to a sideboard Logan would have drooled over. "That Chippendale is exquisite."

Chippendale. Of course it was.

"Thanks." Bea pulled her arms away and pointed to it. "I never liked it all that much, but my ex did so I insisted on getting it in the divorce."

Jack stole a glance at Ellie, who chuckled politely but was clearly horrified. It made him wonder if he saw that because it was an opinion he shared or because he knew her so intimately. Not that it mattered, at the rate they were going.

Someone called Bea's name. She turned to go but stopped and looked squarely at Jack. "We should grab a drink sometime, now that I'll be around more."

Jack nodded vaguely, and Bea flashed a flirtatious smile. She walked away without so much as a backward glance at Ellie.

"You can, you know. If you want to." Ellie's tone was casual, but sadness shadowed her eyes.

"Of course I don't want to," Jack said, more sharply than he'd intended.

"She does seem like she'd be a handful."

He wanted to poke at how much of a handful she was being, but snark wouldn't help anything. "She's obviously not my type, but that's not even the point. I want to be with you, Ellie. Exclusively."

Ellie stared at her drink before looking into Jack's eyes. "I want that, too."

"But I need you to want it enough to trust me with all of you, not just the neat and tidy and happy parts."

She opened her mouth but closed it without replying.

"I know it isn't the time or place to have this conversation, and I'm not going to pressure you. Just know I'm here. And for the foreseeable future at least, I'm not going anywhere."

Ellie nodded this time. Again, she didn't say anything, but her eyes were glassy with tears.

"For the record, I mean that metaphorically and not literally. If I stay at this party much longer, I'm going to stab myself with a cheese knife."

She laughed then. "I'm not sure how much damage that would do."

"No, no. One of those ones for hard cheese that has two giant prongs on the end."

"Oh. Well, then." Ellie tipped her head one way, then the other. "That's different."

Did she have to be so fucking easy to talk to? Did his heart have to thud in his chest like that every time they stood less than two feet apart? Jack sighed. Yeah, she did. And yeah, it did. Because he was head over heels in love with this woman even though it was entirely possible they wouldn't make it through the next month, much less a lifetime.

"Do you want to go for a walk?" she asked.

"Like, now?"

"I mean, it would probably look bad to leave less than an hour after arriving, but, I don't know, I'd love to talk."

The thudding in his chest took on a fight-or-flight edge, but no way in hell was he giving up a chance to maybe, finally, get somewhere. "Sure."

She smiled with a look of relief that said she hadn't been sure he'd say yes. "Sneak out the back with me?"

He gave a little salute. "I'm right behind you."

They emerged into the parking area behind the house. Like the big circular drive at the front, it had been finished with pristine edges and pea gravel. No doubt it would be a bitch to maintain, but it looked good.

"Garden?" she asked.

The daffodils were up, and the forsythia had burst with a riot of yellow. He liked both—for their symbolism that spring was springing but also their low-maintenance, perennial vibes. "Sure."

The moment they started on the small path that wound through the partially planted garden beds, Ellie folded her arms. Since the air still had a chill, Jack tried not to read into it. She continued walking, so Jack did, too.

Ellie took a deep breath. "My mother had her first nervous breakdown when I was seven. Well, not first. First I remembered. She had her first when she was a teenager, several throughout her early twenties, and one right after I was born because she'd had to go off all her meds when she was pregnant and that combined with the hormones was just too much."

He floundered for the right response to acknowledge the magnitude of what she was sharing—what she'd been through—without overreacting. Since he didn't know what that was, even after doing his homework, he settled for Clover's tried and true, "That sounds really hard."

"It was." Ellie nodded. "Is. But I got used to it, you know? My dad was around when I was little. And even after he left, he kept an eye on things and helped when she had an episode and needed to be hospitalized. I was fifteen when he passed away, so I was old enough to help around the house and, eventually, navigate her care."

It killed him that she spoke about it so casually, but he knew she needed to. At least for now. "And you always lived with her? Until recently?"

"I lived on campus in college, shared an apartment with friends after I graduated. Home was still my home base, though. It was nice. I got to live my life but be close to her, too. I was really lucky that we had the financial resources to make that work."

It still sounded like a huge burden—or at the very least a huge responsibility—to him. "I'm glad it felt balanced."

"It really was. And my friends were cool. I didn't get too into the weeds about it, but they knew her health was delicate, that she needed me. They never made me feel bad about having to go back and forth."

Not giving her a hard time wasn't the same as being supportive, but Jack did his best to reserve judgment for the time being.

"Anyway. I made it work. And it was easier to keep my worlds separate, you know? Everyone jokes about having crazy parents, but mine actually was. Trying to explain that, trying to educate people without being the heavy? It just felt like more trouble than it was worth." She sighed. "I know that makes me a coward."

"It absolutely does not." He couldn't even fathom trying to navigate it, especially now that he understood what a psychotic episode could look like.

"It feels that way sometimes."

He took her hand, not sure it was the right thing to do but utterly certain he needed to be touching her. "You had to be an adult from a very young age. That requires immense bravery."

She shrugged. "It didn't feel brave. It just felt necessary."

"Sounds lonely."

Ellie nodded, finally ready to own that's exactly what it was. And once she started talking, she couldn't seem to stop. She talked about the time in church when her mom got dizzy and panicked, convinced she was dying. She confessed the shame and embarrassment she felt in middle school and high school about not having a normal mom, and the resulting guilt because her mom loved her and was doing her best. She shared Donna's most recent hospitalization and the new worries about early onset dementia that often happened with people with severe mental illness.

Jack listened with patience and compassion. And with just enough nuance in his replies to make it clear he had tried to educate himself. He didn't ask for a pat on the back. He never looked bored or bothered. He never looked so overwhelmed with pity that she felt compelled to backpedal and minimize. He was just there.

Eventually, she ran out of words. Or maybe more accurately, she ran out of steam. She lifted her shoulders and let them fall, not sure what to do next.

"How do you feel right now?" Jack asked.

What did it say about her that the last thing in the world she expected was that? "Um, drained. But good. Lighter?"

"That's a lot to carry around all by yourself for so long."

"I wasn't trying to keep it secret, you know."

"No?" He seemed curious more than incredulous.

"I guess my point is that I wasn't trying to shut you out. Or not you specifically. I just don't have a lot of practice letting the messy parts of myself show. Other than Rhett, I've never been around anyone where there was room for it, so it's easier to be what other people want. Or at least what makes them comfortable." Ellie stopped walking. Jack did, too. He turned to face her and took both her hands in his. She legit thought her heart might pound right out of her chest and land on the pea gravel path, leaving a mess some poor gardener would have to come and clean up.

"I don't need you to make me comfortable," he said.

She frowned. It wasn't as simple as that, but she didn't have it in her to say so.

"Or maybe it would be more accurate to say that what I want, what would make me comfortable, is knowing you felt like you could be your whole self around me."

"I think sometimes I'm not even my whole self around me." It was a weird thing to admit.

"What do you mean?"

She might not have resolved it, but she'd had enough therapy that she could explain it. "I'm really good at compartmentalizing my feelings, especially when they're bad or even just inconvenient. And like, I'm not bottling them up and biting my tongue, in danger of exploding. I tuck them away, and it's like they're not even there."

"Oh." Jack nodded slowly, like he was having an epiphany.

"Yeah. So, that's me. I'm working on it, but obviously I'm a work in progress."

He chuckled. "Aren't we all?"

"I don't know. You seem to have yourself pretty figured out." A fact that felt both ironic and yet deeply true.

"I like to get most of my dysfunction out in the open from the get-go. I'm cranky, occasionally antisocial, and set enough in my ways to give the average eighty-year-old a run for his money."

Ellie laughed. And then she laughed harder. As in, doubled over, tears running down her cheeks hard. Probably all those pent-up endorphins. "It's true," she finally managed.

Jack gave a small bow. "Surely you didn't think you had a monopoly on emotional baggage."

The laughter stopped, and she studied him. "Do you have emotional baggage? I figured that was just your personality."

He tipped his head one way, then the other. "Some of it is. Some of it comes from being the middle sibling, being trans. From having a super supportive family, but still feeling like the black sheep sometimes."

She put a hand on his chest. "For what it's worth, you seem remarkably well adjusted."

"Thanks." He smiled. "I had to have a letter from a therapist to get top surgery. I decided to make use of the time instead of just going through the motions. Turns out we're all a little fucked up, one way or another."

"So comforting."

"And here's the thing. If you let some of your mess hang out, it makes it easier for me to do the same."

She hadn't really thought of it that way before, but it echoed Rhett's words with almost eerie verisimilitude. "You make it sound so simple."

"It is. Well, saying it is. Doing it?" Jack shrugged. "Not always so much."

Not simple, but maybe not impossible. "I want to try."

"Yeah?" Jack seemed pleased if not entirely confident.

"I'm not saying I won't fuck it up on the regular, but yes. And I want you to poke at me when I don't." Practice made perfect, after all.

"I do feel like you're due for some after all the poking you did in the beginning."

She laughed again. Not borderline hysterical this time, but it felt authentic. Real. "I'll take that."

"Does that mean you'll come home with me tonight?"

"For the record, I never didn't want to go home with you. Or have you come home with me. You know what I mean." It felt so good to admit that, to own that she never stopped wanting him. Wanting to be with him.

He nodded. "I'm sorry if it felt like I was digging my heels in."

She shook her head. "Don't apologize. You did because it mattered so much. I see that now."

"I hope you'll dig your heels in too, when you have things that matter."

"I'm going to remind you that you said that next time you give me a hard time about being stubborn."

He lifted both hands. "Okay, I meant when it comes to matters of the heart, not like whether or not we should go to some social function."

A little part of her wanted to joke about social functions being near and dear to her heart, but the rest of her was so grateful and relieved to be where they'd managed to get, she didn't want to fall back on teasing. "Noted."

"Good. So, should we go back to the party?"

She made a face. "I think we should bail."

He raised a brow. "Not worried about disappointing Bea?"

"I think she has enough minions and acolytes around to keep her busy for the evening. Besides, if she's going to miss anyone, it's you."

Jack pressed a hand to his chest. "And I, in true curmudgeon form, couldn't care less."

Chapter Twenty-seven

Jack kept glancing in the rearview mirror, half expecting Ellie's car to peel off from following him and disappear. Not that he didn't trust her—or the soul-baring intensity of the conversation they'd had meandering the grounds of Hampstead House. He simply didn't think of himself as one of those people who got exactly what he wanted. At least not when it came to relationships.

Of course, he'd never wanted a woman the way he wanted Ellie. In his bed, obviously, but in his heart and his mind. In his life.

He chuckled as he pulled into his driveway and cut the engine, Ellie right behind him. Logan and Maddie were going to have a field day.

Inside, Dot and Sophia all but ignored him, doing their geriatric version of a happy dance around Ellie's feet. He couldn't blame them. His insides were doing a happy dance of their own.

"Can I get you something to drink?" he asked. "Have you eaten today?"

Ellie looked up from the pets and belly rubs she continued to dole out. "You'll be pleased to know that I eat my feelings rather than skip meals. I had breakfast at my apartment and then a massive Italian sub after visiting my mom."

He was glad she ate, if not for the underlying stress that fueled it. "Does that mean I can or can't interest you in dinner?"

"Oh, definitely dinner. Nothing fancy, though. And wine. Please. Between my mother and having to watch Bea hit on you, I need one."

"She wasn't hitting on me," he said instinctively, then realized it was a blatant lie. "Okay, maybe she was, but I'm not even a little bit interested."

Ellie smirked. "Too rich or too toppy?"

It was a no-win question, but seeing Ellie back to herself—or close to—made it impossible to care. "Neither and both. How would you feel about grilled salmon on a spring salad? And a glass of zin?"

Her smile softened. "I'd feel like the luckiest girl in the world."

"Make yourself comfortable. I'll be right back." He poured them each a glass of wine, bringing hers to the sofa where she'd settled and heading back to the kitchen to prep dinner.

It took longer to preheat the grill than it did to cook the salmon, which was one of the reasons it was a go-to for him. The salad didn't take much more effort, and he'd taken to keeping the crostini crisps Grumpy Old Goat sourced from a bakery in Amherst on hand. It all came together in about twenty minutes.

Jack came in from the grill to find Ellie clutching her glass of wine with both hands and a vacant look on her face. He joined her on the sofa and put a hand on her knee. "You okay?"

"Huh? Oh. Yes. Sorry." She blinked at him a few times and smiled. "Zoned out there for a second."

"You're entitled. It's been an intense day."

"I guess so." She laughed. "I feel like I've run a marathon."

"An emotional marathon for sure." It made him wonder if she'd ever unloaded as much as she had with him today. She'd mentioned confiding in Rhett, but they'd been friends so long, she'd probably been around for at least some of what Ellie shared in real time.

"Just as freaking exhausting." She rolled her eyes. "Still. Didn't mean to space on you."

"I really don't mind. I was coming in to say dinner is ready."

Ellie let out a big sigh. "You're so freaking sweet to me."

He couldn't decide if he should take that as a compliment or feel offended that her bar for being taken care of was so low. "Thank you for letting me. And I promise I'll let you return the favor when I've been put through the wringer."

She nodded, suddenly serious. "I'd like that."

They ate in companionable silence, and Jack got the sense they both could use the quiet. After, Ellie asked if they could put on a movie and cuddle. Given everything, the simple prospect of physical closeness sounded like the best idea ever.

He put on an old Hepburn and Tracy rom-com that Ellie had mentioned liking. Ellie curled against him and seemed to melt into his arms. Not that she hadn't relaxed around him before, but this was different. Deeper. She got quiet, and enough minutes ticked by that he figured she'd fallen asleep.

"Do you want to meet my mom?" Her voice was soft but fully alert.

"Of course I do." He reminded himself not to be frustrated that she felt the need to ask.

"She's not going to be like your parents."

He had no illusions about how hard he'd lucked out in the family department. "She's your mom, which means she's a part of you. And if she's someone you've decided deserves a place in your life, then I want to spend time with her."

Ellie nodded against his chest. "Okay."

"As much or as little as you want, okay? The point is to share, not feel like you've got more piled on your plate."

She lifted her head and looked him in the eye. "I know."

Jack kissed her. "Good."

"So, I know my timing is really weird, but…"

When she didn't finish, Jack braced for something bad. "But we just agreed to talk about stuff, so it doesn't matter if the timing is weird."

"Right." She nodded, suddenly serious. "The thing is, I love you."

He waited a beat, then another. Waiting for the but or the caveat or the whatever else would water down the intensity of those three little words.

Ellie cringed. "So, yeah. No pressure to do anything or say it back, but after everything else today, not saying it was making me feel like a fraud."

"I'm glad you told me. I want to know." He took a deep breath. "I love you, too."

She shook her head. "Please don't feel like you have to say that just because I did."

"I don't. If you could see how fast my heart is beating, you'd know that."

"Really?" She looked genuinely surprised.

"For all my big talk, I've held back saying it. Not because I didn't feel it but because I wasn't sure how things were going to go. It didn't feel fair to put it on the table while you were deciding whether or not you were going to give me a chance."

She chuckled. "It might have moved things along a little faster."

"Okay, fair. Maybe I didn't want to own it when it felt like there was a very good chance you were going to walk away." He hadn't wanted to admit how terrified he was that would be the outcome—not even to himself.

"We're quite the pair, aren't we?"

He normally resisted sayings like that because they sounded so cliché. But between his gruff exterior and her easygoing personality, his squishy middle and her tightly guarded one, it felt more than apt. And as unlikely as it might have seemed in the beginning, he couldn't imagine finding someone he wanted to spend his life with more. "Indeed we are."

Despite the exhaustion of the day, saying "I love you" to Jack—and hearing it back—gave Ellie a second wind. And maybe a third. They'd barely made it halfway through the movie before she was asking him to take her to bed, where they proceeded to keep each other up half the night.

Fortunately, neither of them had anywhere to be and the dogs let them sleep until quarter of nine. It was lazy in the most luxurious way and utterly satisfying. As was the first cup of coffee Jack brought her in bed, the second cup she sipped while Jack made French toast, and the third he poured her to go with breakfast.

She couldn't remember a time she felt more spoiled and had already started concocting ways she might show her appreciation.

Blow jobs sat pretty high on the list, but she was pretty sure she enjoyed them almost as much as Jack did, so they didn't really count.

"Should I be worried about that extremely serious look on your face?" he asked in between bites.

"Of course not." Ellie smiled, feeling a little silly for how much thought she was putting into it.

Jack drummed his fingers on the table and looked uncomfortable.

"I swear." She lifted her chin. "What about you? You look pretty serious yourself."

"How do you feel about weddings?"

She pressed her lips together, wanting to appear neither surprised nor amused. "My own or in general?"

His eyes went wide. "In general. Going to them, I mean. As a guest."

She hadn't meant to tease him, but at this point it was too easy to resist. And she genuinely felt lighter than she had in as long as she could remember. "I enjoy them a great deal. Declarations of love, hopefully good music, and an open bar. What's not to like?"

"I don't have anything against love and good drinks, but you know. So many people. And dancing." Jack shuddered.

"Was that a test, then? Did I fail?"

He had the grace to laugh. "No. Sorry. I just, well, my uncle is getting married in a few weeks and I need a date. I mean, I don't need one, but it would be nice to have one. Not anyone. You. It would be nice to go with you."

He was obviously uncomfortable, and it felt almost mean to continue poking fun, but did he have to make it so damn easy? "Date to a wedding, huh? That is serious business."

Jack's shoulders dropped, and he suddenly resembled a pouty little boy. "It's not serious."

She clicked her tongue. "Of course it is. All that talk of having and holding 'til death do you part."

He scowled. "I can't decide if I'm supposed to argue that it's not a big deal or admit that I see how it could be but ask that you don't read too much into it or…"

When he didn't continue, Ellie ventured, "Say you changed your mind and rescind the invitation?"

"Yes. No. I mean no. I don't want to rescind."

"Because?" She had a feeling he could take the teasing. More, that he'd respect her for it in the long run.

"Because I want you to be my date."

She hadn't actually meant anything by it, but now that he was filling in the details, it was starting to feel like maybe a big deal after all. "Okay, note for future dealings with women. The right answer is, 'I think we'd have fun together and I trust we won't get bogged down in the wedding-ness of it.'"

"Wedding-ness?"

Ellie lifted a finger. "Note number two. Do not critique a woman's word choice when you're asking her to do you a favor."

Jack scrubbed both hands over his face and through his hair.

He was so damn cute when he was flustered. Since she knew better than to say that out loud, she gave his forearm a squeeze. "Sorry. I don't know why I'm giving you a hard time."

"It's in your nature." Jack closed one eye and gave her a sideways look. "And it was kind of funny."

"You weren't laughing a minute ago."

He opened both eyes and rolled them. "Yeah, but that's because I'm mucking it all up."

"You didn't muck anything up. I was being weird, and I'm sorry."

"Sorry enough to say yes?" he asked.

"I would have said yes either way."

He smirked then. "Do I get to cash that sorry in for something else?"

"Sorries have no cash value." She straightened her shoulders, feigning haughtiness.

"Yeah. It would be gross if they did."

God, he was so damn earnest. "But you've been such a good sport, I feel like it's only fair to do something nice for you."

Jack folded his arms and leaned back in his chair. Like he'd just won something or suddenly realized he had the upper hand.

"What?" she asked.

"Maybe you could do another striptease, and we could call it even."

She'd been so busy feeling like a jerk, she'd walked right into that. But despite being caught off guard, she loved everything about it. "I think that could be arranged."

Jack nodded slowly, but his expression turned serious once more. "To tell you the truth, there's something I'd like even more than you dancing around and taking your clothes off just for me."

Ellie waggled her eyebrows. "Ooh, kinky."

Jack closed his eyes, and she regretted being glib. But when he opened them, he looked at her with an intensity that took her breath away. "Not that there aren't about a thousand things I'd still like to do with and to your body, but that's not what I meant."

Hyperbole or no, her body responded in full force. She tried to speak and failed, then cleared her throat. "What did you mean?"

His expression softened, but somehow the intensity remained. "What I meant was I'd like it if maybe you did get caught up in the wedding-ness."

"Oh really?"

"Yeah. Like, not expect a proposal next week level of caught up, but maybe let me know you'd be open to considering that sort of arrangement eventually."

Ellie's heart flipped in her chest. It probably shouldn't be a surprise that Jack would be the one to be looking ahead, the one to broach the idea of taking things to the next level. But it was. A wonderful and glorious—if ever so slightly intimidating—surprise. "I'd definitely be open to that."

He narrowed his eyes slightly. "In general or with me?"

Not a phrase she expected to have turned back on her. And certainly not like that. But again, how glorious. "In general." She waited a beat. "But especially with you."

Jack's smile started slow, but it crept all the way to his eyes. "I'll take it."

CHAPTER TWENTY-EIGHT

Ellie signed herself in, then walked Jack through the process. "You have to leave your phone and keys. Sorry, I should have said that before we got here."

"No worries." He pulled both from his pocket and put them in the little plastic bin the woman at the desk held out.

They stepped back from the desk and waited for an attendant to unlock the door into the ward. "It might have been easier if we'd waited until she was back at her residence."

Jack grabbed her hand and gave it a squeeze. "I don't need it to be easier."

She couldn't explain why that meant so much more than dismissing or downplaying the experience of visiting a psychiatric unit for the first time. It did, though. It made her feel seen and understood and respected. It made her feel loved.

They were shown into the room, the same one as the last time she'd visited. She appreciated that the visiting areas were private. That hadn't been the case a couple of times, and it had been a struggle to keep her focus where it needed to be.

A few minutes later, a member of the staff wheeled Donna in. She wore a floral top and a pair of loose-fitting capris with the slide-on sneakers Ellie had picked up specifically for her hospital stay. "Hi, Mom," Ellie said, tone as bright as she could make it.

"Hi, sweetheart." Mom spoke slowly, but her speech no longer slurred, and her eyes seemed clear.

"How are you feeling today?"

"Oh, I'm well and blessed. Can't complain."

The use of one of her signature phrases made Ellie smile. Definitely a good sign. "I'm glad. I brought someone who's been wanting to meet you."

Ellie stepped to the side and Jack came forward. "It's a real pleasure to meet you, Mrs. Lancaster. Ellie has told me so much about you."

Mom turned to Ellie, eyes wide. "Sweetheart, is this your boyfriend?"

She nodded. "It is. You remember me telling you about Jack, right?"

Her mom's gaze returned to Jack. "But you didn't tell me he was so handsome."

Jack let out a guffaw but recovered quickly. "Thank you, ma'am. But I've got nothing on your beautiful daughter."

Donna beamed. "Thank you. She is beautiful, isn't she?"

Ellie squirmed, as she always did, when her mom went overboard with the compliments when talking about her to others. Jack didn't seem to mind, though. In fact, he seemed perfectly at ease. He asked lots of questions and listened attentively to Donna's rambling answers. Donna blossomed under the attention, and Ellie felt miserly for being so reticent about them meeting.

She'd worried about her mom getting into the weeds of Jack's gender, but it didn't even come up. And when Mom started peppering him with questions about his religion, Jack spoke eloquently about being raised Methodist but living his spirituality in a more general way that focused on connecting to nature and showing kindness to others.

It disconcerted her to be learning new things about him in such a context, but she was coming to terms with the fact that her expectations were rather crap at this point.

"God's wonders abound." Donna nodded knowingly. "If you slow down enough to pay attention."

Ellie chuckled. It was a phrase her mom used a lot, and one Ellie sometimes lost sight of in her quest to squeeze everything she could into whatever time she had for this or that.

Jack glanced at her briefly and winked, as though he knew the vein of her thoughts, before turning back to Donna with a smile. "They most certainly do."

They stayed about an hour, until a nurse came in and said it was time for lunch. Since lunch was also code for medication, Ellie took that as the cue to say their goodbyes. Mom got a little teary, though it had more to do with lunch times back when Ellie was a kid, and her dad would come home from work midday, and they'd all eat together.

Ellie couldn't fault her mother for remembering those times with such sentimentality. As a teen, it filled her with a mix of embarrassment and resentment that Donna couldn't manage her emotions in front of others. Now, she was simply grateful that there were so many good memories to conjure. And that experiencing them as memories meant her mom was rooted in the realities of the present.

"I'll come again tomorrow," Ellie said after her mom had wiped her eyes and managed a smile. "I'll talk with the staff and see if I can stay for lunch so we can eat together."

Without missing a beat, Mom turned her attention to Jack. "Would you like to come, too?"

"I'm sure Jack has to work," she said quickly. "Tomorrow is Monday."

Mom nodded. "Of course."

Jack, who'd hovered off to the side during the trip down memory lane, stepped forward. "But I'd love to have lunch with you next weekend if you're not too busy."

For all the crying a moment before, Donna's eyes lit up. "That would be lovely."

"I hear you have a sweet tooth. I'll see if this one lets me sneak in some cookies from my favorite bakery." Jack jerked his head in Ellie's direction with the subtlety of a bulldozer.

"I'll ask to make sure it's allowed." Ellie smiled. For all the times she resented—or simply struggled with—having to be the adult in situations with her mom, this time she didn't mind.

Jack tsked but shot her a wink. "Rule follower."

She was pretty sure this was the only scenario in which Jack played the rebel to her enforcer, so she didn't mind that too much, either. "Someone has to be."

Jack told himself he'd wait until they were back at his place to ask questions, but he'd no sooner pulled onto the road than the quiet made him twitchy. "How was it? How are you?"

Ellie looked at him with a wry smile. "I'm pretty sure I'm supposed to be asking you that."

He shook his head. "It was harder for you. I could feel the energy you expended staying completely tuned in to both of us."

She chuckled. "No one's ever described it like that before. I mean, my therapist and I talk about hyper vigilance, but that feels different."

That attunement had been one of the things he learned about growing up with a mentally ill parent. Clover had warned him against assuming anything was one size fits all, but it had given him a perspective—not to mention some language—that helped him to do some tuning in of his own. "Well, either way, I hope you know you don't have to do that with me."

Ellie frowned. "Did you feel managed?"

"No." He reached across the console and grabbed her hand. "But I know there's power in telling you out loud I can manage my emotions, and that I'll tell you if I'm not okay."

"Yeah." Ellie gave an exaggerated nod. "Yeah."

"It's good to remind myself, too. I wouldn't be the first guy, trans or otherwise, to equate stoic with strong. I want to be better than that for you."

Ellie chewed her lip. "I want to be that for you, too."

He shot her a side-eye without taking his attention from the road. "The managing your emotions part or the telling me when you're not okay?"

"Both." She pouted for a second, then cracked a smile. "Both."

"Good answer. I think that means we're going to do okay."

Ellie chuckled, as though it might be some sort of novelty. "I like the sound of that."

"What do you need now? Food? A nap?" He was weirdly energized but had a feeling Ellie wasn't.

"Food would be great." She looked down at her stomach. "More than great, actually. I was all nerves before and now I'm starving."

Jack smiled, more than a little pleased with himself for being tuned in correctly. "Requests or do you want me to pick?"

When Ellie didn't answer right away, he glanced over, only to find her staring at him with a wide-eyed blink. "Are you serious right now?" she finally asked.

The self-satisfaction evaporated. "What do you mean?"

"You're like a relationship book personified. Do you have a little therapist on your shoulder instead of an angel or a devil?"

Jack laughed. "More like a little Clover."

Ellie laughed, too. "Remind me to thank her. Or if we ever break up, to date her."

"Hey, now."

Ellie slid her hand behind his neck and gave it a squeeze. "Kidding. I like 'em masc. Besides, I don't have plans to let you go anytime soon."

For not the first time that day, emotion swelled in his chest, pressing against his ribs like a balloon blown up too big for the space. "I'm glad to hear it. Now, about that food…"

"I would love for you to pick." Ellie pulled her hand back and linked her fingers together in her lap. She lifted her shoulders and let them fall. "Thank you."

The gesture—relief, laced perhaps with contentment—said as much as her willingness to take him along to the hospital in the first place. Like she wanted him to be part of her team. Like she trusted him. "I know just the place."

Technically, the Little Gem was out of the way. Only by about fifteen minutes, though. And while he wouldn't call the meal they shared after digging out from the blizzard a date, it held a special place in his heart. Besides, he knew there'd be at least one thing on the menu Ellie liked and wouldn't have to think too hard about.

Ellie must have zoned out on the ride because it wasn't until Jack pulled into the parking lot that her eyes lit up and she let out an "aww."

"Is this okay?" he asked.

"More than." She undid her seat belt and lifted her chin. "Is this you being sentimental?"

"Maybe." That first morning, he might have taken the question as a dig—some implication that he was in fact too sentimental or perhaps not sentimental enough. Things were different now, though. He knew Ellie. More, he trusted that she knew him and liked him exactly the way he was.

No. Not like, or at least not only that. Love. She loved him and he loved her. And as much as they felt like a bit of an odd couple, he believed in his heart of hearts that they might be made for each other.

Unlike that first time, only a few of the tables were occupied. Since he was already on a sentimental streak, he asked the woman at the register if they could have the booth by the front window where they'd sat before. Ellie lifted a brow. Jack shrugged. She grinned, and then he did, too.

Ellie had no sooner opened the massive menu before she peered over it. "You're going to be a heathen who eats pancakes in the afternoon, aren't you?"

"I've been known to, but probably not today."

Ellie nodded and returned her attention to the menu.

Jack had just enough of a view to see her frown. "Would you like me to order you a patty melt and a Diet Coke so you don't have to think about it?"

Her gaze darted to his. She smiled, but her eyes were glassy. "Yes, please."

The server—Liz, the same one they'd had the first time—came over to check in, and Jack decided to take a page from Ellie's book. After the requisite pleasantries, he asked for two patty melts. "A Diet Coke for her and regular one for me."

"You got it, sweet cheeks."

With Liz gone and the menus out of the way, Ellie folded her arms on the table and leaned forward. "You know, I expected it to be hard, but it wasn't."

"Deciding what to eat or letting me order for you?"

Ellie laughed. "Neither. Both."

Jack waited, trusting there would be more.

She took a deep breath and blew it out, then stared at the ceiling for a few seconds before making eye contact. "Letting you do things for me, decide things for me."

"For the record, I only want to decide things for you if or when that's your preference."

"I know."

"As for the doing things, I think the whole point is that it's mutual." He certainly liked all the random little things she'd done for him in the last couple of months.

"Totally. I guess I've always thought of it as fifty-fifty though. Equal."

"I think that's the point overall. But not as a daily tally. Some days or weeks even, you've only got thirty to give and I can make up the difference. Sometimes, that'll be reversed."

Ellie nodded but didn't say anything.

"I'm never going to feel okay taking extra if you don't do the same."

"You make it sound so simple."

"It is." Jack smiled. "Which isn't to say it's always easy."

Ellie laughed again, but it was the full, genuine laugh that he hadn't heard enough of lately. "I'll remember that."

"For what it's worth, I'm more inclined to figure out tradesies with you than anyone else I've been with."

"Tradesies?" Ellie's raised brow reminded Jack of the way he'd described her to Logan back when they first met—full of mirth.

"It's a technical term. I definitely heard it on a relationship podcast."

Liz appeared with their drinks and a promise the food would be out soon. When she'd gone, Ellie lifted her glass. "Well, then, here's to tradesies."

Jack clinked his drink to hers. "Cheers."

Chapter Twenty-nine

As much as Ellie loved weddings, she didn't have much occasion to attend them. As an only child without many cousins, there weren't a lot of family nuptials to celebrate. And aside from Rhett, none of her friends had yet made the decision to tie the knot. So even though she was Jack's plus-one—who'd technically never met the bride or the groom—the prospect of Rich and Cherry's big day filled her with joy.

To be fair, she was pretty full of joy most of the time these days. She'd loved a handful of her boyfriends and girlfriends through the years, but never like this. Never like Jack.

Jack loved parts of her she'd never shown anyone. It was all rather humbling, to be honest. To be loved so deeply and so wholly. But also to admit that the big, open-hearted personality she showed to the world was only one piece of her whole self.

She'd decided to embrace it, though. Just like she embraced Jack's stubborn streak and antisocial tendencies. And the way his siblings took her in as one of their own. And the way her own mother had started to tease her about getting married and giving her a grandbaby. Not that she was in any rush, but she felt open to it, which was a revelation.

"You're looking dewy-eyed and the wedding isn't for two hours still." Jack caught her gaze in the mirror as he tied his tie.

Ellie smirked. "Is that a problem?"

He shook his head without breaking eye contact and smiled. "Not even a little."

"I promise I'm not one of those women who cries at every wedding."

"Good to know." Jack finished tightening the knot, then immediately tugged at it. "Are you just about ready?"

Satisfied with her hair and makeup, she turned and pointed to the dress hanging from the door of Jack's closet. "I just need to put that on."

"Pity." He came close and slipped his arms around her waist. "I kind of like you like this."

She glanced at the swell of cleavage peeking out of the pale blue lace of her bra. "Maybe if you're real nice, I can go back to this when we get home."

"Nah." Jack shook his head. "By the time we get home, I'll need you completely naked."

"And under you?" Ellie quirked a brow, loving the surge of arousal and the fact that Jack seemed to want her all the time.

"Under, over. I'm not picky."

Images of both flitted through her mind. She gave his tie a gentle pull. "I love that about you."

They arrived at Jack's parents' house just as Maddie and Sy did. She'd actually gone dress shopping with Maddie, since Maddie apparently hated that sort of thing. It made Ellie smile to see the emerald and ivory stripe she'd promised wasn't too bold. "You look so great," she said in lieu of a hello.

"You, too." Maddie pulled her into a hug without hesitation. "I'm taking you shopping every time I need something fancy. I love wearing it, but God, picking it out is such a nightmare."

Ellie laughed, but not as loud as Jack. Or Sy. "I accept this responsibility," Ellie said.

They made their way to the backyard. A massive white tent took up more than half of it, and rows of folding chairs facing a wooden arch took up the rest. "Oh, wow," Sy said.

"Agreed," Kathleen said with something resembling reverence.

Ellie turned to find her and Logan behind them. She hadn't spent much time with Kathleen yet but hoped that would soon change.

"We can have this exact setup, you know." Logan made a sweeping gesture. "I can make that happen for you."

Kathleen blushed, but a gleam in her eye made Ellie think she might be considering it.

"Wait, are you two engaged?" Sy asked. "Like, officially, I mean."

Logan lifted both hands. "Hey, now. Don't go spreading rumors. I have not been given the green light to propose."

Everyone laughed, and Kathleen rolled her eyes. "You make me sound like a control freak."

"No, no." Maddie draped an arm around Kathleen's shoulder. "That's me. Just ask Sy."

Sy grimaced, then grinned. "You are headstrong and fierce and delightful."

Clover joined them, and the teasing continued as they found their seats. Ellie delighted in all of it—in being welcomed in like she'd belonged there all along. She also found herself wishing Rhett was there and not for the first time, she imagined how well Rhett and Clover would get along.

The ceremony started and she turned her attention to the happy couple. Despite Jack's low-grade grumblings about his uncle, it was obvious that Rich and Cherry were smitten with each other. The idea of the two of them finding each other, of choosing each other, after previous marriages and kids and careers and everything else life had thrown their way gave her hope in the universe to get things right sometimes.

During the vows, Ellie sniffed, trying to blink fast enough to keep any tears from spilling over.

Jack regarded her with an affectionate smile. "Are you crying?"

"No," she said, reminding herself of an obstinate toddler.

He squeezed her hand. "I thought we agreed we wouldn't hold back our feelings."

She sniffed again and laughed. "Yeah, but I also promised not to turn into a romantic sap at the wedding."

Jack canted his head. "Maybe a little sappiness would be okay."

She narrowed her eyes. "You're not going to tease me about it later?"

"Oh, I didn't say that." Jack winked. "I just said it was okay."

He pulled her hand into his lap and gave it another squeeze. She rested her head on his shoulder. The universe, it seemed, was on a roll.

❖

The wedding might have taken place in his brother's backyard, but otherwise Uncle Rich spared no expense. Legit catering, open bar, and a band he hired to come all the way from Bennington. The vibe was casual but classy—traits Jack never would have ascribed to his uncle but Cherry clearly possessed in spades. The food was out of this world and the bartender Clover had recommended, courtesy of someone she'd dated down in Amherst, whipped up cocktails interesting but subdued enough to tempt even his beer-inclined palate.

Rich and Cherry cut the cake, and the music started. Danceable oldies kicked things off, the kind of songs that had his parents and their friends on the rented dance floor in the middle of the tent. When the music shifted to something more modern, even more people joined. Jack realized it was one of those songs whose lyrics basically directed the made-up dance designed to accompany it.

Fierce debate over the merits of line dancing ensued. Kathleen mostly shook her head and lamented being alive when the Electric Slide was in its heyday. When the bouncy beat stopped, the lead singer made a joke about being too old for that sort of thing and announced that it was time to slow things down a bit. She called out the count and the strains of "At Last" began.

Shy smiles and goofy looks ensued, and both his siblings made a beeline for the dance floor with their respective girlfriends. Even Clover caught the eye of one of Cherry's nephews and agreed to dance. Jack looked at Ellie and tried not to cringe.

Ellie chuckled. "We don't have to."

She'd instantly perceived his hesitation and shifted her body language to take any modicum of pressure off him. Did she even know she did it? Something to talk about, for sure. But not today. Today was for happiness and sentimentality, and maybe even a little romance.

"I want to." Jack stood and extended a hand. Ellie's smile softened and her eyes sparkled as she took it. He led them to the parquet floor, and they joined the other couples swaying close to one another.

"Thank you," she said.

"I'm not going to lie, I'll take pretty much any excuse to pull you into my arms. Even if it requires dancing."

"I'll remember that."

For all his grumbling—internal or otherwise—it felt good to hold Ellie close in such a public way. Like they were announcing to the world that they'd decided to forge ahead together. Symbolic, but also concrete and real.

When the song ended and another fast-paced oldie began, Jack shook his head. "I do not, however, do the twist."

Ellie laughed. "I accept these terms."

It turned out, however, that Kathleen did. Kathleen convinced Logan, who didn't require much convincing, and Sy promptly joined them. It took exactly one encouraging look, and Ellie offered him a parting wave to join them. He found himself leaning against the bar with Maddie, watching.

"You know, I think we did all right for ourselves," Maddie said.

Jack shook his head. "That is literally the most elder sibling thing you've ever said."

"Not true. I know for a fact I've said 'I'm right' many times and I'm pretty sure that's the most elder sibling thing one can say."

"Nope. Using that as your retort and example now officially holds the title. It's kind of meta."

She elbowed him in the ribs. "Don't even with that."

"Whatever. I'm using that word correctly."

Maddie rolled her eyes. "I never said you weren't."

"Well, now that we've got that all settled, yeah, we did."

"Did what?" she asked.

He rolled his eyes. Not annoyed so much as accepting that this was how they had conversations. "Did all right for ourselves."

Maddie's features softened and she smiled at Sy. "I can't believe I'm going to be the one rocking the white dress soon."

"I do love a winter wedding," he said without having any legitimate opinion on the subject.

"I thought you disliked all weddings."

His gaze drifted to Ellie, twisting and turning herself on the dance floor with abandon and joy. "I've reconsidered."

"The curmudgeon has gone soft." She bumped her shoulder lightly to his. "Wonders never cease."

He swallowed the retort that came naturally because it was a matter of habit more than his true feelings. "I've been told recently that wonders abound, if you're willing to slow down enough to see them."

"Wise words."

Donna's smile, her frail hands and fierce spirit, flashed in Jack's mind. Along with it, so much gratitude to Ellie for breaking down her walls and letting him in. They both knew it wouldn't be an overnight fix—as evidenced by her immediate acquiescence about the dancing—but he had hope and more than a smidgen of confidence. And he had plenty of learning and growing of his own to do. But he genuinely believed they could do it together. And he believed Ellie did, too.

The song ended and dancers came and went from the crowd. His crew laughed and hugged and decided to take a breather. "I think some bubbles are in order," he said, more as a general declaration than to Maddie in particular.

Rather than bothering with another round of glasses, Jack snagged a full bottle of champagne from the cooler they'd set up behind the bar. He brought it over to the table he and his siblings had claimed along with Clover, who'd wound up coming alone since her latest attempt at a relationship had imploded. He topped off the empty and half-empty flutes, then lifted his. "I'd like to propose a toast."

Logan and Maddie looked dubious, but everyone else at the table seemed happy to go along. "This ought to be good," Maddie said.

Sy elbowed Maddie in the ribs. "Be nice."

"Yeah." Jack gave her a pointed look. "Be nice."

Maddie made a sweeping gesture with her hand. "Go on."

"I feel like a lot has changed in the last year, especially in the falling in love department."

"Understatement," Maddie said, though she disguised it in a cough.

"Some of us were looking, most of us weren't." He looked at Clover. "Some of us got a little bruised."

Ever the optimist, she winked at him. "Comes with the territory."

He gave her a little bow. "Still, I can't stop thinking about how much better all of us are because of the amazing people who've found their way into our lives and our hearts. Sy, Kathleen, you make my sisters happier than I've ever seen them. And you manage to keep them in line at the same time."

Maddie grumbled, and Logan laughed.

Jack cleared his throat and turned his attention to Ellie. "Ellie, I thought a nice easy woman would stroll into my life eventually and everything would fall into place."

"Ha," Logan said.

Ellie grinned and gave a little shrug. "I didn't get that memo."

"You weren't what I was looking for, but you're everything I want and, maybe even more, you're everything I need. I love you."

"I love you, too," Ellie said.

"So, I wanted to raise a glass to us. To learning and loving and all that good stuff." He'd wanted an eloquent end, but words failed.

"To all that good stuff," Kathleen said, raising her glass.

"To all that good stuff," said everyone else.

They laughed and clinked and sipped. Conversations resumed, and Jack felt a quiet happiness settle over him. He looked at Ellie, who regarded him with amusement and affection and love. "Hi," he said.

"Hi." She smiled. "Nice toast."

He winced. "I lost it a little at the end."

"Nah. The sentiment was there."

It had been. For everyone at the table. But mostly for her. "Thanks."

"Thank you," she said, emphasis on the you.

"For what?"

"For loving me, for helping me learn so much about myself." She shrugged. "For not giving up on me."

He took her hand, ran his thumb back and forth across her knuckles. "You might be surprised to learn this about me, but I can be pretty stubborn."

"No," Ellie said, feigning shock.

"I was so damn resistant to falling in love with you that, once I did, there was no going back." And if he'd had to go forward without Ellie in his life, he'd have done it, but not without being a miserable wretch.

"I'm glad you didn't."

He thought about the future, all the possibilities it held. No absolute certainties, of course, but trust. Trust that things would turn out okay, trust that they'd find a way to weather the storms together. And trust that they'd have fun doing it. As far as he was concerned, there was little more he could ask for. "Girl. Same."

She laughed at the phrasing, mostly because he'd picked it up from Rhett. "I love you, Jack Barrow."

Jack's gaze traveled over her face before locking back on her eyes. "I love you too, Ellie Lancaster."

About the Author

Aurora Rey is a college dean by day and award-winning lesbian romance author the rest of the time, except when she's cooking, baking, riding the tractor, or pining for goats. She grew up in a small town in south Louisiana, daydreaming about New England. She keeps a special place in her heart for the South, especially the food and the ways women are raised to be strong, even if they're taught not to show it. After a brief dalliance with biochemistry, she completed both a BA and an MA in English.

She is the author of the Cape End Romance series and several standalone contemporary lesbian romance novels and novellas. She has been a finalist for the Lambda Literary, RITA®, and Golden Crown Literary Society awards but loves reader feedback the most. She lives in Ithaca, New York, with her dog and whatever wildlife has taken up residence in the pond.

Books Available from Bold Strokes Books

Coming Up Clutch by Anna Gram. College softball star Kelly "Razor" Mitchell hung up her cleats early, but when former crush, now coach Ashton Sharpe shows up on her doorstep seven years later, beautiful as ever, Razor hopes the longing in her gaze has nothing to do with softball. (978-1-63679-817-2)

Firecamp by Jaycie Morrison. Going their separate ways seemed inevitable for two people as different as Fallon and Nora, while meeting up again is strictly coincidental. (978-1-63679-753-3)

Fixed Up by Aurora Rey. When electrician Jack Barrow and artist Ellie Lancaster get stuck on a job site during a blizzard, close quarters send all sorts of sparks flying. (978-1-63679-788-5)

Stranded by Ronica Black. Can Abigail and Whitley overcome their personal hang-ups and stubbornness to survive not only Alaska, but a dangerous stalker as well? (978-1-63679-761-8)

Whisk Me Away by Georgia Beers. Regan's a gorgeous flake. Ava, a beautiful untouchable ice queen. When they meet again at a retreat for up-and-coming pastry chefs, the competition, and the ovens, heat up. (978-1-63679-796-0)

Across the Enchanted Border by Crin Claxton. Magic, telepathy, swordsmanship, tyranny, and tenderness abound in a tale of two lands separated by the enchanted border. (978-1-63679-804-2)

Deep Cover by Kara A. McLeod. Running from your problems by pretending to be someone else only works if the person you're pretending to be doesn't have even bigger problems. (978-1-63679-808-0)

Good Game by Suzanne Lenoir. Even though Lauren has sworn off dating gamers, it's becoming hard to resist the multifaceted Sam. An opposites attract lesbian romance. (978-1-63679-764-9)

Innocence of the Maiden by Ileandra Young. Three powerful women. Two covens at war. One horrifying murder. When mighty and powerful witches begin to butt heads, who out there is strong enough to mediate? (978-1-63679-765-6)

Protection in Paradise by Julia Underwood. When arson forces them together, the flames between chief of police Eve Maguire and librarian Shaye Hayden aren't that easy to extinguish. (978-1-63679-847-9)

Too Forward by Krystina Rivers. Just as professional basketball player Jane May's career finally starts heating up, a new relationship with her team's brand consultant could derail the success and happiness she's struggled so long to find. (978-1-63679-717-5)

Worth Waiting For by Kristin Keppler. For Peyton and Hanna, reliving the past is painful, but looking back might be the only way to move forward. (978-1-63679-773-1)

Flowers and Gemstones by Alaina Erdell. Caught between past loves and present secrets, Hannah and Vanessa must each decide if the other is worth making difficult changes for a shot at happiness. (978-1-63679-745-8)

Foul Play by Erin Kaste. Music librarian Kirsten Lindquist knows someone is stalking the symphony musicians, but can she prove that a string of murders and suspicious accidents are connected, all without becoming a victim herself? (978-1-63679-689-5)

Hollywood Hearts by Toni Logan. What happens when an A-list actress falls for a paparazzo, having no idea her love interest is the one responsible for the photos in a troublesome tabloid scandal targeting her? (978-1-63679-695-6)

Ride It Out by Jenna Jarvis. When the COVID-19 lockdown traps Mick and Katy in situations they'd convinced themselves were temporary, they're forced to face what they really want from their lives, and who they want to share them with. (978-1-63679-709-0)

Scarlet Love by Gun Brooke. Felicienne de Montagne is content with her hybrid flowers and greenhouses—until she finds adventurer Puck Aston on her doorstep and realizes nothing will ever be the same. (978-1-63679-721-2)

The Hard Stuff by Ana Hartnett. When Hannah, the sales manager for a big liquor brand, moves to Alexandra's hometown and rivals her local distillery, sparks of friction and attraction fly. It turns out the liquor is the least of the hard stuff. (978-1-63679-599-7)

The Hunter and Her Witch by Rachel Sullivan. When an ex-witch-hunter falls for a witch, buried pasts are unearthed, and love is placed on trial. (978-1-63679-830-1)

Trustfall by Patricia Evans. Devri and Shiv never expect their feelings for each other to linger, but sometimes what you've always wanted has a way of leading you to who you've always needed. (978-1-63679-705-2)

All For Her: Forbidden Romance Novellas by Gun Brooke, J.J. Hale, Aurora Rey. Explore the angst and excitement of forbidden love few would dare in this heart-stopping novella collection. (978-1-63679-713-7)

Finding Harmony by CF Frizzell. Rock star Harper Cushing has to rearrange her grandmother's future and sell the family store out from under her, but she reassesses everything because Gram's helper, Frankie, could be offering the harmony her heart has been missing. (978-1-63679-741-0)

Gaze by Kris Bryant. Love at first sight is for dreamers, but the more time Lucky and Brianna spend together, the more they realize the chemistry of a gaze can make anything possible. (978-1-63679-711-3)

Laying of Hands by Patricia Evans. The mysterious new writing instructor at camp makes Grace Waters brave enough to wonder what would happen if she dared to write her own story. (978-1-63679-782-3)

Seducing the Widow by Jane Walsh. Former rival debutantes have a second chance at love after fifteen years apart when a spinster persuades her ex-lover to help save her family business. (978-1-63679-747-2)

The Naked Truth by Sandy Lowe. How far are Rowan and Genevieve willing to go and how much will they risk to make their most captivating and forbidden fantasies a reality? (978-1-63679-426-6)

The Roommate by Claire Forsythe. Jess Black's boyfriend is handsome and successful. That's why it comes as a shock when she meets a woman on the train who makes her pulse race. (978-1-63679-757-1)